The LRS is .5 km north. My port track is damaged Cheng-Sze fired and the pace and upped its speed, gaining on the fleeing herd of pogos ahead. *It is larger than I, but it is damaged. I will eliminate it before its Hellbore is repaired. My main cannon has destroyed its front sensor pod.*

The pogos plunged around the Kai-Sabre, clanging against its hull, squealing. They blocked all possibility of pinpointing the Bolo. It shot. Shot again. *There—no, another pogo. It is in this herd of creatures and if I must shoot them all to find it, I will.* It had full power and even if it did not have infinite ammunition, it had plenty enough to exterminate this herd.

Close. A minute flash of light? Yes. There. Stupid beasts. The Bolo was slowing, allowing the herd to pull away from it, the human halfway into the top hatch. One pogo between it and them—with one shot, the Cheng-Sze blew it away. The Bolo's turret swivelled as the human dropped down into the hatch but . . .

Its Hellbore is still five degrees below horizontal. The human has not succeeded. I have it.

Then the Hellbore smoothly angled up, locking on.

It is repai—

Dark and rain turned to blazing white, white as the heart of a lightning bolt, outlining the Kai-Sabre for a fraction of a second like a black speck on the surface of the sun. A second shot sent the Bolo recoiling back on its own locked tracks and then . . .

Where the Sabre had been was a smoldering mound, streams of metal hissing as they flowed and cooled in the rain. The air was thick with steam. All sounds faded, except the creak and ping of overheated duralloy, and the crackle of fires in vegetation dried and ignited in one moment.

"Tag," the LRS said on an external speaker.

"YOU'RE IT."

Baen Books by Keith Laumer

The Compleat Bolo
Bolos, Book 1: Honor of the Regiment
Alien Minds
Retief and the Rascals
Judson's Eden
Back to the Time Trap
Earthblood (with *Rosel George Brown*)

CREATED BY
KEITH LAUMER

EDITED BY
BILL FAWCETT

BOLOS: THE UNCONQUERABLE

This is a work of fiction. All the characters and events portrayed in this book are fictional, and any resemblance to real people or incidents is purely coincidental.

A Baen Books Original

Baen Publishing Enterprises
P.O. Box 1403
Riverdale, N.Y. 10471

ISBN: 0-671-87629-5

Cover art by Paul Alexander

First printing, November 1994

Distributed by
SIMON & SCHUSTER
1230 Avenue of the Americas
New York, N.Y. 10020

Printed in the United States of America

Table of Contents

Ancestral Voices, *S. M. Stirling*........... 1

Sir Kendrick's Lady, *S. N. Lewitt*..... 37

You're It, *Shirley Meier* 71

Shared Experience,
   Christopher Stasheff 115

The Murphosensor Bomb,
   Karen Wehrstein 175

Legacy, *Todd Johnson* 215

Endings, *William R. Forstchen*........ 243

ANCESTRAL VOICES

S. M. Stirling

"Shall I provide a map display of the tactical situation?" The Mark III Bolo sounded slightly hopeful.

"Who needs maps?" Lieutenant Martins said. "Take a goddamn piece of paper, crumple it up, and you've *got* a map of this goddamn country, and the towns are worse."

"My optical storage capacity extends to 1:1 mapping of this entire hemisphere," the tank said.

It didn't add that the street-maps of this particular Central American city were hopelessly obsolete. Unchecked fires and squatters almost as destructive had altered it beyond recognition over the past decade.

The Mark III Bolo still used the sultry-sweet female voice poor Vinatelli had programmed in; Martins told herself that the hint of injured pride was her imagination. The plump newbie's bones were pushing up the daisies—or bougainvillea—back in the Company's old firebase in the now-defunct Republic of San Gabriel a few hundred miles to the south, but the Mark III was still with them. Being sent a giant state-of-the-art tank had seemed right on schedule with the general madness and decay, a couple of months ago. They'd been virtually cut off from even routine resupply, and then the Pentagon had delivered a mobile automated firebase instead of ammunition or replacements. Now . . .

If the Company had any chance of getting back to what was left of the USA, the Bolo would be the key. It was also much more comfortable than sitting outside in a UATV, an Utility All-Terrain Vehicle. A nice soft crash-couch, surrounded by display screen that could register data in any format she chose; there was even a portapotty and a cooler, although the supply of Jolt had given out. You could fight a major battle in this thing without even cracking a sweat—and with 150 tons of density-enchanced durachrome armor, about as much risk as playing a video game.

Bethany Martins hated it. She hadn't joined a Light Infantry unit to sit in a cramped moving fort. Still, you used what you had. She shifted in the crash-couch restraints at the next message.

"Target two hundred sixty degrees left, range one thousand forty-three, target is bunker. Engaging."

A screen slaved to the infinite repeaters showed an aiming-pip, sliding across the burning buildings. Bars of light snapped out as the coils gripped the depleted-uranium slugs and accelerated them to—literally—astronomical speeds. Where they struck, kinetic energy flashed into heat. What followed was not technically an explosion, but the building shuddered and slid into the street like a slow-motion avalanche.

The Company's troopers advanced across the shifting

rubble. Screens focused on them, or showed the jiggling pickups of the helmet cameras. Part of that was the ground shaking under the Bolo as it advanced, maneuvering with finicky delicacy.

"Give me a scan of the area right of our axis of advance," she said to the machine. "Sonic and thermal." The computer overlaid the visual with a schematic, identifying sources of heat or hard metal, sorting shapes and enhancing. Martins nodded to herself and switched to the unit push.

"Right four-ten, Captain," Martins said. "Heat source."

She could see the M-35 in the commander's hands turn. Then the picture tumbled and the weapon went skidding across the stones, catching on a burning windowframe. Bullets flailed the ground around the Americans, and a hypervelocity rocket streaked out at the Bolo. Intercepted, it blew up in a magenta globe of flame halfway across the street. The first screen showed a tumbling view of dirt as someone dragged the Company commander backwards.

"Captain's hit, Captain's hit—medic, medic!" a voice was shouting.

"Suppressing fire!" Martins shouted, cursing herself. *It's not alive*. But it gave such a good imitation you could forget it had no judgment.

"Acknowledged," the tranquill sex-goddess tones replied.

BRAP. That was audible even through the armor; the main ring-gun mounted along the axis of the vehicle cutting loose. The impact was half a mile away; evidently the machinery had detected something important there. The infinite repeaters opened up all at once, threading with needle accuracy around the pinned-down troopers of the Company. Enemy fire shredded and vanished.

"McNaught's out cold, broken leg, doesn't look too

bad otherwise," a voice said. Sergeant Jenkins, the senior NCO.

Martins nodded. "We're pulling out, Tops. Northwest, transmission follows." She traced the Bolo's idea of the optimum path, then transmitted it to Jenkin's helmet display with a blip of data.

Silence for a moment. Then: "Ma'am—" That was a bad sign, Tops getting formal. "—we're awful short of supplies, fuel too, and there's nothing much there."

That was why the Captain had taken the chance of coming into an urban area; better pickings. The problem was that pickings attracted predators.

"Do it, Tops. We've got enough firepower to level this place but we don't have enough troopers to *hold* it long enough to get what we need."

"Wilco."

The Mark III turned and headed northwest. A building was in the way, but the great vehicle only heaved slightly as it crushed its way through in a shower of beams and powdered adobe. The sensation of power would have been more intoxicating if Bethany Martins hadn't been quite so hungry.

Two days later, she popped the hatch and stuck her head out. There was no point in talking to an AI, after all; it wasn't conscious, just a bundle of reflexes. Although a very *good* bundle of reflexes.

For once the air outside wasn't too hot; they'd climbed a ridge above the jungle and they were a couple of thousand feet up. The line of volcanoes ahead of them shimmered blue and green in the morning light, densely forested, patches of mist on their sides. This forest smelled different from the dry scrub and limestone back in San Gabriel, intensely green with an undertang like spoiled bread or yeast. It reminded her of childhood, the time her father had tried making beer in the basement. The barrel had shattered in the night, leaving the floor two inches deep in half-fermented suds, and the smell had never come out of the concrete. The jungle smelled a little like that.

There was the odd patch of smoke, too, where the locals burned off the cover to plant their crops. Her tongue touched her lips. Supplies were short, now that they'd gotten out of the inhabited country.

"Anything new on the net from back home?"

That was Captain McNaught. He was sitting in one of the UATVs, a light six-wheeled truck built so low to the ground it looked squashed, with six balloon wheels of spun-alloy mesh. His splinted foot rested on the dashboard, beside the muzzle of his M-35.

"Nothing I can make sense of, Captain," she said. "California just left the Union. San Francisco just seceded from California. And that's not the worst of the weird shit coming down."

They'd called the United States *Reality* back in San Grabriel, while they'd been fighting the Glorious Way guerrillas. Since the recall order, that was beginning to look like a very sick joke. Things had been going to hell *before* some crazed Russian shot down the President, the Veep and the Chairman of the Joint Chiefs over Alaska.

"Well, if you can bear to leave the air-conditioned comfort—" McNaught said.

"Yeah," Martins muttered, tucking the printout into a shoulder pocket of her armor and picking up her helmet and M-35.

The climb down was a long one. The Mark III weighed 150 tons, and looked it—the Bolo was essentially a four-sided pyramid with the top lopped off, bent and smoothed where the armor was sloped for maximum deflection, jagged with sensor-arrays and weapons. Two sets of double tracks underlay it, each nearly six feet broad and supported on eight interleaved road wheels, underlying nearly half the surface of the vehicles. She dropped to the ground with a grunt— her body-armor weighed about a tenth of her mass— and walked over to the commander's vehicle.

The ten UATVs of the light infantry company were parked around the perimeter of the scrubby clearing. They'd all turned off their ceramic diesels, and the loudest noises were the buzzing of insects and the raucous cries of birds. Everyone was looking at her as if she knew a solution to their problems; all seventy-five of the troopers, and the half-dozen or so hangers-on, mostly girls. Everyone looked hungry. They *were* hungry.

"There *was* a road through here," she said to McNaught. "Problem is, I don't think anyone's used it since before either of us was born. Since things started going bad—and they went bad there first."

"Big Brother can use the route?" Sergeant Jenkins flipped up the faceshield-visor of his helmet. The path behind them was crushed flat and hard; the Bolo pulped hundred-foot trees as if they were stalked of cane.

"Oh, sure—but if there isn't enough traffic to keep it open, where are we going to get food or fuel?"

The Mark III was powered by ionic batteries; it could travel thousands of miles on one charge, and carried acres of monomolecular solar film in one of its dispensers. The UATVs were combustion powered; their ceramic diesels would burn anything from raw petroleum to bathtub gin, but they needed *something*. So did their passengers.

The three leaders looked at each other. McNaught had freckles and thinning reddish hair, and a runner's lanky body; Jenkins was the color of eggplant and built like a slab of basalt; Martins was wiry and olive-skinned, with short-cropped black hair and green eyes. All of them had been together through the

Glorio war and its aftermath; they could communicate without much need for words. *We can't go back.* They'd left a hornet's nest behind them, one way and another, and gringos had never been too popular down here. *We can't stop.* This jungle wouldn't feed a coatimundi, much less ninety human beings.

"*Why* do the locals keep fighting us?" McNaught asked.

Because they're starving themselves, Martins thought irritably, then forced herself to relax. The Captain was hurting and pumped full of painkillers. The locals were hurting too; first the world-wide collapse, a slow-motion catastrophe that had gone berserk in the last year. Chaos with that, and the famine that usually followed anarchy, harder than any drought. At that, things seemed to be going down the tube even faster back home. When worst came to worst people around here could go back to being subsistence farmers, and try conclusions with the hordes of cityfolk-turned-bandits. That wasn't much of an option in the USA.

They were going home because there didn't seem to be much alternative. And they couldn't go forward without something to run on.

"Hey, Top," Martins said meditatively. "Doesn't Carmody's squeeze come from around here?"

The big black man frowned, then grinned. "Now that you mention it, El-Tee, she does. Most recent intelligence we're likely to get."

"Lord of the Mountain, First Speaker of the Sun People, there is no doubt."

The cool whitewashed room was empty save for the old man and the messenger. The man who had once been Manuel Obregon leaned back in his chair and examined the youngster who sank to one knee before him, still panting with his run, trim in cotton culottes and sandals. Seven-Deer was one of his best; a steady young man, and reliable.

"Go on," Obregon said, stroking his chin reflectively.

Pleasant sounds drifted through the tall arched windows; masons' chisels, the clack of a loom, a woman singing. There were smells of tortillas cooking, flowers, turned earth, and underneath it a faint sulphur reek. He used them to cut free of worry and thought, making his mind a clear pool for the scout's words. He would absorb it, and then analyze.

"Sixty, perhaps seventy of the *yanqui* soldiers, and with them some *Ladino* women from the south. A dozen little trucks with six wheels each, some pulling carts."

"They are *yanqui*, beyond doubt? Not government soldiers of San Gabriel, not terrorists of the Glorious Way?"

"No, Lord of the Mountain, First Speaker of the Sun People." Seven-Deer touched the jade plug in his lower lip for emphasis. "The farmers I spoke with saw them closely and heard them speak English. Also . . ."

He hesitated, his eyes sliding aside for the first time. "Go on," Obregon said, schooling impatience out of his voice.

"They said the *yanquis* had with them a mountain that walked."

Obregon's age-spotted hands tightened on the arms of his chair. The scout swallowed: "I only repeat—"

"Yes, yes."

The old man stood and walked to the window. Across the plaza and the town, over the patchwork fields of the basin, a thin trickle of smoke rose in the air from the notched summit of the Smoker.

"I saw myself great tracks and crushed jungle," the

scout went on, gathering confidence. "Like this." He unfolded a paper.

So. A tank, Obregon thought, surprised. It had been a very long time since heavy war vehicles came into these remote uplands. Then he caught the neatly drawn scale. Each of the tread-tracks was wider than a man was tall, and there were four of them impossibly close together.

"A mountain that walks," he said to himself—in Spanish, not Nahuatl. "But does it *burn?*"

Seven-Deer's eyes flicked sideways to the sky-pillar of dark smoke that reached upward from the mountain, and he shuddered with awe and fear and worship.

"Your orders, Lord of the Mountain, First Speaker of the Sun People?"

"Report to One-Coyote that the Jaguar Knights are to be mobilized, and the border guards strengthened. We cannot allow outsiders to prey upon our people."

"Lord of the Mountain, First Speaker of the Sun People," Seven-Deer said, greatly daring, "they are only Ladinos beyond the mountain—and perhaps the *yanqui* will turn aside before the pass."

Obregon nodded. "Yet they pay us tribute," he said. "And their blood is ours." His own face showed more Europoid genes than the scout's did, or than most of the people in the valley. "In time, they will return to the ways of the Ancestors; as we did, after many years of following the false gods of the Ladinos. This valley is our base, not our prison—we must be ready to expand beyond it. Now go."

And, Obregon thought, looking up at the darkening sky, *Venus is nearing the holy place.* The favor of the gods was not bought cheaply. The *yanqui* troops could be valuable, in their way.

Outside, the masons shouted cheerfully to each other as they worked on the last level of the stepped pyramid—small, but brilliant with whitewash, gaudy along its base with murals in the ancient style he had reconstructed from books and disks. It would be ready soon.

And in the end you must go, he thought regretfully, looking at that library. In a way, he would miss the ancient videos more than the anthropological texts. The latter held the voice of the ancient gods, but they would live—live more truly—when they existed only as words spoken among the people. The videos were his only vice; he was not a man who needed much in the way of women or wealth or luxury. In a way, it was sad to think that they must die with him . . . for he too could never really be a part of the world he was bringing to birth.

He selected his favorite; viewing it would calm him, and it was a minor indulgence, after all.

"The Wicker Man," he read from the spine, as he slid the chip into its slot and pulled the goggles over his eyes.

Me and my big mouth, Martins thought. The problem was that she *was* the best one for the job; her Spanish was better than Jenkins', since she'd grown up in Santa Fe.

The view through her faceshield was flat and silvery, as the sandwich crystal picked up the starlight and amplified it. The fighting patrol eeled through the undergrowth from tree to tree, their heads turning with lizard quickness as the sensors in their helmets filtered light and sound. These were *big* trees, bigger than she'd thought survived anywhere in the isthmus. Not too much undergrowth, except where one of the forest giants had fallen and vines and saplings rioted. Not much light either, stray gleams through the upper canopy, but the faceshield could work with very little. The Americans moved quickly; every one of them had survived at least three years in the bad bush, where you learned the right habits or died fast.

Martins made a hand signal, and the patrol froze. They went to ground and crawled as they neared a clearing. Thick bush along the edges, then scattered irregular orchards of mango and citrus and plantains. She felt saliva spurt over her teeth at the sight, and somewhere a cow mooed—steak on the hoof. And where there were people and food, there would be some sort of slash; distilling was a universal art. The UATVs could run on that.

"Careful," she whispered on the unit push. "We don't want to off any of the indigs if we can avoid it."

Not that lifting their stuff was going to make them feel very friendly, but there was no need to put them on a fast burn.

Planted fields, maize and cassava and upland rice. Then a village, mud-and-wattle huts with thatch roofs. It smelled cleaner than most, less of the chicken-shit-and-pigs aroma you came to expect. Nothing stirring; through the walls she could see the faint IR traces of the sleeping inhabitants. A man stumbled through one door, fumbling with the drawstring of his dingy white-cotton pants. A trooper ghosted up behind him and swung his arm in a short, chopping arc. There was a dull sound—a chamois bag full of lead shot does not make much noise when slapped against a skull—and the indig slumped into waiting arms.

"*Proceeding,*" she whispered on the unit push. Captain McNaught would be watching through the helmet pickups.

She wasn't quite sure which was worse; being out here at the sharp end, or being stuck back there helpless with a broken leg. Call-signs came in as the squad-leaders took up position.

"Right." She raised her M-35 and fired a burst into the air, a short sharp *braaap* of sound.

Voices rose; a few at first, enquiring. Then a chorus of screams. Martins sighed and signaled; a flare popped into being high overhead, bathing the village in actinic blue-white light. That was for the benefit of the locals, to let them see the armed soldiers surrounding them.

"Out, out, everybody *out*!"

That and slamming on doors with rifle-butts was enough to get them moving. Martin's mouth twisted with distaste. *Robbing peasants wasn't what I joined up for either.* There had been altogether too much of that, back in San Gabriel, after the supply lines back to the US broke down.

Although when it came down to a choice between stealing and starving, there wasn't much of a dispute.

The noise died down to a resentful babbling as the two hundred or so of the little hamlet's people crowded into the dirt square before the ramshackle church. Very ramshackle; the roof had fallen in, and goats were wandering through the nave. That was a slightly jarring note; mostly the people in this part of the world took churches seriously. And it wasn't one of the areas where everyone had been converted by the Baptists back in the '90s, either.

Jenkins trotted up, flipping up the faceshield of his helmet. There was a slight frown on his basalt face.

"Not a single goddam gun, El-Tee."

She raised a brow, then remembered to raise her visor in turn. A village without a few AKs was even more unusual than one that let its church fall down.

"Not just rifles—no shotguns, no pistols, *nothing*."

Something coiled beneath her breastbone. They might have hidey-holes for the hardware that would defeat the sonic and microray sensors in the Americans' helmets, even the scanner set Sparky was packing, but they wouldn't have buried every personal gat and hunting shotgun. In fact, since they hadn't known the soldiers were coming, they shouldn't have hidden anything. You keep a gun for emergencies, and a gun buried ten feet deep is a little hard to get to in a hurry.

She looked at the peasants. Better fed than most she'd seen over the past half-decade, and almost plump compared to what had been coming down recently, with the final collapse of the world economy.

"If the indigs can't defend themselves, bandits should have been all over them like ugly on an ape," she said meditatively.

"Right," Jenkins said. Which meant that the locals—or somebody—*had* been defending this area.

The locals were murmuring louder, some of them trying to sneak off. She was getting hard stares, and a few spat on the ground. That was wrong too. Far too self-confident . . .

Well, I can fix that, she thought, keying her helmet.

"Front and center," she whispered.

It took a while for the sound to register over the frightened, resentful voices. When it did it was more of a sensation, a trembling felt through the feet and shins. A few screams of *earthquake!* died away; the ground was shaking, but not in quite that way. Harsh blue-white light shone from the jungle, drawing their eyes. Trees shivered at their tops, then whipped about violently and fell with a squealing, rending crackle. What shouldered the forest giants aside like stems of grass was huge even in relation to the trees. The steel-squeal of its four treads grated like fingernails on a blackboard, crushing a path of pulp stamped harder than rock behind it. The snouts of weapons and antennas bristled . . .

Now the villagers were silent. Martins walked up to the huge machine and swung aboard as it slowed, climbing the rungs set into the hull until she stood at its apex. When it halted, she removed her helmet.

When she spoke, her voice boomed out like the call of a god:

"BRING ME THE *JEFE* OF THIS VILLAGE!"

Best to strike while the iron was hot. Eyes stared at her, wide with terror. A whisper ran across the sea of faces; *the mountain that walks.*

"I don't like it."

Martins also didn't like the way McNaught was punishing the tequila they'd liberated; the bottle wavered as he set it down on the rough plank table beneath them. Liquor splashed onto the boards, sharp-smelling in the tropical night. Big gaudy moths fluttered around the sticklight she'd planted in the ceiling, taking no harm from its cold glow. A few bugs crawled over the remnants of their meal; she loosened the tabs of her armor, feeling it push at her shrunken and now too-full stomach.

He'd always been a good officer, but the news from the States was hitting him hard. Hitting them all, but McNaught had family, a wife and three children, in New Jersey. The broadcasts of the bread riots—more like battles—had been bad, and one blurred shot of flames from horizon to horizon before the 'casts cut off altogether.

"Plenty of supplies," he said carelessly. Sweat trickled down his face and stained the t-shirt under his arms, although the upland night wasn't all that hot. "More than we can carry."

"It's the indigs," Martins said, searching for words. "They're ... not as scared as they should be. Or maybe not as scared of *us*. The Mark III sure terrifies the shit out of them."

McNaught shrugged. "It usually does; whatever works."

Martins nodded. "Sir." Somebody had to be boss, and her misgivings were formless. "We'd better scout the basin ahead; according to the maps there's a fair-sized town there, San Pablo de Cacaxtla. We won't get much fuel here, but there should be some there even if the town's in ruins."

McNaught shrugged again. "Do it."

Six hundred men squatted together in the circular ball-court, ringed by the empty seats, a stone loop at each end where the hard rubber ball would be driven during the sacred game. Now it served as a rallying-ground. They were young men mostly, leanly fit, their hair bound up on their heads in topknots; they wore tight uniforms of cloth spotted like the skin of jaguars. Those and the hair and the jade plugs many wore in lips or ears gave them an archaic cast, but the German-made assault rifles and rocket launchers they carried were quite modern. So was the electronic equipment hung on racks by one end of the enclosure.

One-Jaguar finished his briefing; he was a stocky-muscular man, dark and hook-nosed, still moving with the stiffness of the professional soldier he had been. He bowed with wholehearted deference as Obregon stood, and gestured to his aides to remove the maps and display-screens from the stone table.

Obregon was in ceremonial dress this time, feathered cloak, kilt, plumed headdress, pendants of jade and gold. He raised his hands, and absolute silence fell.

"Warriors of the Sun," he said. The armed men swayed forward, eyes glittering and intent. "When the mother of our people, the holy Coatlicue, was pregnant with Left-Handed Hummingbird, his four hundred brothers conspired to kill him—but Standing Tree warned him. As Seven-Deer has warned me of the approaching enemy."

In the front rank of the Jaguar Knights, Seven-Deer

looked down at the ground, conscious of the admiring eyes on him.

Obregon continued: "And Left-Handed Humming-bird—Huitzilopochtl—was born in an instant; his face painted, carrying his weapons of turquoise; he had feathers on the sole of his left foot, and his arms and thighs were striped with blue. He slew the four hundred Southern Warriors, and our people worshipped him, and he made them great."

A long rolling growl of assent. "That was in the day of the Fifth Sun. Huitzilopochtl showed us how to greet enemies—and made us great. Yet when the new invaders came from the sea, the First Speaker of the Sun People, Montezuma was weak. He didn't take up his weapons and kill them, or send them as Messengers. So the Fifth Sun was destroyed. Now the Sixth Sun has been born here; we have returned to the ways of our ancestors. While all around us is starvation and desolation, we grow strong.

"Will we follow the word of Left-Handed Hummingbird? Will we kill the invaders?"

This time the growl grew into a roar, a savage baying that echoed back from the empty seats of the auditorium.

"Before we go into battle, we must appeal for the help of the gods of our people. Seven-Deer, bring out your beloved son."

The young scout bowed and walked to the entranceway. His role was symbolic, like the cord that ran from his hand to the prisoner's neck; two priests held the bound captive's arms, their faces invisible behind their carved and plumed masks. The prisoner was a thin brown man with an acne-scarred face, naked and shivering. His eyes darted quickly around the ampitheatre, squeezed shut and then opened again, as if he was willing the scene before him to go away. He was neither old nor young, wiry in a peasant fashion, a farmer from the lowlands driven into banditry by the collapse.

"Come, my beloved son," Seven-Deer said, his face solemn. "Hear the messages you must take to the land beyond the sun. Be happy! You will dwell as a hummingbird of paradise; you will not go down to Mictlan, or be destroyed in the Ninth Hell." He bent to whisper in the man's ear.

Evidently the lowlander spoke a few words of Nahuatl, or he recognized the stone block for what it was, because he began to scream as the Feathered Snake priests cut his bonds and stretched him out over it on his back. That too was part of the rite.

Obregon—*Lord of the Mountain, First Speaker of the Sun People,* he reminded himself—stepped up and drew the broad-bladed obsidian knife from his belt. There had been enough practice that he no longer feared the embarrassing hacking and haggling of the first few times. His original academic specialty had been geophysics, not anatomy, but the sudden stab down into the taut chest was precise as a surgeon's. There was a crisp popping sound as the knife sliced home, its edges of volcanic glass sharper than any steel. Ignoring the bulging eyes of the sacrifice, he plunged his hand into the chest cavity, past the fluttering pressure of the lungs, and gripped the heart. It beat one last time in his hands like a slippery wet balloon, then stilled as he slashed it free of the arteries.

Blood fountained, smelling of iron and copper and salt, droplets warm and thick on his lips. He raised the heart to the Sun, and felt the pure clean ecstasy of the moment sweep over him. The Jaguar Knights gave a quick deep shout as he wheeled to face them, red-spattered and gripping heart in one hand, knife in the other.

"We have fed the Sun!" he proclaimed. "And so

shall you, Our Lord's knights, be fed." The priests were already taking the body away, to be drained and butchered. "Our Lord Smoking Mirror shall fill you with His strength, and you will destroy the enemy— take many prisoners for the altar. Victory!"

The Knights cried him hail.

"Looks good," Martins murmured under her breath.

The jungle thinned out around them as the UATVs struggled up the switchback road. Grassy glades and forests of pinion pine and oak replaced the denser lowland growth; the temperature dropped, down to something that was comfortable even in body armor. After years in the steambath lowland heat, it was almost indecently comfortable. The air carried scents of resin and cool damp soil and grass; for a moment she was back in the Sangre Del Christo, longing like a lump of scar-tissue beneath her breastbone. Then she caught a rotten-egg tang underneath it.

"Air analysis," she keyed, on the Mark III's frequency.

The tank was back downslope with McNaught and the other half of the Company, but it should be able to tell her something through the remote sensors she carried.

"Variations from standard: excess concentrations of sulphur, sulphur dioxide, dilute sulfuric acid compounds, ozone," the Bolo said. "Seismic data indicate instabilities." A pause. "My geophysical data list no active vulcanism in this area."

Which means it's as out of date as the street maps, Martins thought.

She leaned a hand against the rollbar of the UATV, the long barrel of the autocannon on its pintle mount swaying about her, tasting the dust and sunlight, eyes squinting against it. The landscape looked empty but not uninhabited; the grass had been grazed, and there was animal dung by the side of the road—goat and cattle, from the look of it. It was a different world from the ghost-grey limestone scrub of San Gabriel, or the thick moist jungles they'd been passing through since. Telltales in her faceplate gave a running scan of the rocky hillsides. No indications of metal concentrations, no suspicious E-spectrum radiation. She cracked one of the seals of her body armor to let in the drier, cooler air.

"Our athlete's foot and crotchrot will die if we're not careful, El-Tee," Jenkins said. "Doesn't look like much else in the way of danger so far."

Martins nodded. "Objective A deserted," she broadcast.

That was a small town near the top of the pass; a couple of thousand people once, maybe more in shack-tenements at the edges that had long since slumped into weed-grown heaps. There was the wreckage of an old colonial Baroque church and town hall near the center, and both might have been impressive once. The snags of a couple of modest steel or concrete structures stood nearby. The buildings looked positively crushed, as if toppled by earthquake, but they had also been quite comprehensively looted. Stacks of girders and re-bar hammered free from the concrete stood in orderly piles; there wasn't much rust on cut ends and joints, which meant the work had been going on until the last few weeks. Rubble had been shoveled back out of the main street.

"Halt," she said. *This is serious*. Bandits would steal food and jewelry, but this was *salvage*. That implied organization, and organization was dangerous.

"Take a look. Make it good, troopers."

She collated the reports. Everything gone, down to the window-frames. Truck and wagon tracks . . .

"You," she said. It was her private name for the Bolo; she couldn't bring herself to give it the sort of nickname Vinatelli had. "How many, how long?"

"I estimate that several thousand workers have been engaged in the salvage operation for over a year, Lieutenant Martins."

Martins' lips shaped a soundless whistle.

"You catch that, Captain?"

He grunted. "We need more data."

"Damn, that's impressive," Jenkins said.

The cut through the lava flow wasn't what he meant, though it showed considerable engineering ability. The view of the valley a thousand feet below was. The road switchbacked down forest slopes; much of the forest was new, planted. The valley floor beyond was cultivated, with an intensity she hadn't seen in a long, long time. A rolling patchwork quilt of greens and yellows and brown volcanic soil rippled with contour-plowing. She cycled the magnification of her visor and saw the crops spring out in close view; corn, wheat, sugar-cane, roots, orchards, pasture. There were people at work there, some with hand-tools or oxen, but there were tractors as well. Irrigation furrows threaded the fields, and so did power-lines.

"Damn," Martins echoed. "They've got a grid working down there."

"Geothermal plant, I think," Jenkins said. "Over there by the town."

There were several villages scattered through the valley, but the town was much larger. It lay in a semicircle around the base of the conical mountain, tiny as a map from this height. The usual *hispano* grid centered on a plaza, but very unusual otherwise. The buildings were freshly painted, and there was *new* construction off to one side, a whole new plaza ringed by public structures and some sort of monument, a stone heap fifteen meters on a side and covered in scaffolding.

"Well, we ought to be able to get fuel here, right enough," McNaught's voice said in her ear, watching through the helmet pickups. "All we want. Maybe even spare parts."

"If they'll give us what we need," Martins said slowly. They looked as if they could afford it, much more so than anyone else the Company had run across. But it was her experience that the more people had, the more ready they were to defend it. "I wish we could pay for it."

"Maybe we can," McNaught said thoughtfully. "I've been thinking . . . the computer capacity in the Beast is pretty impressive. We could rest and refit, and pay our way with its services. Hell, maybe they need some earth-moving done. And if they won't deal—"

Martins nodded. "Yessir."

We have the firepower, she thought. Using it hadn't bothered her much before; the Company was all the friends and family she had. These people looked as if they'd hit bottom and started to build their way back up, though. The thought of what the Mark III could do to that town wasn't very pleasant. She'd seen too many ruins in San Gabriel, too much wreckage on the way north.

"Well, we'd better go on down," she said. "But carefully. One gets you nine they're watching us with passive sensors; Eyeball Mark One, if nothing else."

"No bet," Jenkins said, his voice returning to its usual flat pessimism.

"Right, let's do it." She switched to the unit push. "Slow and careful, and don't start the dance unless it looks like the locals want to try us on. We fight if we have to, but we're not here to fight."

* * *

"Surely you see that precautions are reasonable," the old man said to her. "In these troubled times."

He looked to be in his seventies, but healthy; white haired and lean, dressed in immaculate white cotton and neat sandals. The "precautions" consisted of several hundred mean-looking *indios* spread out along the fields behind him, digging in with considerable efficiency and sporting quite modern weapons, along with their odd spotted cammo uniforms. The helmet scanners had detected at least one multiple hypervelocity launcher, and the Mark III thought there was an automortar or light field-piece somewhere behind.

This close the town looked even better than it had from the pass. The additions upslope, near the black slaggy-looking lava flows, looked even odder. The building beneath the scaffolding was roughly the shape of her Bolo; a memory tugged at her mind, then filtered away. There was a delegation of townsfolk with the leader, complete with little girls carrying bouquets of flowers. It made her suddenly conscious of the ragged uniforms patched with bits of this and that that her Company wore. The only parts of them that weren't covered in dust were the faceshields of their helmets, and those were kept clear by static charges.

The spruce locals also made her conscious of the twenty-odd troopers behind her in the UATVs; if the shit hit the fan the rest of the outfit and the Mark III would come in and kick butt, but it could get very hairy between times.

"Hard times, right enough, *señor*," she answered politely. Some of the crowd were murmuring, but not in Spanish. She caught something guttural and choppy, full of *tz* sounds.

"You've done very well here," Martins went on, removing her helmet. A face generally looked less threatening than a blank stretch of curved synthetic.

The old man smiled. "We seek to keep ourselves isolated from the troubles of the world," he said. "To follow our own customs."

Looking around at the rich fields and well-fed people, Martins could sympathize. The well-kept weapons argued that these folks were realistic about it, too.

"You've also got a lot of modern equipment," she said. "Not just weapons either, I'd guess."

The *jefe* of the valley spread his hands. "I went from here to the university, many years ago," he said. "There I had some success, and returned much of what I earned to better the lives of my people here. When the troubles came, 1 foresaw that they would be long and fierce; I and my friends made preparations. Luckily, the eruption sealed the main pass into the valley of Cacaxtla when the government was no longer able to reopen it, so we were spared the worst of the collapse. But come, what can we do for you?"

That's a switch. "We're travelling north, home," she said. "We need fuel—anything will do, whatever your vehicles are running on—"

"Cane spirit," the local said helpfully.

"—that'll do fine. Some food. We have spare medical supplies, and our troops include a lot of specialists; in electronic repairs, for example."

Actually the self-repair fabricators of the Mark III were their main resource in that field, but no need to reveal everything.

"You are welcome," the *jefe* said. "The more so as it is wise to—how do you say in English—speed the parting guest." He looked behind the brace of UATVs. "I notice that not all your troops are here, señora, or the large tank."

Large tank, Martins thought. *Nobody really believes in that mother until they see it.*

She inclined her head politely. "Surely you see that

precautions are reasonable," she said. "In these troubled times."

The *jefe*'s laugh was full and unforced. "I am glad that we understand each other, *teniente* Martins. If you will follow me . . ."

Fearless, he stepped into her UATV; the children threw their bouquets into it, or hung necklaces of flowers around her neck and those of the other troopers. Martins sneezed and looked around. The *jefe* noted her interest.

"As you say, a geothermal unit," he said, pointing out a low blocky building. "The waste water is still hot enough for domestic use, and also for fishponds and other uses. Very simple. We have a few machine-shops, as you see, and small workshops to make what household goods we need."

There were actual open shops along the streets, selling clothing and leather goods, tools and food—something she hadn't seen for years. And people selling *flowers*. That shook her a bit, that anyone could still devote time and energy to a luxury like that.

"We issue our own money, as a convenience for exchange; but everyone contributes to things of public worth," he went on. "As our guests, your needs will be met from the public treasury; and first, since you have travelled far, baths and refreshment. Then you must join us for dinner; tomorrow, we will see to the fuel and travelling supplies you need."

Martins and Jenkins looked at each other and the spacious, airy house the Americans had been assigned.

"Is it just my sour disposition, Tops," she said meditatively, "or does what looks too good to be true—"

"—probably too good to be true, El-Tee," the sergeant said.

"See to it."

"All right. Listen up, shitheels! Nobody gets out of reach of his weapon. Nobody gets out of sight of his squad—washing, crapping, I don't care what. Nobody takes more than one drink; and you keep it in your pants, I don't care what the local señoritas say, understand me? Michaels, Wong, you're first guard on the vehicles. Smith, McAllister, Sanchez, overwatch from the roof. Move it!"

"Omigod," Jenkins muttered. "*Beer*. Real, actual, honest-to-God-not-pulque-piss *beer*."

The *jefe*—he'd answered to Manuel Obregon, but the locals called him by something unpronounceable—smiled and nodded and took a swallow from his own earthenware pitcher. There were more smiles and nods from all around, from the tables set out across the plaza. Much of the town's population seemed to be taking this chance for a *fiesta*. They were certainly dressed for one, although the clothes were like nothing she'd seen in the back-country, and very fancy. The food was good enough that she'd had to let out the catches of her armor—nobody had objected to the troopers wearing their kit, or seemed to notice their M-35's and grenade launchers—roast pork, salads, hot vegetable stews, spicy concoctions of meats and tomatoes and chilies.

Obregon sat at their table, and quietly took a sampling of everything they were offered, tasting before they did. Martins appreciated the gesture, although not enough to take more than a mug or two of the beer; Jenkins' eagle eye and the corporals' made sure nobody else did either. It was intoxicating enough just to feel *clean*, and have a decent meal under her belt.

"I notice you don't seem to have a church," she said.

Obregon smiled expansively. "The Church always sat lightly on the people here," he said. "When the *campesions* prayed to the Virgin, they called her Tonantzin, the Moon. Always I hated what the foreigners—the

Spaniards—had done here. Since my people made me their leader, I have spoken to them of the old ways, the ancient ways of our ancestors; what we always new, and what I learned of the truth in the university in my youth, things which the *Ladinos* and their priests tried to suppress."

Can't argue with success, Martins thought.

The helmet beside her on the table cheeped. She took another mouthful of the coffee, thick with fresh cream, and slid it on.

"Lieutenant Martins," the Mark III's voice said.

"What *now*?" she snapped. *Damn, I'm tired.* It had been a long day, and the soak in hot water seemed to be turning her muscles to butter even hours later.

"Please extend the sensor wand to the liquids consumed."

Nothing showed on Martins' face; except perhaps a too-careful blankness, as she unclipped the hand-sized probe and dipped it into the beer.

"Alkaloids," the computer-voice said calmly. "Sufficient to cause unconsciousness."

"But the *jefe*—"

"Partial immunity through sustained ingestion," it said. "Have you any instructions, Lieutenant Martins?"

Bethany Martins tried to shout and pull the knife sheathed across the small of her back in the same instant. Somewhere a single shot cracked; she was vaguely conscious of Jenkins toppling over backwards, buried under a heap of locals. Her tongue was thick in her head, and hands gripped her. Obregon stood watching, steadying himself with one hand against the table, his eyes steady.

"Basser sumbitch," Martins slurred. *"Help—"*

The helmet came off her head, with a wrench that flopped her neck backward. Blackness.

*   *   *

A confused babble came through the pickups. Captain McNaught stiffened in the strait confines of the Mark III's fighting compartment. His leg knocked against a projecting surface in a blaze of pain.

"Get through, get me through!"

"None of the scouting party are responding, Captain," the tank said in its incongruous sex-kitten voice.

The pickups from the UATVs showed bustling activity, and a few bodies in American uniform being carried by unconscious or dead—until thick tarpaulins were thrown over the war-cars. The helmets showed similar blackness; IR and sonic gave the inside of a steel box and nothing more. Until one was taken out.

"Greetings, Captain," Manuel Obregon's voice said.

His face loomed large in the screen, then receded as the helmet was set on a surface and the local chieftain sank back in a chair. The voice was slurred, but with tongue-numbness, not alcohol, and his black eyes were level and expressionless as a snake's.

"Release my troops and I won't kill anyone but you," McNaught said, his voice like millstones. "Harm them, and we'll blow that shitheap town of yours down around your lying head."

Obregon spread hands. "A regrettable ruse of war," he said. "Come now, *mi capitan*. I have more than a third of your personnel and equipment, and your second-in-command. It is only logical, if distressing from your point of view, that you listen to my terms. I cannot in all conscience allow a large armed body—which has already plundered and killed—to operate in the vicinity of my people."

"I repeat; release them immediately. You have no conception of our resources."

"On the contrary," Obregon said, his voice hard and flat. "You have forty men, light weapons, and one large tank—which must be short of fuel. Abandon the vehicles and the tank, taking only your hand weapons, and you will be allowed to leave, with your advance party. For every hour you refuse, one of the prisoners will die. And, *Capitan*—do nothing rash. This valley is protected by forces which are stronger than anything you can imagine."

Flat sincerity rang in the old man's voice.

Something seemed to have crawled into Martins' mouth and died. She tried to sit up and stopped, wincing at the pain, then doggedly continued. She was lying in a row of bodies, some of them groaning and stirring. They were all wearing white cotton tunics; a quick check showed nothing else underneath. The room was bare and rectangular, with narrow window-slits along one wall and a barred grillwork of iron at the other end, the holes barely large enough to pass a human hand and arm. Fighting weakness and a pain that made her sweat, she staggered erect and groped along one wall to the end. Beyond the grillwork was a plain ready room, with a bench and nothing else except a barred window and steel-sheet door.

And a guard in the jaguar-spot local uniform, with an assault rifle across his knees. He gave her a single glance and turned his eyes back to the wall, motionless.

Oh, this is not good. Not good at all, *Bethany,* Martins thought to herself.

More groans came from her troopers where they lay like fish on a slab—an unpleasant thought she tried to shed. Jenkins was sitting with his head in his hands.

"Goddam native beer," he said, in a painful attempt at humor.

"Check 'em, Tops," she said.

A minute later: "Wong's missing."

Martins chewed a dry tongue to moisten her mouth, striding back to the grillwork and trying to rattle it.

"I demand to speak to your leader," she said in a calm voice, pitched to command. "Where is Private Wong?"

The guard turned, moving very quickly. She was just quick enough herself to get her hand mostly out of the way of the fiber-matrix butt of the man's weapon, and take a step back sucking at her skinned knuckles.

Jenkins unhunched his shoulders as she turned. "What's the word, El-Tee?"

"For now, we wait until the Captain and the Beast get here," she said quietly. "We—"

A rising swell of noise from outside interrupted her, muffled by the high slit windows. Then it cut off, replaced by chanting. One commanding voice rose above the rest. Then a scream; words at first, in English, followed by a high thin wailing that trailed off into a blubbering *don't . . . don't . . .* and another frenzied shriek.

Jenkins bent and cupped his hands. Martins set a foot in the stirrup and steadied herself against the wall as he straightened, then raised his hands overhead until her compact hundred-and-twenty pounds was standing on his palms. That put the bars on the slit windows just within reach. Grunting and sweating with the effort and the residual pain of the drug, she pulled herself up.

Brightness made her blink. They were on one side of Cacaxtla's new square, the one with the odd-looking building. Her mind clicked, making a new association; the one with the unfinished stepped pyramid. Because it was unfinished, she could see quite clearly what went on on the flat platform atop it, over the heads of the crowd that filled the plaza below and the gaudily-costumed priests on the steps. When she realized what was happening, she wished with all her heart that she could not. A dry retch sent her tumbling toward the floor; Jenkins' huge hands caught her with surprising gentleness.

"What's going on, Lieutenant?" he said—the formal title a sign of *real* worry.

"Wong," she said. "They've got him on the top of that pyramid thing. They're—" She swallowed, despite years of experience in what human beings could do to each other. "They're skinning him."

"Enemy in blocking positions two thousand meters to our front," the tank said. "Shall I open fire?"

Captain McNaught felt cold sweat leaking out from his armpits. The narrow switchback up to the pass had been bad enough, but the passage through the recent lavaflow was worse, barely any clearance at all on either side of the Mark III. Every once and a while it scraped the cutting, and sent showers of pumice rock bouncing downslope toward the UATVs.

"Not yet, we'll wait until we can do 'em all at once," he said, and switched to the unit push. "Take up covering positions."

Damn, damn. It was his fault. He'd let things slide, gotten apathetic—and the wound was no excuse. There *were* no excuses. The Company was his.

Obregon's voice came though. "This is your last warning," he said.

"Fuck you."

If they thought an avalanche would stop the Mark III, they could think again. Or an antitank rocket. They might damage one of the treads, but that was a worst-case scenario; there was no precipice they might hope to sweep the tank off, not here.

"Follow when I've cleared the way," he went on to the waiting troopers. Some of the guilt left him. He might be behind a foot of durachrome alloy, but he was leading from the *front*, by God.

The tank trembled. "Seismic activity," it said helpfully. "Instructions?"

"Keep going! Bull through. We're going to rescue Martins and the others *at all costs*. D'you understand, you heap of tin?"

"Acknowledged." Rock ground by, pitted and dull, full of the craters left by gas-bubbles as it hardened. "Anomalous heat source to our left."

There was no view, but the rumbling underfoot grew louder. "What the hell are they doing?"

"Insufficient data," the tank said. "Estimated time to firing position—"

Obregon's voice: "You are in the hands of Xotl-Ollin," he said regretfully. "Feel his anger while I dance for Xipe Totec. Better if this had been a Flower War, but the god's will be done."

The indig chief had clearly gone nuts. The problem was that the world seemed to have done so too. The restraints clamped tighter around McNaught as the Mark III shook. Rocks and boulders and ash cataracted down around it, muffled through the armor but thunder-loud in the pickups until the guardian AI turned it down. Something went off with a rumbling *boom*, loud enough for the noise alone to make the tank vibrate slightly.

"What was that, what was that?" McNaught shouted.

"No weapon within known parameters," the Mark III said. "Searching."

At first McNaught thought that the wall of liquid was water, or perhaps thick mud. It wasn't until he saw patches of dried scrub bursting into flame as it touched them that he recognized it. That was when he screamed.

It was not entirely the lava that made him bellow and hammer with his hands at the screens. The one slaved to Martins' helmet was showing a visual; it was showing Obregon. He was dancing, and he was covered in skin—Trooper Wong's skin, skillfully flayed off in one piece and then sewn on to the old man like an old-fashioned set of long-johns. Hands and feet flopped empty as he shuffled and twirled, his eyes staring through holes in the sagging mask.

The molten stone swept over the Mark III in a cresting wave.

The guard proved unbribable, to anything from promises of gold to offers of more personal services; and he never came within arm's reach of the grillwork.

The attendant who brought them water did. Martins' eyes met her NCO's; from the man's frightened scurry, they both did an identical, instant evaluation of his worth as a hostage. He was old, older than Obregon and withered with it, nearly toothless.

Somewhere between nada and fucking zip, Martins decided.

"*Aqua*," he said.

Martins crouched to take the canteens through the narrow slot near the floor.

"*Gracias*," she whispered back.

That seemed to make the man hesitate; he glanced over his shoulder, but the guard was staring out the window at the pyramid. The screaming had stopped long ago, but the chanting and drumming went on.

"It is a sin against God," the servant whispered fearfully. "They worship demons, demons! It is lies, but the people were afraid—are afraid, even those who don't believe in Obregon's lies."

"Afraid of what?" Martins whispered back, making the slow drag of the canteens on the rock floor cover the sound. "His gunmen?"

"The Jaguar Knights? No, no—they fear his calling the burning rock from the mountains, as he has done. As he did to cut us off from the outside world."

Oh, great, one sympathizer and he's another loony, Martins thought.

The man went on: "It is lies, I say. I saw the machines he brought, many years ago—machines he buries all about the valley. He says they are to foretell earthquakes, but he lies; he *makes* the earth shake and the lava come! It is machines, not his false gods!"

The guard shouted in the local language, and the servant cringed and scurried out.

"What'd he say?" Jenkins asked.

"We're in the hands of the Great and Powerful Oz, Tops," Martins said with a bitter twist of the mouth. "But I don't think this one's a good guy—and this sure isn't Kansas, anyway."

"No shit."

This is where we're supposed to make a rush, Martins thought. *If this were movieland. One of us would get a gun . . .*

She'd seen an old, old vid about that once—some snotnose got a vid hero into the real world, and the stupid bastard got himself killed, or nearly.

In reality, a dozen unarmed soldiers with automatic weapons pointed at them were simply potential hamburger. The door in the grillwork was too narrow for more than one person to squeeze through at a time, and there were grenade launchers stuck through the high slit windows on either side of the prison chamber.

Jenkins muttered under his breath: "We could crap in our hands and throw it at them."

"Can it, Tops. Wait for the Captain. I got us into this, no reason more should get shorted than have to."

Although it was taking an oddly long time for the Mark III to make it. The ground had trembled after Wong . . . died . . . and then nothing, for hours.

She walked out from the huddle of prisoners. Hands pulled her through the slit door and clanged it behind her, pulled off the tunic and left her nothing but a loincloth. Others bound her hands behind her back and led her out.

The sun was blinding; no less so was the fresh paint on the pyramid, the feathers and jade and gold and bright cloth on the priests. She ignored them, walking with her eyes fixed on the horizon and the smoking volcano above the town. Her heart seemed to beat independently of herself.

Crazy bastard, she thought, as she trod the first step. The stone was warm and gritty under her feet; twenty steps up it started to be sticky. She could smell the blood already, beginning to rot under the bright sun, and hear the flies buzz. Sheets and puddles of it lay around the improvised altar; she supposed they'd build something more imposing when the pyramid was finished, but the block of limestone would do for now.

At the top, Obregon waited. They'd washed the blood off him—most of it—when he shed Wong's skin.

Like a snake, she thought, light-headed.

"Lord of the Mountain," she said in a clear, carrying voice. He frowned, but the chanting faded a little—as it would not have for screams. "The Mountain that Walks will come for me!"

Obregon gave a curt sign, and the drums roared loud enough to drown any other words. Another, and the priests cut her bonds and threw her spread-eagled back across the altar, one on each limb pulling until her skin creaked. Her skin ... at least they didn't have the flaying knives out.

"You are brave," the old man said as he stepped up to her, drawing the broad obsidian knife. "But your tank is buried under a hundred feet of lava, and the valley sealed once more." The plumes nodded over his head, and his long silver hair was streaked and clotted with crusty brown. "Tell the Sun—"

"That you're a fucking lunatic," Martins rasped, bending her head up painfully to look at him; the sun was in the west, and she could just see Venus rising bright over the jagged rim of the valley. "Why? Why the lies?"

Obregon replied in English, slowly raising the knife. "My people needed more than tools and medicines. More even than a butterfly-effect machine that could control venting. They needed to *believe* in their guardian." A whisper: "So did I."

The knife touched the skin under left breast and then rose to its apogee.

Braaap.

The ultravelocity impact that smashed Obregon's hand cauterized the wound. It twirled him in place like a top, until his head sprayed away from the next round.

One of the priests released her left foot and snatched for his own knife. Martins pivoted on the fulcrum of her hips and kicked the other at her feet in the face. Bone crumpled under the ball of her foot. Something smashed the man with the knife out into the shadows of gathering night. One hand slacked on her wrist; she wrenched it free with a brief economical twist and flipped erect, slamming the heel of her free hand up under the last priest's nose. He dropped to the blood-slick stone deck, his nasal bone driven back into his brain.

Martins stood and walked to the head of the steep stairway down the pyramid, the only living thing on its summit. Below her the crowd screamed and milled, and behind them . . .

Mountain that Walks. It looked it, now, with the thick crust of lava that covered it from top deck to the treadguards. Cooling and solidifying, smoking, whirled and dripping like hot wax. A few antennae poked through, and the muzzles of the infinite repeaters.

Two treads were gone, and the machine kept overcorrecting for their loss.

"Light," she whispered.

Actinic glare burst out from the Bolo, making it a hulking black shape that ground forward and shook the earth. The same searchlight bathed her in radiance; she couldn't see much detail of the square below, but she saw enough to know that townsmen and Jaguar Knights alike had fallen on their faces.

Bethany Martins raised both hands, fists clenched, her body spattered with blood and bone and brains. She remembered treachery, and Wong screaming. One word, and everyone in ten miles' space would die.

She remembered famine and bandits, and bodies in ditches gnawed by rats or their own kinfolk.

"They do need a guardian they can believe in," she muttered to herself. "A sane one." Whether she was still entirely sane was another matter, but she had more to think of.

A statue stood at the base of the stairs, squat and hideous. Her right fist stabbed at it, and stone fragments flew across the square, trailing sparks. It was important to know when to stop. The rest of the Company wouldn't take much talking around—and it was best to get things straight with the locals right from the beginning. Hit 'em hard and let 'em up easy, as her father had always said.

"Amplify."

"YOU HAVE FOLLOWED FALSE GODS," her voice bellowed out, relayed at an intensity enough to stun. "BUT THERE WILL BE MERCY."

The people of Cacaxtla shuddered and pressed their heads to the ground, and knew that a god— a goddess—stronger than the Lord of the Mountain had come.

He had brought fire from the stone. She had made stone walk.

SIR KENDRICK'S LADY

S. N. Lewitt

Like they were making us do this really stupid thing. I mean, sure our parents and their parents and all that believed in all that garbage, but I sure didn't buy into it. They could have all the honor and self-sacrifice and sheep they wanted. Not for me. No way.

I'm a modern girl and I can't wait until the day I can leave Camelot. Make tracks. Get gone. This isn't even a backwater. Nothing gets here, nothing at all. And the local restrictions. You'd think we were living in some time before there was even spaceflight or something. Like we didn't have Dover Port twelve klicks away, even if it is nearly a whole day trip by horsecart. Who are they trying to kid? A horsecart. Get real.

No one my age wants to stick around here. At least not any of my friends. Elizabeth and Susannah have already got their appointments to take their Merchant

Spacer's Exams. I'm a year younger so I still have to wait until I turn eighteen. As if that will change anything.

Robert Redson already got out and he's the same age as me. I don't know how he did it, exactly, and I miss him like crazy. Not that we were an item. Not even possible.

But Robbie went down to the port one day and never came back. He never wrote to me or told me what happened, but I know how much he hated this place and how nice Mr. Penney was to him. Said that a smart boy like Robbie wouldn't have any trouble finding a spacer berth and a new life in the big universe waiting out there. How Robbie and I used to love to go down to the Port together and dream of the day when we would leave everything about Camelot behind.

Our parents would kill us if they knew how often we go down there to watch the merchant ships come in. Luckily, Mr. Penney thinks it's a good thing for us to know a little more about the civilized universe, and he always invites us in on his shift. Mr. Penney is about the only grownup I think remembers what it's like to be young.

Anyway, if my folks think I'm sticking around after my majority, they're in for one big surprise. So it really bothers me that they're making me do this.

"But all the girls your age on the whole planet are invited," my mother said.

Yeah, right. I know. Like the whole planet is more than twelve villages, three towns and a spread of farms. At least I don't live on a farm. That would be totally the worst! My father is the town silversmith and my mother draws up his designs.

We're pretty well off, really. We have a two-story house with a slate roof and a stone floor and even a rug from somewhere off world on the dining room table. I have eight dresses, five everyday, two for Sundays and a blue velvet one for holidays with embroidered roses at the neck and sleeves. None of the other girls in my class have anything like my clothes, or my house, or anything else.

"I don't know what you've got to complain about," Elizabeth said when we were making our plans to take the Merchant test. "It isn't like you have to muck out the chicken house every day, or eat eggs and bread and cabbage every single day."

Bess makes too big a deal of my family. I think because she was hot on my brother Andrew and admitted that she went too far with him. And then he went off and got betrothed to Annie Carpenter. But I think Bess just went after Andrew because she wanted to live in our nice house and have all the silver plates and pretty clothes she wanted. She never liked Andrew at all, not really. She just got to be friends with me because she wanted to hang around with Andrew. But at least it got me in a position to suggest that she take the Merchant Spacer test and get offworld (and away from my brother).

So the call came around for this competition for the Queen of Love and Beauty and all young virgins (I hate how we're always called virgins, and even if I am it isn't anyone's business, thank you very much) under the age of twenty were welcome to the tournament and to sit on the dais and everything.

It's really stupid. I wouldn't do it. I mean, who wants to be a Queen of Love and Beauty, like it means anything anyway. Just another way for our parents to make us buy into this whole Camelot fantasy they've tried to create.

I really wouldn't do it at all. Except Mother said I could have a new dress made, anything I wanted. And they said Sir Kendrick would be there, and he would be the one to chose the Queen of Love and Beauty.

Now, you think that a bunch of pastoral dorks like the idiots who settled Camelot about a hundred years ago wouldn't have any psychotronics. And in general we don't. But Sir Kendrick is, well, Sir Kendrick. A Mark XXIV Bolo who is all that stands between the fantasy universe of Camelot and the whole real live high-tech universe out there.

I'd never seen Sir Kendrick. I've only heard stories. But I wanted to see the one honest piece of tech in the whole let's pretend fairy tale. Seeing Sir Kendrick alone was enough inducement.

And, of course, there was the dress.

I read the invitation while sitting in the draper's shop. There were at least five girls ahead of me, all with their mothers and sisters, giggling and gossiping with each other. Bunch of Camelot sell-outs, willing to play all the little Camelot games in hopes of marrying well or maybe bringing more money into the family. I thought they were all creeps.

Also, of the five only one could really be counted pretty. Joan Talmadge has a very big nose and no chin, Mary Featherdown is just plain fat and Kathryn Hollis has bad skin. Susan Talmadge isn't too bad to look at, only she has no personality at all. Nope, no competition here. I could safely ignore the losers and read the information instead.

The invitation had been calligraphed by Sister Bridget, who had spent four years despairing of my handwriting. And it had been illuminated in the borders with unicorns and gold crowns and silver spurs, I suppose in honor of our only knight.

Of All the Virgins Young and Faire, the invitation started. I hated when they played around with spelling. Mr. Penney said Camelot was the only Trading Port in the whole sector that has free spelling.

Of All the Virgins Young and Faire, the gentlemen defenders of Camelot would have the honour of your presence at a tourney on the Fifteenth Day of Maye, in the hope of selecting one of your Glorious Company to be our Queen of Love and Beauty, to Reigne over our poor hearts and effort and to inspire us to greater valour in your gentle eyes.

I read it over twice. All that gross overstatement. And what was a Queen of Love and Beauty supposed to do, anyway? Inspire who to greater valor? There was only one gentleman defender of Camelot and he was rather impervious to feminine charm, I should think.

The rest were just boys with pretensions, or those who couldn't make the rating on the Merchant test and had to do something or go crazy. So they play their little defense games, knowing full well that Sir Kendrick is there to back them up. If and when they deserve backing up, which I suspect is near never.

"Ooooh, that yellow is so pretty," Susan Talmadge said. "Don't you think so, Abigail?"

Hearing my name, I snapped around. Susan Talmadge is a total idiot. I hate yellow. And the fabric she had spread between her hands was sickly and uneven, like a healing bruise.

"I don't know, Susan," I said, trying to be nice to her even if she didn't deserve it. "I think you'd look better in the pink, I really do."

And I was being honest, too, not trying to cut down the competition. I mean, not that they were any competition. But I didn't want to be on a dias and be the only one there who looked even just a little decent.

"But Mary is getting the pink," Susan protested feebly.

"Then why not get one of the prints?" I suggested. "One of those summery flower things with lots of pink in it? And it could have yellow, too, if you really want. But it'll look much better."

"Thank you." Susan seemed so cheered up at the

thought, as if she couldn't figure out to ask for something that was right in front of her face.

"What color are you getting, Abigail?" Kathryn asked.

"Oh, I haven't decided yet," I replied. This time I was lying though. I had seen exactly the fabric I wanted and I wasn't about to tell Kathryn. "What about you?"

"Oh, I think the eyelet," she said. "White over pink. That's so feminine."

They went on talking about patterns and stuff, and my mother was in it as much as the rest of them, but I took out my school slate and began my homework. Not that I care all that much about homework, but it's better than talking to that bunch.

I ignored them while they made their selections and walked out. Honest, I'd done my best, and I couldn't be bothered. Then I showed my mother the burgundy brocade that I had in mind for myself.

"It's too old for this kind of thing," my mother said. "It should be some pastel, or white. You're a young girl, you should look like one."

I groaned. "But I look ugly in those washed out colors. And you know I look great in red. Especially burgundy. If you want, we can do an underdress of white, maybe with some silver. That virginal enough for you?"

My mother couldn't argue the facts. I do look great in jewel colors and I look something like a corpse in anything else. Besides which, it's her fault, I have her coloring and she knows it. I've never seen her wear some baby blue or other appropriate color. Not with that blue white skin and black hair.

I wish I didn't have black hair, that's another thing I don't like. I wish I was a redhead like Joan Talmadge, because then when I got into a temper everyone would just blame it on my hair and leave it be. Now when I get angry I get a rep for being stubborn and bad tempered. When I get off planet, the very first thing I'm going to do is dye my hair bright red.

So I ended up with the red brocade, and a pretty white chiffon with silver stripes, and wide silver ribbon with a pattern of red roses on it. Mother was happily planning the style while we walked the block and a half home.

I was so worn out with playing the nice girl that I was ready to quit the whole farce there and then. Maybe if I told my parents what I really planned to do they'd let me off on all the Camelot games. Next year . . .

But my folks are real Camelot people. We don't have a single electronic in the house, let alone anything post-prehistoric. They'd probably ground me just for having gone over to the Port those few times. I couldn't tell them about going offworld. They wouldn't understand. They never wanted to go anywhere themselves. They're happy just because they can afford this house and have a nice shop and Andrew's getting married, all this stuff that isn't important. They don't understand important things. But what could I expect? They are my parents, after all.

The next few days all the girls at school talked about nothing but the tourney, or, more precisely, about their new dresses for said event. I was half-dead of boredom when Margaret Rose and Peter Smith and Will Davidson invited me to skip school and go along to the Port with them. Will's father was sending him to drop off a shipment of wool and pick up a package that included cloth and genetech equipment for the flock.

It was a beautiful spring day. None of the kids whose parents had planting to do were in school. And some of the sheep families, like Will's, had the kids all working on shearing and lambing and spring sheep chores. Only us town kids who weren't yet apprenticed in trade had time to sit and listen to off-world chemistry and math. So it was no contest. I didn't even think, just threw my pack with the slate and my lunch in the back of the cart and heaved myself in after it.

At least we're not so primitive that the roads are rotten. We passed a road crew working with new 'tronics and good grade plasfalt, repairing the cracks of winter. There was a bit of traffic as we drove. Three other carts at least were filled with fluffy wool bags, and the draper's boy had only one package wrapped in his lap, but that was good embroidered cutwork that he could trade for bolts and bolts of offworld cloths.

Mother sometimes designed cutwork and embroidery pieces when we've got enough silver to do. Technically I'm not apprenticed, but actually she's been teaching me design since I can remember. I'd done a few embroidery and lace patterns in the past year that Mother sold to pieceworkers, and I knew that she had been very excited about my work. She said that when I finished school I would only have to spend a few months to finish the bits of apprenticeship that the guild required, since I had never worked in stained glass or fine jewelry. But that wouldn't take long and Mother nearly promised that I'd make journeyman by the time I was eighteen.

In fact, there were moments when I was being ultra practical and I thought about waiting to finish my apprenticeship until I left for deep space. Even people on modern planets need design. Do we ever know that here on Camelot. That's one reason why we can sell so much, even if it is expensive. Our goods all look good. I figured with the right background I would never have to worry about work offworld. Of course, I only think that way when I'm in a very practical mood and things have been going well with Mother and Dad and I think I could maybe stick it out a couple more months. Most of the time I think I'd rather get away first and figure out what else I'm doing with my life later.

Even though there's always traffic in the spring, there seemed to be more than I remembered from earlier years. When I was ten or so we could drive down nearly to Ashbury before we saw another cart. Now there was practically a solid line of drovers and peddlers making their way to trade with the offworlders.

Maybe it's just that we got populated. That's what they say at school. Life on Camelot is good and we've grown rapidly. But I'd also bet that people want more trade and have more and we're working on becoming part of the bigger economy. Time for isolation is past. Either we join the future or we remain some stupid nowhereville forever.

It was a great day to travel in an open cart, though. The weather was perfect, just warm enough to smell green everywhere, and the fields blazing with young plants. The sky was full of puffy clouds like fleeces falling out of a bag. I lay back against the soft wool, not thinking too much about anything except how beautiful the day was and how glad I was to be alive and on the road, not stuffed in a classroom with Sister Bridget trying to get my Italic strokes even.

Margaret lay beside me in the back of the cart. The boys were up front driving. I could drive, but I didn't have the experience of a farm kid, and Margaret never did any normal Camelot thing she didn't have to do.

"I'm going," Margaret said to me. "This time for real I'm going to take the test and leave."

That made me open my eyes wide and study her. "But you aren't packed, you don't have anything with you." Then I thought for a moment. "And you're not eighteen, either. They're real strict on their age of majority thing over at the Port."

Margaret sighed. "I'll lie. What are they going to do for a few months, anyway? And if I don't go now ..." She began sobbing into her hands, trying to keep quiet so the boys wouldn't hear.

"What's the matter?" I asked. "Are your parents getting you married off?"

"I hate him," she said, maybe louder than she wanted. "That Simon in the Defenders. He thinks he's just the hottest, strongest, smartest ... I can't stand him, Ab. I can't do it. I've got to go now."

I rubbed her back and didn't say anything. Margaret was too smart, too good, for Simon. My mother had said something about her making the match because they were afraid that no one would want Margaret with all her crazy ideas. That was when she wanted me to drop Margaret entirely.

"She's not quite all, there, you know," Mother said delicately, like when she tried to tell me about things like sex and menstruation. "She's got, well, problems."

"You mean you think she's not a virgin?"

Mother turned bright red, just the color of cherry paint. "No, no nothing like that," she sputtered. "I only meant that she's got some strange ideas about things. People don't like the way she talks, the way she won't help around the house. She won't weave, won't sew, doesn't do anything useful on the farm. All she does is sit and read. Which would be fine if she were headed for the nunnery. But she's not."

"I'll say," I agreed. Margaret said bad things all the time in religion class. She didn't believe in anything except her books and the Port and *away*.

So I patted her on the back again and handed her my handkerchief. Margaret had already soaked hers through. "You can wait until you're eighteen, can't you?" I asked. "It's not that long, and your parents can't plan to marry you off before then. Because they're really strict about that age thing at the Merchant Spacers Guild. They won't even let you in the door if you can't prove you're of age."

Margaret blew her nose into my clean hankie. "If I don't get in the guild, I'll stow away," she said. "I'll hide in the Port, maybe Mr. Penney will let me be his assistant until I'm old enough. But I can't stay around Simon. Ugh."

Silently I agreed, but I couldn't approve of her plan. Margaret might be bolder than I am, but I have the common sense. Margaret doesn't have a lick of it.

"What about Peter and Willie? Do they know?"

She blinked twice. "Willie knows. I told him that I wasn't coming home. I don't know about Peter. I don't trust Peter."

It wasn't really my business. I just knew that if the boys didn't know, they'd tear apart the port looking for her before we could get home to a decent dinner.

"You know," Margaret said after a little silence. "I have this idea. I think if I could work things out, I'll try to help you. Get you out of that stupid tourney. I was so insulted I just couldn't believe the whole thing."

I shrugged. "It's not so bad, really. I mean, just a games day, and we'll see Sir Kendrick. He's got to be worth something."

"That's what our parents say," Margaret said darkly. "But I don't buy any of it. They just want us to stay here, to pretend that this is the center of the universe and that we even have our own Bolo. Have you ever seen Sir Kendrick? Do you know anyone younger than your parents who has?"

Margaret had a point there. "But isn't that the point of the tourney, for us all to see him in action?" I asked.

Margaret laughed. "Are you crazy or what? The point of the tourney, of everything that happens here, is to keep us all in line. To turn us into good little subjects of Camelot. It's even working on you. Look at you, Abigail. Once upon a time, you would have been ready to jump with me. Now you're talking like you're going to the damn tourney."

"Well, I *am* going," I said. "I want to see Sir Kendrick. If he doesn't exist, then at least I'll know for sure. And besides, I'm getting a new dress out of it."

"I can't believe that you'd sell out your whole life, all your friends, for a new *dress*," Margaret said. "Oh, Ab, I'm sorry. And I won't let it happen, I won't let them destroy you, too. I promise."

I pulled my hand away from her gentle pats. I didn't want her to touch me. Margaret could be unreliable. And promising to keep me away from the tourney, what right did she have, anyway, to live my life. She was making a bad enough mess of her own. And if she did run off, we'd have to wait for her and figure out whether she made her exams and was leaving or if we had to find her to come back with us.

Suddenly the whole day looked like a bad idea. I should have known before I'd said yes. We would get home real late, after dinner, and I'd be in real trouble and have no dinner besides. All of which did not appeal.

And all because Margaret has to have her way in everything and just won't be reasonable.

We got to Dover Port by midmorning. The Port is surrounded by a high wall, like a city would be if we had one. Like the Castle, the administrative and technological center for all Camelot. Only the wall there is just for show, and because the view from the observation towers is so good that people are willing to pay five pennies each to go there. Lots of extra income for the government and no extra taxes. My parents always take me up one of the observation towers when we go there.

But the wall is the last part of Dover that belongs to Camelot. There was a line on the road waiting to be checked in to the Port and issued day ID. Not that the Merchanters or anyone else in Dover requires it, but because Camelot doesn't want to make things too easy.

So we waited in line for what seemed like hours. Finally I was too hungry to wait, so I opened my lunch bag. Mother had packed thick sliced cheese and bread and an apple. I ate the cheese with the apple, they taste good that way. Then I traded my bread to Peter for his pear.

Finally we were at the head of the line. One of the Port workers in the pale grey Merchant Guild uniform went over all our papers and slid them under the 'tronic tester to make sure everything was authentic. Then they inspected the wool, and took down our personal data again on another machine that spit back picture IDs with retinal patterns on the back and the date stamped across the whole thing in huge black numbers. It was not a date I recognized. The Port ran on a different calendar than the rest of the world.

From the inside, the Port was fairyland. We were surrounded by three story buildings with blank faces, all made out of the same featureless white concrete. The roads were all paved in black. The only color was from the neon, but even in the middle of the day there was so much colordazzle that it seemed obvious that the blank white buildings had been created as a backdrop for the dense advertising.

I wanted to enter that maze of glitter and light immediately. But Will said we should maybe get rid of the wool first.

"What about your goods?" I asked. "Won't we have to carry them around all day anyway?"

"We'll get a locker at the Port," Will said like he knew what he was talking about. "My father said I could."

"And besides, we could see Mr. Penney right away," Margaret said.

I shrugged as Peter took the reins and turned the old bay away from the glory zone and into the plain white open. Here the buildings were only two stories high and spread far apart. Far in the distance was a huge white open field with a few protrusions. I realized that I was seeing the actual landing zone at the Port from a great distance. It made my heart sing. Margaret sighed and reached out as if to stroke the narrow ships gingerly supported in the docking rig.

We didn't get much chance to look with Peter doing the driving. He turned to the left, to a giant block of a building with "Merchandise Mart" painted in big black letters over a puny door. In front were a zillion carts coming and going. Camelot horsecarts along with the autocarts the offworlders use. People screamed and jostled to get into that one tiny door, and others outside offered black market deals for goods.

No matter how many times I saw it, I was thrilled by the sharp contrast between cultures. And how, oh how it made me long to be one of those competent women in a grey uniform who got up on the autocarts and did everything the men did. I'll bet they had never been invited to parties as "virgins."

"If you don't mind, I think I'll go see Mr. Penney now," Margaret said so quietly I could barely hear her. Then she slipped off the back of the cart and darted between the sellers and buyers in the yard. I watched her veer over to the Guild building, off past the paved mercantile area and past the warehouses.

The Guild building was the only one on the Port painted, a pale grey like the uniforms with the Guild glyph in blazing color across the entire expanse of the front. I stared at it, thinking that perhaps the glyph would work in well to an embroidery design. We could even create a Guild lace, that should sell well enough.

"What's going on?" Peter asked.

"Margaret just went off to see Mr. Penney," I snapped. "You did know about that, right? That she doesn't plan to come back."

"Well," Will said, "we'll have to see if she passes her test. And if she does then she should buy us all a drink. Maybe some Port whisky."

My hands balled into fists before I realized it. Now I understood why the boys had been willing to take Margaret, knowing that she planned to run. Port whisky was bad enough when it came into the ale-house. I didn't want to be alone in a cart with two whisky drunk boys driving.

The whole day was a mistake. I knew it. I was miserable, and it was the first time I had ever felt unhappy at Dover. I always thought of it as fun and exciting, fuel for dreams and the center of my ambition.

Now it was just tawdry and plain. The courtyard with people yelling and trying to advance their places in line was no different from Market Days during St. Anthony Fair. Margaret was gone, like so many of my friends, swallowed up by the giant building with the Guild colors all over the front.

We waited at least two hours, maybe longer, until we got inside and got our goods into a locker. One that could be accessed by an outside code, so we didn't have to enter the building again. The loading dock on the other side of the building was less crowded and we had it easy.

"Why don't we drop in on Mr. Penney?" I found myself asking. Anything to keep the boys out of the bars. They were too young by spacer standards, and besides, I had to drive home with them.

"Yeah," Will agreed. "We can see how Margaret is doing."

"And if she'll take us out after she's all done, like Robert did," Peter added. Peter had hated Robert, except when Robert bought drinks. I wanted to kick them both.

So we stowed the cart along with the goods in the locker on the loading dock and took off across the courtyard to the Guild hall. We found Mr. Penney in his usual place behind a bank of grey screens in an office with no title on the door. We used to wonder what his title might be, before we realized that it might be better if we didn't know.

"It's very good to see you again," he said warmly, extending a hand. "Abigail, of course, and Will. And you're . . . Peter?"

I was pretty impressed. Peter had only been to the Port twice before, when he was much younger. Mr. Penney was something for names.

"How's Margaret doing?" Peter blurted out. "She said she was going to take her exams today."

"Margaret?" Mr. Penney looked surprised. "I haven't seen her. Isn't she a little young for the exams, though? We won't even look at someone who isn't eighteen, and doesn't she have at least three months or so until her birthday?"

That was kind of creepy. How did he know when our birthdays were? And then I panicked even more. Did he know mine?

"That's just like Margaret," Peter complained. "She knew she couldn't take the exams and she'd come here anyway and now we don't know where she is. And we can't just go off leaving her. She owes us, Margaret does. She probably wouldn't pass the exams anyway, she isn't responsible enough to bother studying."

I hated to agree with Peter, but it was true.

"Look, why don't we go into the shopping district?" I suggested. "If she didn't come here, she would have gone there. So we can find her and then decide when to go home."

"She still owes me a drink, at least," Peter mumbled.

"I could try to track her down," Mr. Penney said. "She isn't in our registry, but I could do a body audit in the strictly spacer areas."

"You can do that?" Will asked, awed.

I was revolted. "Doesn't it bother you?" I asked Mr. Penney. "I mean, don't people have the right to go where they want to go? It doesn't have to be your business."

Mr. Penney looked concerned for a moment, then the shadow passed from his face. "We're spacers, and most of us are on call," he said smoothly. "If a Captain needs to gather a crew quickly, this is the best way to do it."

I bet. I didn't say anything, though. What Mr. Penney said made sense, but I just didn't like the idea that they could track Margaret down if she didn't want to be found.

Mr. Penney turned to his bank of screens. His fingers flew over various combinations of keys and knobs that I didn't understand. Maps and wire-grid diagrams flew by, and I couldn't help but be fascinated. Then Mr. Penney's hands rested and he smiled.

"There she is," he said softly. "In the Black Star cantina." He looked up at us and his face was sad. "Not a place I would recommend anyone go into, let alone an underage kid from Camelot. I don't think you should go there."

We left the Guild Hall. Of course we were going

to go there. Saying it was bad was like telling Peter this was the place of his dreams. Peter always likes to think he's bad even when he's just obnoxious. I don't get it.

Honestly, I didn't want to go to the Black Star. I liked Margaret, but it sounded to me like she was up to something stupid. I didn't want to get involved, myself. I just wanted to go home and eat dinner and pretend to my parents that I'd been in school all day. But of course we had to go to the bar and find Margaret and make sure that she wasn't planning to come home with us now that she was dead drunk and would puke all over me the whole way home.

The Black Star was way down past the heavy neon. There were a few streets that wound around the back of Dover Port, where the hookers and the croupiers lived. A couple of late night groceries dotted the residential buildings, and only a few cheap monocolor signs indicated a place of business.

The Black Star didn't even have that much. It had windows painted out black and the name written in silver over the darkened glass. We passed it twice wandering the back alleys, and only when someone stumbled out drunk and singing did we notice it at all. Peter smiled and we went in.

To be very honest, this den of offworld evil wasn't much different from the alehouse back home. Oh, there was black glitterdust on the walls and ceiling, the bar and tables were made of mirrors, but that was just gloss. The smell of cheap stout and cheaper whisky mingled with stale perfume and smoke. I was very disappointed. I'd expected something really dangerous looking, maybe with armed guards sitting with their boots up on the bar ready to blow my head off as we came in the door. No such luck.

There weren't even many patrons yet, except a fairly large group in the back who were making all the noise that the rest were not. They were obviously all to that stage of inebriation where they couldn't stand but could still sing and swear. I couldn't hear anything over their constant rendition of songs I didn't know.

I only wanted out of there. And then Margaret stood up with the crowd in the back and waved us over. We went. Even Peter realized that he had better be on good behavior with these folk, and he kept his expression blank and his walk respectful.

"These are my shipmates," Margaret said, her words so badly slurred that I had to think twice to make them out. "I got an apprentice berth. Lucky, huh? No tests, no age requirement. I just signed the papers."

"Margaret, you can still come home," I told her, hoping all the time that she wouldn't. I didn't want her to be sick all over me, and she didn't look like she could handle the rough cart ride back.

"No!" she said, flinging her arm up and to the side in negation. She nearly hit one of her new crewmates in the head. "I'm going. And I'm coming to get you, to that tourney. End the restrictions, end the whole thing."

"Let's get out of here," Will said.

"I want a beer," Peter protested.

"Then you can get a beer at some other establishment," Will said. "We're not staying. Margaret made her choice. It's not our business any more."

I wanted to get out of that place, and hoped only that Peter would give in decently. There was nothing at all going on here. For all its bad reputation, the Black Star was pretty dull. But I couldn't look at Margaret, already wearing a bright yellow jumpsuit with the word "apprentice" stenciled across her chest. I wondered where her dress had gone.

But Peter looked disappointed and followed Will. I

knew that he was going to say the same thing I would say—*yeah, I've been to the Black Star. Well, I wasn't afraid. Of course, it was early, but it was just a bar, you know? No big deal.* Only it was a big deal.

We didn't stop at another bar. Instead we went in to one of the little late-night groceries and bought packaged salami and cheese already sliced on bread. Peter got a six-pack and we paid and went off with our supper. I hoped we'd be home in time for real dinner, but from the look of the sky I didn't think it likely. The sun was already resting on the horizon and the all white buildings of Dover Port reflected the red/pink/apricot tinge of light.

It was faster going back. Maybe the horses were better in the evening cool, maybe it was that there was so little traffic, maybe it was our collective will to get home to where we didn't have to think about Margaret.

I sat alone in the back of the cart. It wasn't nearly so comfortable as it had been when it was filled with fleece. And I tried not to envy Margaret the courage to leave, to wander off and talk someone into taking her on without Guild papers.

But I didn't have any luck. If only I had the nerve I could have done it. I'm smarter than Margaret by a good bit, and I can be charming when I choose. And if I'd have any nerve at all it would be me that was free of all this ancient trapping, and not returning to a two story house with a shop in the front downstairs and the only 'tronics in the lights and the heat service. And the plumbing. I hadn't seen any offworld plumbing yet.

My parents didn't say anything when I got in late. I took the dish of warmed over stew that was waiting for me and ate it all, even though I didn't think I was that hungry. Maybe it was just because I was all confused and sad and jealous of Margaret at the same time.

The next day Mother asked me about a device. "All the young ladies have to have a sleeve or some token to give to their Defender," she said. "I remember when I did it. I must have been a little younger than you, and my older brother had disappeared at the Port. I guess he's a Merchant Spacer now, but I haven't seen him in all that time."

I looked at her, astounded. No one ever went off-world in her generation. I knew that. All the old people believed in those virtues and everything and they never ever did things like that. Let alone my own uncle. If I had an uncle. I figured Mother was just letting me know that she knew about yesterday, about Margaret, and that it just wasn't going to change anything.

"Anyway," she went on, "you have to come up with something lovely. Original. That will help you in the competition, you know. I know you'll be the prettiest girl there, but showing off your talent doesn't hurt."

"What should I make?" I was completely stymied.

Mother giggled. I swear she did. "Something that Sir Kendrick might like to tie around his turret," she said. "He might not fall in love with human ladies, but he does appreciate aesthetics."

I thought about that one for a long time. And I began to embroider a cloth belt and embellish it with beads and bits of stone that my father said weren't fine enough for jewelry or plate. I even enjoyed the work, knowing full well that none of the other girls had either my skill in design or my resources. I could even run silver thread through the pattern, which made it look rich. I never thought I would enjoy embroidery this way, but it was something to create and it was quiet and well paced. And it filled up my mind so I didn't have to think about Margaret and the Port and offworld, so I didn't have to think about the decisions that were just ahead.

It was real Camelot time, each day just like the one before it. All the rhythms of the sun and crops, of water and wheat, carried us. My own inner rhythms, my impatience to be gone, had somehow been swallowed up by the embroidery project and the new dress and all the little details of living. So I did not realize how time passed until it was Wednesday and that Saturday was the tourney.

My dress was ready, hanging in Mother's press. I had seen it on and it transformed me into some fantasy princess of the old days, when Camelot was a place on Earth and men fought each other to the death for someone like me. Honestly, I loved the feeling.

The belt was not quite ready, but it would be done soon, very soon. I concentrated on it over the last few days the way I concentrated on a new design piece, or something I was doing for one of Mother's clients. I thought of when I would become a journeyman designer, before I would leave forever and design stained glass for starships and embroideries for spacer uniforms.

And then the day of the tourney was on us. I didn't feel real, dressing up in the white and silver under dress, and then the slit burgundy brocade over that. It looked rich and quite adult, and in the mirror I didn't look like me at all. Mother adjusted the ribbon with a pearl drop on my forehead, and threw the veil over it all.

"Now keep it neat," she admonished me as we left the house.

Dad had hitched the buggy, not the cart to the horse, so we rode in style. The road was far more crowded than it had been going to the Port. Indeed, there were even some spacer vehicles in the throng.

I stared at them, for once grateful for the veil so I wouldn't get caught. Mother held the belt I had made on her lap, not examining it or unfolding it the way I would. She likes to keep work neat before turning it in to a client, a thing she says I have to learn.

The market grounds were beautiful, I thought. No match for the neon of the Port, of course, but still there were multihued pavilions and pennants fluttering in the light breeze. And there were booths for various vendors with ribbons flying from the top, as good as a market day but more festive. And everyone from town and all the surrounding villages and countryside was dressed in their finest, so the muddy grass was dotted with groups in bright moving colors.

Dad took care of the buggy and horse while Mother rushed me off to one side, her invitation clutched in one hand. "This way," she told me. "This is where the young ladies are."

There was nothing at all I could do but follow. The crush was near threatening, with the wall of people getting thicker as we neared the canopied platform with all the young women of the area. Mother thurst me up the steps and I found myself among them, no one saying anything at all.

What could we say to each other? These were not the girls I had gone to school with. These were strange creatures in splendid confections of fabric, all uncomfortable as the strangers who had been our neighbors stared up at us. Trying to figure out if a special day and dress could really make a town girl into a Queen of Love and Beauty, if only for the afternoon.

Mother had been right, I was the only one in such a dark jewel color. Several of the girls were in white, and with the many others in pale pink, half the dias looked like a flutter of cherry blossoms. The effect, I had to admit, was stunning.

All our devices, sleeves, belts and banners, were laid out over the high fence on the far side of the field. So that the competitors and audience could see them clearly, I supposed. We surely couldn't. Though that did cut down on bickering over who did the best embroidery work and who couldn't keep her threads straight on the back.

It was really boring. I knew it was going to be boring, but I didn't know how long we were supposed to wait around for anything to get started. I wouldn't have minded so much if we could have wandered around the booths on the Market field, or if we could gossip. But that wasn't possible because everyone I'd want to gossip about was right here. So I had to make do with simply watching. At least there were chairs that we could use, though they crushed the more delicate dresses. Some of the girls were doomed to stand.

It was well past noon when the loudspeakers in the trees gave off the trumpet blast indicating that really, something was almost ready to happen and people ought to finish up their purchases and start to drift over. Which meant it was past one when the herald announced the Parade of the Defenders to honor their ladies. I yawned before I pulled back my veil.

They came in from the open side of the fence, each one on a high-spirited horse, each of them dressed as sensibly as were the girls on the dais. I recognized Piers Goodman and William Spencer. And Simon, who didn't look nearly so vacuous and stupid with all the others in the field. They formed up in a single rank.

Then we could feel him before we saw him, Sir Kendrick Evilslayer, who was the biggest thing in Camelot. I had not realized how big that was. I could fit in the space between his treads. I could easily believe that this being, this Bolo, could crush cities.

He was better than anything at the Port, even. His

speakers were playing something lovely with a flute, and the silver spurs of his knighthood glittered atop his turret, along with his other battle honors. He rode into the tourney field as if he meant it, as if this little ragged imitation of a tournament was grand and noble and not to be taken lightly.

"The gentlemen in attendance shall each take a token from the fence, and shall compete for the honor of the lady whose device he wears. At the end, the gentleman who wins the most events shall have the honor of crowning his lady the Queen of Love and Beauty."

The herald on the loudspeaker gave out the rules. There were contests in archery, running, swimming, fighting (electrified, non-contact only) and the composition of a poem to his lady.

This was going to be dull dull dull, I figured. Like having to stand around and cheer on the boys at school. Why did I always have to sit on the side and cheer them on while they had all the fun and all the glory? Offworld that never happened, I was sure of it.

Now all the Defenders, Sir Kendrick among them, went to the fence and chose their devices. One thing on that method—the ugly girls had as much a chance as the pretty ones, and the ones like me were up as much as any little Camelot lady. I figure that if someone really wanted one of the Defenders to choose her, she would let him know what her device would be.

All around me on the dais, girls yelled and went silent and pale as their devices were chosen by Defenders. Or left on the fence. Like mine.

Not that I'd care if it was never taken. I didn't want to be any Queen of Love and Beauty. There was nothing, nothing at all in Camelot I wanted. This was all a farce, pretending that we had some culture, some life worth living. If I wanted to do anything real at all I was going to have to leave. Margaret had been right.

My belt still hung on the fence, the largest and most intricate of the pieces. All the Defenders had chosen their token, and now Sir Kendrick went before them. I held my breath, not really hoping. After all, what did I want with a Bolo, right? I'd seen him, that's what I'd come for. But he was one more part of the whole Camelot package, and I didn't want any of it.

He chose my belt. Maybe because it was the only thing long enough to tie around the nozzle of his Hellbore, maybe he just liked the design or the colors. I never did ask.

I gasped. I was Sir Kendrick's Lady. Me. And I couldn't care less about Camelot or the way anything was done on Camelot. I was leaving as soon as I could. That was final.

Sir Kendrick came over to the dais and lowered his guns toward me. "May I come up and ride you?" I asked, wondering if he could even hear me.

"My Lady's desire is my command," he said.

It was not easy to climb onto his fender in my fine dress. Someone eventually brought over a ladder so I could attempt it with some dignity.

What joy, what freedom riding on the fender of a Bolo. It had looked giant from the platform. From up here I could easily believe that I could touch the clouds.

This is how it must feel on a starship, I thought. This is power. I felt like a goddess, omnipotent. I could see over the fence, past the village and the competition fields. I could make out the shape of the monastery huddled apart in the middle of its fields. I could make out the double line of brown-habited brothers filing through the cloister into the chapel. And in that great vision, with the infinite power of the greatest fighting machine ever conceived in the mind of humanity, I knew there was nothing, nothing ever, I could not do.

They were setting up for the archery competition. I thought watching the various games was boring. I'd watched them all before, and it's only fun if I get to play. So I looked out over the horizon, over the stretch of citron field of dainty new wheat and the stunted, gnarled apple trees on the hills.

And I saw them coming. Spacers. In autocarts, wearing their tight-fitting uniforms and carrying power arms.

For a moment, shocked, I assumed they were merely coming to join in the festivities. But there was something about the line of carts, the stance of the free riders, the presence of weapons, that didn't fit the image of peaceful neighbors.

"Offensive light attack force approaching at eight o'clock. My orders are to destroy immediately," the Bolo beneath me rumbled.

And suddenly I was scared. My brain froze in my skull. There had never been any problem with the Port. Spacers never came into Camelot. What could they want with our lives? I couldn't think.

"All personnel shall stay in the current enclosure," Sir Kendrick ordered. "This is possible intrusion. It is my duty as Knight-Defender of Camelot to protect this population. You will not move from your present position." Then he rolled over to the dais. "My lady," he said very elegantly.

"I'm going with you," I said. How could anything hurt me when I was with Sir Kendrick. I was invincible, untouchable, immortal. There was nothing at all to fear.

"My lady, it is my duty to protect you. And to serve you," he said.

"But a true knight obeys his lady," I reminded him, wishing now that I had paid more attention in Sister

Claire's course on The Literature and Practice of Courtly Love.

"That is so," Sir Kendrick agreed. And he turned and rolled out of the enclosure and onto the open road where eight autowagons at least of motley clad spacers approached the tourney grounds.

And then we were in front of them looming over their path like a mountain. I looked down from my high perch on the fender. And I realized that I recognized at least one of the faces in spacer's gear. This was the band Margaret had joined. And there she was, right in front, just as she promised. To save me from the miseries of dull old Camelot. She looked miserable.

"You told me it was a myth," one of the spacers was saying. "You told us there was no Bolo. And that there would be plenty of merchandise ready." The spacer who spoke was familiar, too, but it took me a moment to recognize him outside his Port clothes. Mr. Penney.

Margaret looked like she was about to cry. "I never saw a Bolo," she said. "Not before now."

"Target acquired," Sir Kendrick said. "Destroy the despoilers of Camelot."

The vibration under me changed as anti-personnel guns fired two bursts. The second autowagon exploded in a wash of fire.

Spacers abandoned their vehicles and ran. Sir Kendrick swung his tower and both fore and aft guns blazed in rapid succession. And brightly clad offworlders lay smoking dead, dotting the road and the new field of wheat.

"Wait, wait," I yelled as the turret swung again, this time bearing down on Margaret and Mr. Penney.

"My mission is to destroy the Enemy. I have never failed in my mission," Sir Kendrick stated flatly.

"No," I yelled. "Your mission is to protect Camelot.

We need to know what's going on. We need to question them."

There seemed to be a jolt in Sir Kendrick's thought that I felt as a physical thing, though I know that's not possible. "Insufficient data," he said. "Mission cannot be achieved without proper data. I have never failed in my mission."

Margaret was crying, sobbing loudly as tears ran down her face. I saw that she was not armed the way the others had been. And that Mr. Penney was pointing his power rifle at her.

"You said there were no defenses," he growled. "Just boys with arrows. You are responsible for this."

He was going to shoot. I could feel it. Looking at Margaret with her eyes squeezed shut and tears on her face, I knew that she was dead already.

Time became still and perception became hyperaware. I could smell the laser-burn in the air, the smoldering of fabric and flesh. And I whispered, "Protect Margaret. Protect Camelot."

Laser light flashed and Mr. Penney lay in the road, a small black burn hole right between his eyes. I stroked Sir Kendrick's turret.

Then I looked down at Margaret. "What the hell were you doing?" I asked.

But she only sobbed harder. I reached down a hand. I couldn't lift her to the Bolo's fender, but she climbed on top of the abandoned autowagon, and from there she could scramble up the two last treads to the fender. I pulled her up the last few feet and put my arms around her as she collapsed against me.

"Mission accomplished," Sir Kendrick said. "Camelot is safe."

We returned to the enclosure to find that no one had moved in our absence. The archery butts were still only half-set, and the Defenders were as quivering silent as the few nuns who had come down to sell honey. Margaret was still quivering against me as we faced the crowd.

"Danger has been averted," Sir Kendrick announced. "The Enemy has been vanquished. Camelot is safe."

"No," Margaret said, and stiffened in my arms. Her voice was barely above a whisper, hoarse over her sobs. No one could hear her but me. "No, we're not safe. None of us. I didn't know, I didn't know," she sobbed.

"Know what?" I demanded.

"It was all a lie," she sobbed. "Everything. The Guild. Mr. Penney. Our friends who left, who went offworld. They weren't accepted into the guild. They were sold to pirates and mining companies and brothels on Miranda. Bess and Robbie, all of them. And me. They made me do it, I swear, Ab. I swear." And she collapsed in a heap on Sir Kendrick's fender.

I shuddered slightly and called for a ladder. Someone, Simon I think, came up and got Margaret. I got down by myself, all distracted and confused.

I could hardly credit what Margaret said. Why would places far more advanced than Camelot need slaves? Weren't there machines to do all the work?

But something in my instinct told me that Margaret was telling the truth. Mr. Penney always so friendly and encouraging, but also always telling us not to tell our parents. And his stories about other worlds, their wealth and opportunity, just seemed too good to be true.

And then I thought about the way Mr. Penney had leveled that rifle at Margaret and I knew she wasn't lying. Maybe it was just cheaper to lure kids offworld than to build psychotronics. And some functions still required humans. I flinched at the memory of the word brothels, but it all made so much sense. It had always been the attractive ones among the disaffiliated that Mr. Penney said had the best chances.

I had wandered far from the Market area while trying to figure out what I had to do. I hugged my elbows close, thinking how ready I had been to jump, to run. It made me angry, made me want to kill everything and everyone.

And I had the power to do that. I was Sir Kendrick's lady. I could tell him the story and we could burn the Guildhall to the ground. Raze the Port. Make them pay for my friends, make them pay for my own stupid, dying dreams.

I had the power to destroy absolutely everything in the whole world.

I turned and ran to Sir Kendrick. He was still near the ladder and it was easy for me to climb up and jump on his fender. He could destroy anything, keep us safe from exploiters forever.

But as I caressed his shining turret, I realized that he couldn't keep us safe from ourselves. Our ignorance could not be blasted away with a Hellbore, and the lies we told ourselves couldn't be burned by a laser.

Robbie, Bess, Margaret, how many others? It must be a very profitable business. And on how many other planets did they play this scam? Anger replaced fear, and I knew they had to pay. The blood on the road wasn't enough for the lies and the pain and the outrage.

I had never questioned the thought that all adults were free. I had heard of other concepts in school, of course, but on Camelot there is only one way to live and one truth. And now I began to see that it wasn't so bad or so backwater as I had thought.

I stood silently on the fender of the Bolo for a long time, until the sun turned the sky ruddy with nightfall.

"Let's show them their dead," I whispered. Sir Kendrick rolled.

We had several of the Defenders pile the dead into their autowagons and hitch the wagons into one long chain. Sir Kendrick pulled them along to the Port. We arrived by early evening when the Port doors were shut.

This was no problem for a Bolo. He hardly slowed down as his massive treads flattened the Port wall.

The glitter of neon reflected off his shiny armored body ominously, and suddenly the blaze of color against the dark no longer looked so romantic. It was a lure, that was all.

"Destroy the Enemy," he said. "Defend Camelot."

"But how do you destroy thought?" I asked. "How do you destroy ignorance?"

Sir Kendrick didn't even hesitate. "Provide useful data."

Obviously. But who would provide it? Margaret was never the most credible witness.

"I suppose we should bring the bodies to the Guildhall," I said. "I can't think of anywhere else to dump them."

We brought the eight wagon loads of dead, pulled by a massive Mark XXIV. Sir Kendrick rolled onto the landing field. Next to his bulk the ships seemed fragile and vulnerable.

And then I knew exactly what to do. And I began to giggle as badly as any of the Talmadge girls.

"Spacers," I yelled. Some came over, and then Sir Kendrick played a flourish from his speakers, and repeated my words.

"We are the Defenders of Camelot and we know that there has been an evil thing here. Young people have been lured into slavery on distant worlds, being told that they could become merchant spacers. If you do not want us to blow your ships to shreds and leave you stranded on Camelot forever, you will all go into every school and church and village grange and you will teach the young people of Camelot about the other worlds in the quadrant and how people really live. And how good life is here. I always thought that wall was to keep us from leaving. Really it was to keep you from seeing how good it is here."

So now Sir Kendrick is a fixture at the Port, and here I am in Mr. Penney's old office, chief Port Administrator. I have two school groups touring today with a lecture series on Miranda and Llorda, and a new Camelot Space Trade building to dedicate and a group of Defenders who are too busy checking imports and running our segment of sector linknet that none of them ever has had time for another tourney.

So I was quite surprised to see an invitation on my desk today, beautifully calligraphed and illuminated with pictures of Sir Kendrick and my belt and spaceships picked out in silver around the border.

All ye goode citizens of Camelot, hail, it begins. We invite the honour of your presence at the tenth anniversary celebration games, where we shall endevour to compete with those people of Camelot in the greate skills of running and swimming and riding. And we shall be pleased to find from among those ladies younge and faire a Queen of Love and Beauty.

I tossed the invitation in the trash. I hate it when people screw around with spelling like that.

YOU'RE IT

Shirley Meier

It was raining on New Newf. Of course it usually was. Tall fern trees waved in the light breeze and the air was full of crashing, crunching noises as pogos browsed on the tree-tops. From a distance, one could imagine a day in old Earth's Late Jurassic period; brontosaurus herds grazing through primitive trees. Except these creatures had gargantuan metallic shells, their gentle curves glinting weakly in the gray light.

The trunk-like forelegs were used mostly to support the long neck and head; the shells rested on a snail-like back-pad. At a hundred tons on average, the beasts had reminded some early settler of a legendary Terran monster, "Ogopogo"; hence the name.

Sensors indicate two drone Enemy scouts approaching. Correction: manned scouts. The Bolo halted, turned, turned back, mimicking the motion of a pogo in its herd.

The LRS 1-8-12 was an old Mark XXIX, now obsolete. Allocation policy hadn't allowed for one of the new standard units, the vastly upgraded Mark XXX, to be deployed on a sleepy backwater planet which was basically six towns, a moderately steady yield of uranium ore, and otherwise, pole-to-pole swamp. Concordiat long-term projections had been that no one would likely notice it, let alone want it.

Now, six fallen garrisons and 20,000 lives later, it was clear Concordiat long-term projections had been wrong. A moderately steady yield of uranium, easily taken, had apparently been exactly what the rebel Xishang Empire wanted. The Bolo's hull was pitted and scarred, the duralloy surface showing swirls of green and purple where it had come close to melting, the result of an atomic warhead's near-strike. That had been part of the Xi-shang's first salvo, intended to soften up resistance before the personnel ships landed. The LRS's main turret's rotational tracking and its Hellbore's vertical angling mechanisms, both, had been jammed by the impact, the great gun's muzzle stuck beyond all the bolo's self-repair capabilities, at minus five degrees, forty-five degrees off median.

Hellbore inoperative, its monitoring signal circuits continued to read; it was programmed not to waste power-pack energy shooting if it couldn't aim. *All other systems fully functional. Ready to lock on targets*.

A two-ton calf reared up on its backpad, its head weaving back and forth as it bellowed at the scoutships streaking through the sky. The herd bull roared an alarm/challenge, drowning out his offspring, and the rest of the herd snapped into their shells, turning the swamp into a field of hundred-ton, metallic boulders. The LRS shut down all but one external sensor and waited.

The enemy scouts circled the herd, came low.

Necessary. My radar trace is identical to a pogo's. The pilots cannot rely on their equipment. They must use their more sensitive, built-in sensors to detect my presence. Eye-balling, humans called it.

The LRS came to life, its infinite repeaters tracking the scouts jittering over the herd. Two heavy coughs shook the ground. The two ships dematerialized into shrieking fireballs, shearing of the tops of the fern trees and plowing up two five hundred meter gouts of boiling mud.

Standing order: Disable and/or destroy enemy equipment through guerilla action, obeyed. As the pogo herd thundered away from the fires, the Bolo mingled with them, staying in the midst of their two hundred metal-laced shells, letting their pads erase all signs of duralloy treads. Gradually it made its way towards the front edge of the herd, to be clear of the radio interference caused by the massive creatures.

It replayed the last transmission from the garrison at Porto Basque again. That tape was worn with repetition.

"The Xi-shang rebels are attacking New Newf ... pr ... for the mines ... Additional information—" the transmission squeal. "1-8-12, activate standing orders, but with evasive action. Do not, repeat, do not be captured. Remain concealed until repaired." Then extraneous noise and unchained commands, end of transmission. Three months and twenty-two days ago.

Static crackled in the ionosphere as Xi-shang ore shuttles launched from the port. Then another burst of static came, as Xi-shang fighters scrambled into orbit to beat off a small flock of four-man ships from the nearby planet Tawa and its moon, Kwivit, where the Concordiat still held. The LRS detected a flurry of chaff covering friendly forces, as they altered formation. It shut down under a tangle of Walking shrubs, drive-train half buried. Above the atmosphere the battle raged.

Xi-shang Mission Commander James Lung leaned back in his chair and listened to the reports pour in. His hands absently finished stripping down his sidearm. As an officer he could indulge himself with carrying a look-alike of 20th-century semi-automatic built by DWM. The cleaning cloth was grey with use.

His off-planet battle was won: whatever Concordiat orbital forces hadn't been destroyed were effectively stranded in space. A well-aimed strike had eliminated the planet's antiquated Bolo base, with everything and everyone in it; he'd made sure to hit during working hours. The Concordiat had its attention on a few larger opponents. Light-years away; that had made this occupation possible. The Emperor was confident enough—and pressed enough elsewhere himself— that he'd called all Xi-shang battleships away, leaving Lung with ground-to-orbit ships only. And the interstellar freights, of course; they were being loaded day and night.

Still, it had been a gamble, a somewhat desperate bid for desperately needed ore, and it was proving a harder nut to crack than the Emperor and War Council back home had expected. The problems were planetside. With the Emperor so sticky about taking every last building and bit of non-military equipment intact, the citizens of New Newf had soon figured out his threat of nuclear devastation was a hollow one, and he'd had to take each town street by street. Sabotage at the mines was rampant. "It's been three months, and I still don't have all of Porto Basque," he said to the screen as if it could hear him. "I'm losing men because they think a groundcar as cover will stop a high caliber round. They're just learning that tin-cans on window sills make dandy mortars."

And then there was the damned Bolo.

He sighed, clicked a magazine into the small handgun before putting it into his desk drawer. He wiped his hands and ran them tiredly over his face. He was a tall, spare man with ice-gray eyes surrounded in a nests of crow's-feet and a powdering of gray in his straight black hair.

At least he still had two working Kai-Sabres, eighty-ton clones of the Bolo Mark XXVIII, built after decades of very sophisticated technical espionage. That had started even before Xi-shang had revolted against what it called excessive taxation and insufficient support from the Concordiat, declared itself independent, and then declared itself an Empire, a generation ago. Kai-Sabre Cheng-Sze patrolled Novo Aklavik, and Kai-Sabre Temujin was in New St. John's, just their presence enough to keep those towns relatively quiet.

He sighed again. The computer chimed at him. "What?"

"Lojtan Smith to see you, sir."

"Send him in." Lojtan By-The-Book Smith. On top of this latest problem, the Lojtan had lost most of his unit ordering them into the sewers—by the book. He made the same error every time, but his family was too close to the Emperor for any commander to do more than slap him on the wrist. He came in, polished as if he were reporting to the Emperor. His salute was razor perfect ... and his commanding abilities matched. Perfect for the High Court; lousy in field conditions.

"I've read your report, Lojtan Smith."

"Sir!"

"You were in command of the Victorious when we invaded." It wasn't a question. The Emperor had "requested" it, personally. As a favor to an old friend.

"I had that honor, sir!"

"You reported the destruction of the Bolo LRS 1-8-12, assigned to the enemy's New Newf garrison."

Smith swelled with a prideful jut of his chest. "I did, sir!"

"And you verified this before landing."

He deflated slightly, puzzled. "Of course, sir. The blast circle was entirely visible from low orbit as we initiated atmospheric flight."

"And was this, in your opinion, sufficient?"

"Sir? We destroyed the Bolo, sir."

"THEN ITS GHOST JUST BLEW OUR LAST TWO SCOUT SHIPS TO FRAGMENTS!" Lung's roar was enough to make Smith step back. The commander pushed himself away from his desk and rose, turning his back on the Lojtan's paling face. "Furthermore," he continued more quietly, "I've just had a confirming report that this 'destroyed' Bolo was responsible for damaging the oreshuttle *Steadfast* before she could lift."

"My observations were by the book, sir."

I guess you didn't see, or credit, the tape the report cited, clearly showing a Bolo's repeater burst at maximum distance, taking the nose assembly off Steadfast. Cretin. At least it hadn't used its Hellbore—meaning you at least damaged it.

But pogos throw radar traces just like Bolos, so it can hide almost indefinitely from any air power I can scrape together, and cause more of the same kind of trouble.

"By the book. Like your last command, Lojtan?"

Smith thrust his chin into the air. "My unit succeeded in rooting out the insurgents, sir."

"At the cost of eighty per cent of its equipment, and seventy per cent of its personnel, Lojtan. Are you aware of what our situation is here, regarding reinforcements?"

"Sir, surely the Empire will support our gains."

Lung sat down and pulled open his desk drawer. "You're assuming, Lojtan. Assuming wrongly, as a matter of fact. You know our support has decreased—since we've done such a fine job of taking this planet, His Majesty's pulled away all battleships to other theaters of operation. It's up to us to dig in, Lojtan, to consolidate our on-planet defenses enough to withstand a full Concordiat attack."

"I'm aware of that, sir." Smith's voice had started to take on an edge.

"We simply can't afford your kind of losses, Lojtan."

"And what do you suppose you're going to do about it?" With a faint sneer, the Lojtan added, "Sir."

"Let me tell you something about the big wide universe, Smith. Your daddy's pal the Emperor isn't always going to take care of you in it." Smith's jaw dropped—just the words were enough to get Lung into very deep trouble, if they ever got back home. He filed them away smugly. "I've considered your report and your record," Lung continued, "and I am going to do something that I should have done long ago."

"What, sir?"

He pulled out the Luger and fired. Smith only had a fraction of a second to register shock as the Commander's shot took him in the left eye and blew out the back of his head. The body fell back against the wall, smearing the spatters of red and gray down the cool green paint.

Lung placed the pistol back in the drawer as his guards ran in, automatics ready, his aide on their heels, sidearm drawn.

"At ease. Lojtan Smith has unfortunately fallen victim to a sniper, Hyotan."

She holstered her weapon and straightened. "Yes, sir." Her eyes flickered across the unbroken window, showing the distant port. "I understand completely, sir."

His eyes swept across the guards, who had re-slung their weapons. Their eyes too had taken in the fact that the window was unbroken. Two good men, survivors of one of Lojtan Smith's moronic forays. He'd seen that they were on duty today. "I trust we understand, privates?"

"Sir! Yes, sir!" They bent to carry the body out.

As the door closed he continued. "Inform sub-Lojtan Simms of his promotion to full Lojtan."

"Sir."

"And send my condolences and apologies to Smith's family when you send back his effects."

"Sir."

"I'll be on the roof, thinking, while you send to get this mess cleared."

"Of course, sir."

One less problem to deal with.

On the roof, Lung paced in the rain. The problem with insurgents and "dumb insolence" in a captive population was one of firepower. The Kai-Sabres were like hammers, that he was using to swat mosquitoes; the only difference, of course, was that he might convince the mosquitoes to stop by showing them his hammers.

"Computer, has Kai-Sabre Sun Tzu been repaired?"

"No, commander. Kai-Sabre repair team is seriously under strength."

"Due to the sabotaging of the maintenance bay."

"Yes, commander. Projected repair date five weeks."

He sighed again. "Status on ground-to-air repairs?"

"Fleet technicians required for combat aircraft repairs, Commander."

We're getting spread too thin. And that damned Bolo, still alive . . . He had to bring in its smoking wreckage. *At least its main gun's knocked out. Or else it could take all three Kai-Sabres, probably. As it is . . .*

He inwardly smacked himself on the head. Why didn't I think of it before?

He keyed his com. "Hyotan."

"Sir."

"Pull Kai-Sabre Cheng-Sze off the port and have it report to maintenance, then to me."

A Mark XXIX could take three Kai-Sabres; but one Kai-Sabre could certainly take one Mark XXIX minus Hellbore. Set a machine to catch a machine.

The water of the swamp rippled for a long moment, then was still again. Skaters walked over the surface, long spidery legs holding the plate-sized body clear of the water, each of the sixteen feet cased in a cup of surface tension. Kai-Sabre Cheng-Sze turned its sensors across the water to the waving sea of purple spear-grass.

I search. The Bolo was three hundred kilometers away when I intercepted the last transmission. The man whose mission is to repair it is nearer.

Its orders had been changed, as soon as it had reported the contents of the transmission between man and Bolo. Destroying the man was now priority. *My sensors are keen. Yet no human heat signature. I will find him.* If it were capable of frustration it would have been. Its treads stirred up the muck, sent ripples across the water, sending the skaters flying into the shelter of the reeds. There were only the plumes of methane bubbling their heat from the mud on the bottom. It churned its way along the edge of the swamp and up onto higher ground, began scanning in the trees growing there.

From below the water surface, the skaters' feet

looked like silver ping-pong balls holding up rippling reflections. The Kai-Sabre's trends had churned the water brown. Sven Todd clung to the hollow reed he was breathing through, his other hand knotted in the roots of the spear-grass two feet down. He tried to stop the pounding of his heart. The water around him shook and the MA-50 dug into his back. Useless as a pop-gun against a Kai-Sabre.

Along his right side, wrapped along with his tool kit in waterproof duraplas, lay the hunk of metal that was the purpose of his mission. If not for his expertise, it would be more valuable than his life. The left traverse stabilizer: four kilos of replacement parts that the LRS needed to get its Hellbore online.

If I pull this off, we'll be able to blow the 'Shang off the ground for keeps. Even if Central Command did decide to pull forces away from its major campaigns, it took time to organize it all, time to move them in, especially to a backwater like New Newf. *We've been on our own from the start.*

It was an incredible stroke of luck that he was still alive to attempt this mission, which the Kai-Sabre's presence had now probably made impossible, in the first place. *The first day I call in sick in a year, and my workplace gets turned into slag. And on a Friday, too . . .* He tried not to think about the others.

Yet the mission still shouldn't have been possible. The 'Shang's plan, of course, had been to destroy all Bolo maintenance equipment and spare parts, as well as all the technicians, just in case they only winged Laura . . . Laura Secord, the LRS's full nick-name, was after an ancient war heroine. The 'Shang hadn't counted on a tech who was such a dedicated Dinachrome Brigade machine nerd, he kept an attic full of Bolo junk, and spent half his spare time molding duralloy toys in his basement.

So here I am. Laura just let me know over the com

what part was trashed, three months to put it together, hey, no problem. He fought not to gasp. Only a thin stream of air could get through the reed, which might break if he clutched it too hard. His lungs strained for a full breath but he stayed where he was, breath burning in and out slowly, slowly. His right leg felt on fire and he tried not to think of the muck working its way into the wound. *I cultivate a fever and find Laura, or else I buy it now and take New Newf with me. I'll take the first, thanks. Where is the Sabre?* It could be heading for him, and he'd have no way to tell. If he showed himself it would just blow him away. It couldn't be sure exactly where he was, thank God, or it would have just boiled that section of swamp.

No, it was probably just waiting. It had to be. Just sitting there, sensors straining for some sign, a heat signature it could recognize as human. He lay still and breathed slowly, listening to the surf-roar in his ears.

The sediment was settling, the ripples on the water surface stilled again. The skaters came out. Was it just waiting for him to surface? Waiting for a clear shot? Another ripple, but not the heavy wash of the machine. One of the pseudo birds, an erkrok, skimming to land on the patch of open water. He forced calm.

They'd snuck out of Porto Basque easily enough. He'd had three people to support him, all Newf reservists: Major Marjo Williams, Lieutenant Me Too (Melvin) Taylor, and Captain George Varsilkov. All to get Lieutenant Sven Todd, Bolo Technician, through the midge-laden swamp in one piece, so he could get Laura into one piece.

It had been the first night that George had started complaining. He wasn't a Newf native. *"Cave Cimex!* Why in hell does every planet under a yellow sun develop flying bloodsuckers?" George slapped the side of his face and looked at the mess on his palm with distaste, his almond-shaped eyes narrowing. "They still have to bite you before they find out they can't use your protein."

"Well, we all know how poisonous you are," Marjo drawled, running a hand over her short cut brown hair. "Even without the Latin lessons."

George glared at her. "I learned Latin before I learned to hate these bugs in basic."

"Oh? How many centuries ago was that?" Me Too asked innocently as he'd swung his pack down were they'd chosen to camp. George had frowned at him, then laughed.

Marjo had gotten them out into open country, and they'd trekked overland—overmuck, Sven thought—with short bursts of radio contact leading them toward rendezvous.

That was when the Kai-Sabre had zeroed in on their signal.

Marjo had had been on point, fifteen meters ahead of Me Too. That put her thirty meters ahead of Sven and forty-five ahead of George.

The Kai-Sabre's beam had burned George into a cinder that managed to walk three more steps before it fell and shattered into ashes.

At the sound of the heavy purr of the beam Marjo had dived one way into the bush and Sven the other.

Weighed down as he was he could run, but slow, too slow. . . . Then Marjo and Me Too had showed themselves, to draw it away from Sven as he lay in the mud, hoping it was enough to hide his heat. *They knew they could only give me time. They knew.* Marjo had disappeared in a gout of mud and blood that fountained thirty meters in the air. Me Too had kept running, but fired backwards over his shoulder. Even though the MA could, theoretically, blow a hole through a concrete bunker, it was a gnat's bite to the Kai-Sabre's lightest guns. As Sven half-ran, half-crawled towards the best hiding-place he could think of, this patch of water, the world seemed to blow up behind him. A heavy, blunt impact on the back of his leg as he'd taken a running dive into the water, hoping it was deep enough.

A sudden trickle of water blocked Sven's breathing tube and he fought to keep from choking. *Swallow, don't breathe it in. Swallow, don't choke.* He ignored the taste of mud and dead worms in his mouth. His heart leaped into a gallop and he struggled not to panic and thrash his way to the surface. Something nibbled him in the cheek, rubbery, and he clamped down on his need to flinch away. Thank God it didn't have teeth. He took a slow breath, tinged with the green sap odor of the reed. His calf was bleeding, drawing the leechoids and nibblers. He couldn't twitch, the ripples would give him away.

Maybe it's not even sure I'm around here, so it's gone away. Then he shook himself mentally. The Kai-Sabre's sensors were too good. Lambourgh built half decent knockoffs. *Even if they aren't Bolos, they're tough.* It was out there.

The LRS moved carefully along the river, stop, start. The feathery bluish fronds of the weeping trees brushed across its scarred hull.

Covert action required. Over the open radio link, passive reception only, the LRS was picking up nothing but static. The com had been open. Data gathered indicated that the repair team, had been destroyed, probability eight-five percent.

Data inconclusive. Proceeding to area of last transmission to confirm. The Bolo left the relative shelter of the riverbank and engaged amphibious mode to cross a bog. A lone Kai-Sabre without air support was the next valid target—but only with a working Hell-bore. *I am damaged. I must find the tech first and then I will grind the Enemy undertread.*

Sven emerged slowly. *It may not recognize just the top of my head and eyes as human.* He blinked slowly to clear his eyes of muddy water. His hair, grown long enough to fall in his eyes over the last two months, trailed a straight brown lock down the side of his nose. "A brown man," one of his friends had called him. "Brown eyes, hair and skin, as if you were carved out of one piece of wood."

She was dead now. They were all dead, as far as he could tell.

A drift of smoke from smoldering vegetation wavered across his sight in the misty sunlight. The crater where Me Too had been running half a day ago was still smoking sporadically around the edges, though the bottom had filled with water. A faint film of brown coated the surface of the new, oval lake.

There was no sign of the Kai-Sabre that he could see, except the chewed up earth and the path of splintered trees off to the left. A trunk as thick as two of him was snapped off clean and crushed.

As his nose cleared the water, his ears ran clear and in the distance he could hear the thunderous growl of the Kai-Sabre.

He drew in his first full breath in what felt like hours. And coughed, struggling to cough quietly, as the smoke and the smell of wet char and sulfur caught the back of his throat. One thing he was glad of: it wasn't a battlefield where Bolos had gone through foot troops. He'd seen that once, as a young tech. What he remembered most was the smell. There had been so many people blown into such fine pieces that the smell was more of seared blood rather than cooked meat. He caught himself gagging as the smell from the crater brought that memory back strong.

Even if the Bolos haven't used diesels in centuries, they still manage to sound as if they do. He'd heard the sound on history tapes. Maybe it was built into the design as a fear tactic against ground troops.

He eased out of the water, spat and slapped a med-patch on his leg. *Looks like most of the muscle just got sheared away.* He drew in his breath as it finally, mercifully, went numb as the local anesthetic hit. Then he checked his toolkit, the plastic casing of the part, and the com which was still clipped to his belt before hauling the MA out of the mud and clearing the barrel. *I might need it against nessies.* An ancient flat photo flashed into his memory: the underside of an old tank, just as it was going over the foxhole the guy had been in.

"Yeah, and they managed to recover the camera from his body afterward," Sven muttered. The text had just mentioned that in passing. He had no intentions of letting a similar sight be his last.

There was a suspicious fuzziness to his thinking and he was cold. Fever? No, probably shock, and the parasites in the mud. *Gotta remember to keep checking the damned part. Mud-lice eat duraplas like it's going out of style.* The mud-lice were almost transparent, ghostly little pin-head sized bugs. *I hope they're giving the Xi-shang royal hell. We certainly planted enough packets of them in their machinery.*

He limped out into a thicket of reddish bushes. The sound of the Kai-Sabre was fading northward and he put some distance between himself and the smoldering forest and, hopefully, the Kai-Sabre.

It was late when he stopped to rest, carefully placing his kit on the ground, wanting to drop it. *Four damned kilos. And my tools, and the damn gun. My aching back.* It was more awkward than heavy, sharp ridges digging into his back muscles as he walked. He sprayed a lice-killer on the plastic, re-coated the fraying edges with another sprayon. *Running out of this stuff.*

The sun was low enough that the nightshrieks were out hunting the bugs. He half-smiled, thinking of George as he slapped a four-inch bloodsucker. *"Ave Imperator . . ."* he muttered. George had been the history buff.

He was talking to himself a lot more now, fighting down the aches in his bones, the shivers that trembled through him. Fever. Another hour and the sun would be down. New Newf had no moons; out here it would be dark as the inside of an asshole.

His calf was burning as if it were being cauterized. Mud-lice ate med-patches too; it was peeling away in long strips of wrinkled grayish pseudo skin, leaving the wound open; a couple of leechoids clung to its edge. He rubbed a dab of salt from his kit on them and got them off. "Damn." He only had one med-patch left. George had been carrying more.

Sven pressed his last patch onto the wound carefully and hissed in relief as the pain faded to an ache.

The MA needed some strip-down before the action would work and he wondered a moment why he kept it, since he only had four rounds left. *Hell, sometimes one round is useful.*

The last fix he had on the LRS was due west. *I need the med-set in that Bolo. Then fix her, and we'll fix those effing 'Shang good . . .*

"Forty-five hundred thousand tons of partially refined ore, including this shuttle." James Lung's voice was quiet as he sat looking down at the computer screen. The feed was coming through the sensors of the Temujin as it patrolled, protecting the loading bay. For the moment it showed the latest shuttle being loaded. He looked up and through the window at the port. He could see the top third of the fifty meter high shuttle over the city buildings. A light rain pattered on the glass, smearing the image. Each shuttle was capable of hauling a hundred and fifty thousand tons into orbit where the megatonner waited. He turned back down to the computer screen. The loading of the shuttle was almost complete.

The occupation was not going well. The computer lists lay on his desk, hardcopy. Munitions stocks were dangerously low. Five squads were extant only because they had one member left alive. The infirmaries were almost at capacity, and most of the equipment was desperately in need of repair. "The problem is," he said, rubbing his chin, looking up at the newly repainted wall. "Any barbarian with a rock can disable a lot of high-tech equipment in seconds. . . ." He smiled ironically to himself. Perhaps not a rock, but chemical explosives and swamp insects let loose in the garages at the very least. "We cannot keep up this rate of attrition."

On screen, Newf slaves operated the loading equipment under watchful eyes and rifles; the work was slow but steady. His eye was caught by a group of children playing near where their parents were working; the only spot of laugher or noise. Life goes on and people learn to live with the new order of things. Then something caught at the back of his mind. His attention swung back to the children who were tossing a ball between them. There was something wrong, something not quite normal . . . The picture swung as the Kai-Sabre tracked across the scene.

One of the children had missed a throw. The ball rolled between two of the guards and stopped near one of the landing struts of the ore-ship. The child who had thrown stood looking at it, then ran. So did the others.

"Dear God." Lung stared helplessly at the computer image of the blue and red striped ball lying in the dirt. Simultaneously, the flash blacked his screen, and, through the window, lit up the metallic side of the oreshuttle for a moment, bright against the grey sky.

Unbelieving, he watched: the nose of the ship was slightly off center, then more so, the angle growing steeper as it fell, ponderously slow, stately, as if through syrup instead of air. "God. The powerplant . . ." A reactor large enough to power a hundred and fifty thousand tons of rock into orbit, he calculated helplessly, hopelessly, would take half the city with it when it blew.

He sprang to his feet, ready to dive into the shadow of the desk, when the floor moved under his feet, as in an earthquake, knocking him to the floor. The shockwave of the ship hitting ground. Everything seemed to become very quiet; he felt the entire building sway, reverberating. He threw both arms over his eyes, and still saw the flash of the explosion, blood-red through his flesh. He stayed down, heard the shatter and hiss as the window blew in across the room, felt the whole building lurch again and the burn of heat. Then he couldn't hear anything . . . *My eardrums, burst.* Slivers of glass slashed into his hands as he crabbed under his desk, felt in his bones the ferroconcrete of floors and walls crack all around and above and below him, tearing. *Oh, shi—*

Sven ran. Everywhere he ran, the Kai-Sabre was there, everywhere he turned, playing with him like a cat. He fired, fired, fired, and the MA clicked empty. He flung it at the machine and ran. It didn't even bother shooting him. It would catch him, looming, crush him under its treads. Its growl sounded like a laugh. It had him, it was rolling over his leg, slowly, slowly . . .

He woke with a jerk, flailing against the belt he'd used to tie himself into the tree so he could sleep. He hung, panting, looking around wildly for the Sabre, sure it was there, convinced that it had him.

The scrubby trees around him hissed in the breeze that was blowing chill through his damp clothes and hair. Clicks and creaks and sounds he couldn't put a name to echoed in the dark, metallic pinging noises like a baby drive-train. *Bugs,* he thought, but went on shaking.

Shit, Sven, you're going nuts. A Sabre would just blow the whole tree away. Get a grip on yourself. It was out there, searching for him. At night it was as if its presence were spread through the dark all around him, everywhere. He laid his cheek down on the rough bark of the tree, closed his eyes, and shook.

Daylight. The Enemy is here. The human is close. The Cheng-Sze ground a nessie shell undertread. There were a number of them scattered about the sodden ground. West by northwest. *For the human to rendezvous with the Enemy machine he must radio. This will allow me to fix on them. It is a stupid machine. It has no honor. I will kill it. For my honor.* It moved into a pinkwood thicket, thick enough to hide a whole herd of pogos, and shut down, waiting. *I have circled around. I am waiting. He will lead the Enemy machine to me and then I will take them both.*

Sven slogged, hefting his pack, over a dryer patch of ground, though he slowed when the wound sent a stab of pain up his leg. He couldn't strain the med-patch, since he had no replacements. It was worn enough that the mud and blood-suckers had been at the wound again.

It seemed to him that the air had gotten foggier, thicker, hotter as he dragged it into his lungs. His clothes felt too tight; his leg was red and puffy up past his knee. There the skin was stretched, shiny red and purple like the skin of an over-ripe plum. He'd caught himself imagining what it would be like if he let the pressure out with his knife, giggling as he imagined his leg flopping and deflating like a punctured balloon. That had managed to scare him cold.

He swallowed another anti-bac tab dry and hoped it would help. The tablet pac was empty; he crumpled it and shoved it into his kit. The dim, gray day was darkening again, light fog and overcast hiding the sun. *Typical lovely day in New Newf.* He had a couple more hours before it got too dark to see. The parts and tools on his back weighed more and more, as if the gravity were increasing on the whole planet. His arms and legs felt heavier as well.

Oh, God. Another night waiting for it to catch up to me. He shivered as he limped past a pocket tree, its basins of leaves full or partly full of rain. *It's out there.* He started at a looming shadow, hit the dirt, waiting to die, dragging at the useless MA. When nothing happened he cursed, realizing it was just a rock outcropping towering out of the rain that had caught his eye. Not a common sight on a swamp world. *Get a grip, Sven.* He re-slung the MA and kept going.

The last radio fix with the LRS had been much closer and he stretched his pace again. This was the highest, driest ground he'd seen in days; he could actually walk rather than wade through mud. The hillock ahead of him turned out to be a dead pogo, half devoured. That explained the nessie remains. A pack had cornered this old bull on the dry ground and taken it down, losing a few of their own in the process. A flock of skinheads hooted and fought over the rotting meat, wings flapping. Ugly things, hook-billed naked greenish heads with pink blotches over a bat-like body.

Since nessie shells were thinner and smaller than pogos', exposing more of the corpse, the scavengers had made more headway with them, ripping out shreads of gray-pink meat. He was just as glad that he'd never run across hunting nessies. *Just a city boy. Never had to go out into the morass.* They travelled in packs of ten to fifty members, fifteen to twenty tons of muscle each. Their long, narrow heads were mostly mouth, fringed with scales and tipped with a horn as long as his leg, a horn strong enough to puncture a pogo shell. Their shells were spiralled and carried on four clawed legs.

He covered his nose with his hand as he moved. Even though he'd been used to the smell in the swamp, this was something else again. Rotting seafood, iodine and melted slugs was all he could think of, making him gag. Thankfully the wind shifted. He stopped to take a swig from his canteen and gauged how much clean water he had left. *God, I'm thirsty.* He wanted to pour it over his head, drink it dry, drink it so it spilled cool out of the corners of his mouth, poured down onto his sweat-soaked shirt. He wanted to swim in clear, cold water, not this mucky beef-broth that had been in the back of the fridge for a month. He shook himself, staggered slightly, and shivered. *God. How'd it get so hot.*

He skirted around an empty nessie shell. It was one of the bigger ones, stretching over his head, maybe five meters. Hell of a thing to see a pack of these take on a pogo.

He glanced around, keyed the new frequency. "LRS, Laura, babe, respond please." As he did there was a momentary gleam of brightness in the stand of pinkwood. His throat went dry, his knees going to water as he realized what it was, his stomach knotting. The edge of flint-steel tread showing.

The Sabre.

He staggered back, one step, two, head bent as he listened. The nessie shell was just one more step back there. If he could . . .

"Responding. Location fix. Remain in the area—"

"Laura, the Sabre's here!" Sven dove into the shelter of the nessie shell.

The Cheng-Sze had begun scanning multiband as it picked up the man on its sensors, and had locked on the LRS's signal. The man was standing well within range. But he dived behind the shelter of the nessie shell and Cheng-Sze's laser shot merely holed the ground. It powered up, moving forward. *If my laser just incapacitates him and I use my waldo arm to capture him, I will still have fulfilled my orders.*

The man's heat signature was already fading in the damp air, but it led clearly back toward the dead pogo.

Sven ran. *Oh shit. Oh shit.* He leaped over a small log, his leg almost buckling under him. Behind him the Sabre growled, close, so close . . . He ducked low and scrambled through the pile of rock downslope. Rock—it would hold his body heat nicely. *No water here. High ground. No water to hide in. Shit, shit.* The Sabre couldn't target him because the nessie shells messed up its sensors, or he'd have been pink mist in the air already. It could only track him, with heat.

The skinheads flapped into the air ahead of him. Nessie shells and . . . the pogo. Pogo shells did an even better number on sensors and radio waves . . . He scrambled around the huge mound of corpse, hit the dirt as the Sabre fired again. The light buzz of the laser came almost simultaneously with the flare of fire off to his right. It was guessing, or it had just nailed a skinhead real good. He ran, hunched low, ignoring the pain in his leg, the weight pounding on his back. *The pogo's my chance. Am I dreaming? Will I wake up? Please let me wake up. No, it's real. Run. Run, dammit.*

Ahead, the monstrous carcass lay flaccid, the tension of living that would have held the neck close to the edge of the shell gone. The webbing of skin was gouged out, lying folded out on the ground like a peel of grayish pink melting wallpaper.

The Sabre was wheeling around, would have him in its sights in a moment—he dug his hands into the rotting wall of meat and climbed into it. The rifle and pack caught up under the lip of the shell; he yanked them free and crawled into the cavity opened up by putrefaction. *I'll puke later, won't make any difference to this stink.*

It was hot inside, with the warmth of decomposition. His hands sank into the mess up to the elbows, with a hiss of gas that made him stop, eyes watering. His legs sank down past his knees. He was coated in it, almost swimming in it. He braced a boot against the inside lip of the shell so he wouldn't slide, then lay still, cushioned in rotten pogo, trying not to breathe. *I wish I had another reed, to the outside, to breathe through.*

As far as he could see, the pogo's body had fallen away from the inside of the shell, and was slowly oozing out both ends. There was an occasional draft of cooler, cleaner air from where he'd crawled in, but he couldn't see out. He could hear the growl of the Sabre, muted through the shell, the thunder of his own blood, the buzz of fever in his ears. *Maybe I am dreaming. This can't be real.* The liquefying flesh of the pogo around him trembled like jelly with the ground-grinding motion of the Sabre.

*   *   *

Commander Lung leaned back, winced as the back brace dug into his skin, and wiped the sweat off his upper lip.

The oreshuttle had landed right on top of the Temujin. Though a Kai-sabre was tough, surviving a nuclear explosion that had leveled a quarter of Porto Basque was a bit much to ask of it.

He tried to stretch, winced again since there was no one to see him and reached for a sip of water. He was still dehydrated. He remembered waking up in thick black, his head leaning against a metal edge of some kind. He'd woken up trying to tell the babbling voices on the com to shut up and leave him alone, the wound on his scalp already clotted dry. But he'd been imagining the voices. It had flung him back to an old battle where as a young corporal he'd been trapped in a disabled battlebridge with the air running out. But then he'd had the ability to communicate.

It had taken his men three days to find and cut him out of the rubble of the building. He drank deep, and shoved the thought of thin air tainted with plaster dust out of his head. He'd been lucky. His desk had saved his hide, mostly, and he only had a mild touch of radiation poisoning.

He would heal. *And I will control this stinking mudball.* He sipped again, savoring the cool water across his tongue. He had to report to the Emperor. He made the connection.

"Majesty." He leaned forward in his chair, very carefully, the closest he could come to a bow in the brace. "My apologies for such an insufficient obeisance. I have been injured."

The image of the Emperor flickered slightly, then firmed. His head nodded in acknowledgement, the gold trim on his cap of maintenance winking in the light. "Report, James."

Drawing a deep breath, Lung summed up, not attempting to hide the severity of the situation.

The Emperor thought for a long moment before responding. "My dear James, you realize that a great deal depends on you." The Emperor waved a hand before him to indicate his holomaps and battle plans. "We have our own agenda, my friend." His voice was cordial but his dark eyes were cold.

"I quite understand, Sire."

"Yet you yourself were injured in the attack on the oreshuttle."

"Unfortunately, yes, Sire. *Steadfast* cannot be repaired, though her metal is salvageable."

"I am not counting the salvaged metal of our own ship as a bonus, James."

Lung bowed again. "Of course, Emperor. There are three hundred thousand tons of ore and one hundred thousand tons of metal coming now."

The Emperor raised one elegantly shaped eyebrow. "Oh? And is this including our own?"

"No, Sire. This is also salvage. If we cannot get what we wish out of the mines, then I am taking it from the population itself."

"Good. However you get it. The cost of equipment and men is almost too high, James-my-friend."

"I understand, your Majesty." He shifted slightly in his chair, trying for a more comfortable position, resisted the urge to run a finger under the brace on his back, chasing that itch. That was nothing to show the Emperor. "Sire, is it possible that the liberation fleet could spare one battleship—"

"No." The Emperor leaned back from the screen. "You have all the men and equipment you are going to get at the moment, James."

"Of course, Sire." He wanted to grind his teeth, but kept his face impassive. One did not show the Emperor one's pique, either.

"Keep the metal coming for as long as you can, James. Consolidate our position there and I'm sure we'll be able to send you reinforcements soon."

"Yes, Majesty."

"Oh, and James . . ."

"Yes, Majesty?"

"Try to keep the casualties by sniper down, will you?" The Emperor's face showed only lordly concern, but James bowed very low.

"I will do my utmost, Your Majesty."

The Emperor reached one manicured fingernail to touch the chime next to him and with the sound both signalled the end of the interview and terminated the call.

The Cheng-Sze was reporting success in destroying three New Newf insurgents as it tried to track the Bolo, relating that MA-50's were apparently still being produced, somewhere. The thing that brought out the sweat on Lung's forehead though was the glimpse it had caught of the man it was now pursuing; carrying a worn Bolo tool bag and a heavy pack. A Bolo Tech? Left alive? Trying to make contact with the machine? The Sabre hadn't yet found the disabled LRS. The locals questioned about the attack on the shuttle had been taking heart from the fact he hadn't caught the Bolo—all the locals were. "Damn that machine."

Sven shifted his position inside the pogo, slowly, afraid that if he moved too much he'd be buried in an avalanche of decomposing meat. He changed his bracing foot and as he did something popped under his shoulders and he sank a couple of centimeters, into the oily liquid of a scent gland. On top of the other stench the sweet musky odor of the scenting gland was almost a relief. He gagged anyway.

God, I'm scared.

*   *   *

The man disappeared. This was not possible. His trail led clearly through to the rocks, more patchily across the ground toward the dead pogo. Near the pogo his trail disappears. This is not possible. There was a heat trace there, downslope; it shot and a few leathery bits of wing drifted down. Another skinhead. With their wings they were approximately the size of a man. It ground forward, then back, chewing up the dirt with its treads. *This is not logical.* It picked up the fading trail. Perhaps the man had moved fast enough to follow his own back-trail.

Sven slid down to the shell opening and gently, slowly fingered aside a desiccated flap of skin. It was almost full dark. He could only tell that the Kai-Sabre was hunting down his back-trail from the distant growl. Now would be his best chance to get away from the pogo shell so he could signal Laura.

He slithered out and down the mound of meat between him and the Sabre, running as lightly as he could, leaving the tools and pack back in the Pogo. Not a mistake, he hoped; he wouldn't be gone long. *Too damn heavy.* The MA bounced on his back, light enough to take, its plastics impervious to mud-lice. Besides, only a fool would go out alone at night on New Newf without some kind of weapon.

He wiped his face and spat, scrapped a hand through his hair and threw the wet mess he clawed out of it back at the pogo. He was coated, head to foot, with decaying meat fluids and the thick, oily yellow musk from the burst gland.

Once he was off the high ground he slowed to a limp, breath heaving. *God, get me out of here.* The wind picked up and it was beginning to rain, which would wash away all heat sign.

He paused and leaned back against the trunk of a weeping tree, listening to the early evening sounds.

He could barely hear the bellows of a nessie hunting pack downwind of him, the continual patter of water on leaves. Water. He wiped the mouthpiece of his canteen and drank. *Thank God for clean water. Funny, the wind must be dying down, though it doesn't feel like it. The nessies are closer.* He fought down a shiver that wasn't from cold or fever. *Getting damn paranoid. Everything in this world isn't after me.* "Can't go too far from the dead pogo," he said blearily to his canteen.

He peeled off his shirt and tried to wring and scrape some of the goo from it but the pogo musk wouldn't dissolve in the rainwater. He dragged it back on, hating the feel of it, knowing he needed the warmth. The nessies were getting very close.

"Laura, come in."

"Roger."

"Short contact. In pogo corpus. Watch out for the Sabre."

"Roger. Out."

The nessies were closer—too close for him to make it back to the pogo corpse. He'd have to wait until they went by, and hope that left him enough time to get back inside the shell before the Sabre showed. *Damn.* To be on the safe side he climbed the tree he was leaning against.

He was half-way up when the first of the pack heaved into sight. In the darkening swamp they were armored shadows, waving their long horned snouts as they scented the air. The frill of spines around their heads rattled as they moved. The air filled with their stink; "snake on steroids," Marjo had called it. They milled around the tree he was in, their many feet shaking the ground as much as any one pogo's, tearing great chunks of dirt with their front claws.

He looked down at his sleeve and wished he could kick himself. "Damn you, Sven." He was covered head to foot in pogo musk, and decomposition fluids. They were after him. The tree was rocking already, two nessies reared up against it, scraping, clattering their neck-spines as they stretched toward him. No, he didn't look or act like a pogo, so small, less than a mouthful for any one of them, but he for damn sure smelled like one, a very sick one.

He frantically shinnied the rest of the way up the tree until he was sure they couldn't reach him. Perching on a branch he peeled off his shirt and pants.

The Sabre's too close. If I start shooting them, it'll target on me. He only had four rounds left anyway.

He was high enough that the tree was bending under his weight, whipping back and forth slowly as the creatures pushed on it this way and that. *Damn. I have to get them off me, somehow.* He wrapped both legs around the whipping trunk. Below him he could see the shine of teeth clomping at the air under his boot, feel the breeze it made. Further down he thought he saw a beady yellow eye. *The Sabre will already be coming to the radio fix; if I shoot, it won't make a difference.* And four rounds might do something; nessies would attack one of their own if it were wounded, which would draw a number of them away into a fight.

He held his breath and squeezed off one shot into that eye. The nessie fell away from the tree, convulsing once, twice, before the others pulled it down. Most of them couldn't reach their wounded packmate and were circling, focussing on the enticing, enraging scent of wounded pogo. Three more shots and half the pack was occupied. He flung the empty, useless rifle after them.

As the tree he was in whipped wildly back and forth he scrubbed at his hair. On one swing he flung his shirt one direction, saw a few of the beasts follow it, flung his pants another direction. That was most of them but the tree he was in was going, its roots tearing out of the ground as the thrashing beasts below battered it over.

As it fell and hung up in the next tree he scrambled into that, then to the next. The one beyond that was too far to grab a solid enough branch. He looked back. The pack wasn't following him, yet.

He bounced on a springy branch, let the bounce fling him into the next close tree, slammed through branches, scraping the skin off his chest, falling until his flailing arms managed to grab a limb and swing up his legs. He clung, feeling the bark digging into his raw chest, stinging. *I'm in a tree, in my underwear. This can't be a dream, it hurts too much.* Scratched and bruised now, he was forcing his leg to work though it didn't feel as if it belonged to him any more, but like a dead weight on his body, a puffy balloon that wouldn't bend. He heaved himself into the next tree.

Four trees later the pack was distant enough. The closest nessie to him snuffled and loped back to the pack, which was tearing his clothes to shreds. He waited a long minute, then risked dropping to the ground. He was shivering almost continuously in the cool rain. From the east came the snarl of the Kai-Sabre's engines, growing closer.

" 'tween the devil and the deep blue sea.' " He chuckled, a hysterical sound. "Laura, get your duralloy and flint-steel ass here." He fell, scrambled to his feet and headed back toward the dead pogo. "Home plate," he said through chattering teeth. "Blue plate special. Yum."

He was just climbing the higher ground when he heard the snuffling of the nessie pack, quieter, but closer. *Damn, have they picked up my scent-trail?* He started rubbing plants and mud on himself as he ran, anything to change his smell. The med-patch was pulling away from his calf but he didn't touch it in the hopes it would still help.

The growl of the Sabre was increasing fast as well. "Shit. It'll shoot me and they'll eat what's left." He was at the rocks, the huge corpse almost in sight. The Pocket tree let go one of its leaf clusters, letting a splash of collected rainwater hit the ground. The moisture on his face could have been tears, or rain, or just plant juices. "Me Too? George? Are you guys hanging around here? Planning a practical joke? No buckets of water over the doors?"

He was babbling. *That's not the way an officer acts, even if I am a civilian in uniform.* "Yes, sir." Half-crazy with fever. Then the idea came to him. He still had his knife, and the com. "Shit, Sven, you're nuts to try this. But what the hell. Fast—do it fast."

The Pocket tree next to the rocks bent nicely and was easy to pin in place, once he'd emptied the pockets of water, shaking it vigorously. The vines near made a dandy trigger. In the dark he couldn't tell exactly where the Sabre was, or the nessies. "Gotta hope. Gotta work. Laura, Laura, if you can't get here just about now, this has to work. Turra-Lurra-Laura, don't want to buy any farms yet." It was a hoarse whisper. He didn't even realize that he was talking to himself. It seemed as if someone else were standing by, talking as he stumbled in the dark. "Shut up and help me, will you?"

He crawled into the pogo and found the rest of the string of scent glands, trying to be careful not to nick them with the knife as he cut them out of the carcass, though one broke and splashed him. "Won't matter in a bit, won't matter." He laid the glands in the pocket-leaves of the tree and set his trigger. "Come from the east. Come from the east, you overrated, knocked-off 'Shang piece of scrap."

He retreated to the pogo and called Laura to give the Sabre a nice long fix on the radio source.

"Laura? Respond please. Laura Secord?"

"Tech, suggest radio silence. I have the fix, but so will the Sabre."

"Doesn't matter."

"I am close, Tech."

"Rog."

He sat in a hollow in the carcass, just under the front lip of the shell. No matter that he smelled like pogo on a dead pogo. "Front row tickets." He could just see over the edge of his "seat," the meat under him settling a bit.

Radio contact. West again. Close. A pack of nessies. The Cheng-Sze wheeled and set off, top speed. As it rounded the rocks it sensed something odd, braked. It turned to allow its sensors more range. The tree snapped forward and though the Sabre reacted, blowing the tree to shreds, the glands burst over its carapace and rained down on its hatch. It identified and ignored the liquid, moving up toward the dead pogo. That was when the nessies came out of the trees.

Inconsequential creatures. Where is my Enemy? There were shots. I will find the man. I will find the LRS.

Nothing on its sensors. Three nessies rammed it at once, driving their horns against its hull, tips striking sparks off the duralloy, or shattering to dust; no pogo shell was this hard. Two more leaped up on it clawing at the hatch, squirming over one another to attack. It blew them apart, but it could only deliver so many anti-personnel mines and laser bolts at once; more kept coming, in a mindless attack frenzy, like sharks. *The liquid. Pogo scent. Clever.* It backed, trying to shake them off, more and more piling on top of it, on top of the heaps of blackened flesh and shattered shells of their fellows. *I must not allow them to stop me.*

The laser-beam, unbroken, arced and whirled, carving the close ones to pieces, mirroring drunkenly off heaving shells. They began slashing at anything that moved. Two external sensors damaged, inoperative. It moved, cracking and smearing a nessie undertread.

The Kai-Sabre turned on its lights, the harsh white glare searing through a misty pink haze. It fired and fired, lasers and main cannon and anti-personnel mines. It spun and flung the creatures off, light and explosions wheeling out into the dark and fog with the thrashing bodies of the nessies, one with a link of duralloy still in its teeth.

They have a scent, and a fight. Their instincts are self-sacrificing, like army ants, or piranha, Sven thought, hunkering down under the edge of the shell, covering his head with his arms, wondering vaguely if the liquid falling on him was rain or nessie blood.

He crawled far back inside the pogo shell as the fight came closer. It was the only thing that would offer him some protection. *Am I dreaming? I'm still in the dead pogo. I must be dreaming.* He curled into a pit in the carcass and held on. His leg wouldn't bend.

The world seemed to rock, the inside of the shell ringing like a hundred ton bell. God. He clung to one of the internal ribs along the inside of the shell as it rang again, and again, explosion-flashes flaring even through the metal of the shell. *Will I ever be able to hear again?* The carcass sloshed, a wave of dead meat and fluid slamming him up against the inside of the shell.

I can't stay inside here. Laura has to come soon. I have to get to her. Sven scrambled back down through the rippling carcass to the opening, clutching the pack to his chest. Its seams were rotting, dropping bits of duraplas as they tore further and further, threatening to spill parts and tools all over the decaying meat and ground. *Hell, hell, where's Laura? The nessies aren't going to hold the Sabre forever.* . . . The battle had moved off again, flashes bursting green through a curtain of leaves. He strained his eyes and ears in the dark. All he could hear was the raging fight, and his hiss and blatt of static in the com as the Sabre blew the nessies away. God . . . God . . .

Then, just for a second, in a flash of the Sabre's beams he caught a glimpse of a mountain moving, downslope. The noise of it was lost in the explosions. "Laura! Open your hatch!" He hoped his shout would get through the static or this was going to be one hell of a short repair mission. He slid down, dragging the clothpack with him. Holding it together, clutching it to his chest he staggered downhill, hit the dirt as another explosion flung him off his feet and jolted the dead pogo toward him. Then the blasts ceased. *Shit. The fight's stopped.* The bellows of nessies were fading to wounded moans and whimpers, like bleeding bassoons. The growl of the Kai-Sabre idling whispered over the muddy landscape. It didn't seem to be moving. *The pogo's in between it and me; it can't sense anything through the shell.* Then its engine revved, pitch rising.

"Oh God, dear God. LRS, Laura . . ." He was almost whimpering, falling against the Bolo's hull, trying to climb the ladder one handed, the other clutching the precious pack; while some part of him shrieked too heavy, drop it! *Drop it and climb into safety before the laser carved him in half* . . .

His fingers closed over the edge of the hatch as the Kai-Sabre blew the exposed forequarter of the pogo out of its way, knocking the shell tumbling downhill. He couldn't see anything, but felt the recoil as the LRS fired back, the repeaters below him almost shaking him off the hull; he dragged himself inside and as the hatch closed felt the heat of the beam scorch his naked legs as he half fell into the LRS's cabin.

The jouncing was making him sick. "More light, here, Laura," Sven muttered, clenching his teeth to keep his gorge down, fighting his hands so they didn't shake.

Was it fever or the hammering of the Sabre? He couldn't tell. There was no time. Fully armed, full powered, it was more than a match for a Hellbore-less old Bolo. No time to use the med-pack built into the couch—that would have to come later. If they made it. His fingers, greasy with slime, trembled with fatigue.

The LRS switched on another set of pin-lights inside the turret control; she jolted over something she couldn't compensate for, he bounced, smacked his head against the backpanel, lost the screw for the third time down into the narrow slot next to the backup motor mount. "Christ, I have no idea how it can be that a machine as big as you are still has to have so many tiny, inaccessible, knuckle-chewing—" He rattled against the sharp corners of the narrow space again as the terrain shifted.

"This is taking an unprecedented length of time, Tech Todd," the Bolo interrupted, barely audible through his earplugs.

A clang, a muffled thud and a stream of curses. "Laura!" Sven crawled out, a layer of grease now covering the layer of pogo-goo, holding his left hand in his right. "I usually have a team of four and a small waldo to position this particular part." His voice rose, almost hysterically. "I also usually have a steady floor. Repairs on the run are somewhat more difficult. In other words, Laura, go piss up a rope!"

"That order is impossible to obey, Tech. I do not have a urinary tract. I do not have a rope. Also, the gravitational properties of this world do not allow urination up. Suggest alternatives—"

"Just shut up!" That she could obey. The fever was singing in his ears, making the cabin shift and sway even more than the battering they were taking from the Kai-Sabre.

He didn't want to think what he smelled like. Luckily his nose wasn't registering it anymore. He staggered, caught himself on the edge of the open panel as the floor bucked. Sven crawled back in and picked up the screwjack he'd been using to try and manually lift the part into place. "Stup ... damn ... shit eating screws ..."

"Tech Todd, may I remind you that the Kai-Sabre is one kilometer away."

That was the best distance the running fire-fight had given them, could give them. "YES! You may remind me. You just did ... Dammit, I can't fix this without a little more stability ... Laura, we're cooked if you don't smooth out, somehow."

"I am somewhat heated from the Kai-Sabre's main cannon."

"That's not ..." He cut himself off. "Laura, sweetheart, find us a pogo herd ..."

"They will be stampeding because the bombardment, Tech."

"WELL, CATCH UP TO THEM!"

"Enhancing power to engines, Tech."

"God-damned most lethal game of tag I've ever been in," he muttered, struggling to reach the screw he'd lost.

"Tech?"

"What?"

"What is 'tag'?" He managed to grab the screw. "What? Oh, a chase game by children, who try to avoid being touched by the one designated 'It.' In this case it's us, trying not to get shot to bits."

"Understood."

His following statements over the next ten minutes were not directed at the LRS so she ignored them. ". . . sumbitch . . . There. Laura, try the traverse now." With a squeal it shifted, halted, shifted again. "Hold it!" He dug down into the bottom of his bag, yelped as the LRS swerved and sent him sliding across the floor, his tools rolling to bang into his legs and the console across the cabin. "Hey! Owww."

"Main cannon burst from the Kai-Sabre. It is making almost eighty kilometers per hour."

"Well, you do ninety then!" His groping fingers found the can in the bottom of his bag. "Got it! You know, Laura, you can do almost anything in the universe with spray lubricant and duct tape? I hope the hell this is one of them!" He sprayed liberally; the mechanism continued to stick. "Damn."

"Tech Todd: suggest impact of one pound at thirty kilometers per hour on left rear corner of traverse stabilizer base shaft."

"Fine!" A precise whack from his fist, and the turret traverse mechanism responded, turning smoothly to the tracking command.

"This is tolerable, Tech Todd." Sven sucked on the cut on his left hand, swaying. "Yeah." He leaned over to pat the small cameo painted next to the manual controls, the portrait of a young, serene woman in victorian garb, the picture surrounded by a lace frill. "Tolerable. Shit!" He staggered and sat down heavily, half-falling into the couch as the cabin trembled; his tools rattling into the corners.

"The Kai-Sabre is .5 kilometers away and closing."

"And I still have to find the glitch in your gun's vertical controls."

"Might I suggest you do that, Tech Todd."

"It was a rhetorical statement!"

A few moments later Sven unclipped his tester from the plug-in patch. "It's not in the electronics. It's physically jammed."

"I have attempted to free it, Tech. I ceased when it appeared to be about to cause internal damage to the motors."

"Damn straight." The extra light he'd brought out of one of the supply packs swung wildly over his head, trying to tear itself loose from where he'd clipped it. He ignored the swaying, letting the couch gimbals take the shocks.

"We are entering a pogo herd of approximately fifty." The Bolo's motion smoothed out.

"Good. Because I can't get at it from the inside."

"Outside is dangerous even for armored personnel, Tech." He ran his hands through his sticky, stiff hair.

"I know. Open the top hatch."

"I advise against this move, Tech."

"Shut up and obey orders, Laura. No Hellbore, and we're screwed—haven't you figured that out yet?"

"Yes, Tech." The hatch un-dogged and slid open a crack, letting in a roar of sound that made Sven cover his ears despite his plugs. The pogos bellowed in terror and rage all around them as they plunged through a forest of Weeping trees. He was seemingly surrounded by a churning field of boulders, clashing sparks off each other. A spark drew an anti-personnel bolt from behind, near the rear of the herd, and a cow pogo squealed in pain, the high shriek as loud as the shot.

He pulled on the toolkit work gloves. "Keep the home-fires burning, Laura, I'll be right back in."

He climbed out into the dark and the rain, the deep wails of the herd battering at him as much as the jouncing of the hull. The darkness swam around him; he wasn't going to be much good for anything very soon, he knew. *Hang on.* He gritted his teeth. *I'm going to finish this. Damn every 'Shang that ever lived.*

He couldn't key his light yet, that would just draw the Sabre. He'd clipped the com into his ear so that Laura could warn him of drastic maneuvers, the alto voice a smooth murmur in the background undercutting the howling blast of bolts as the Kai-Sabre shot away pogos around them. Dirt and mud mixed with the rain pelting down on him and he ducked his head into his shoulders, unable to free a hand to protect his head. For a long moment he just clung to the hull like a bug on a barrel, getting the breath battered out of him; then began inching forward. The rain pounded down on his back and mud splashed up on the LRS's fender skirts, making the hull slippery. It was like riding a wet nessie. Fortunately this particular ride had handholds. Despite the wet, Laura's hull was hot. He sucked in his breath with a hiss as his skin met the searing duralloy. *God knows how many rads I'm taking. Shit, shit, shit.*

He looked up to see the looming stalks of pogo heads swaying above him, darker streaks of black against a cloudy sky. *Maybe this is all a delirium.* He was shaking so hard with cold he could hardly keep his hands clenched as Laura bounced over the rough terrain; his legs left the hull completely for a moment, his weight in midair, then slammed down again. *If I fall off, I'm mincement.* He'd never get up before pogo legs and pads crushed him.

Sheet lightning flickered above the clouds, even thunder drowned out by the din around him. Sven ducked flat again as the LRS slewed around a thick stand of fern-trees, and plowed through a small bog. The herd bull was attacking the Kai-Sabre, judging by its screams. Three massive shots and the night was suddenly full of gobbets of meat raining down out of the sky with the water. Sven gagged.

He groped for the ring-glitch with his gloved hands, found it. Blinking dirt out of his eyes, he strained to see how bad the damage was. He grunted, and risked tonguing his head-light on. In the puddle of yellow light slashed through with rain, he saw the duralloy deformed around the barrel, Hellbore stubbornly locked in the pinch.

"A bigger hammer," he muttered, more to himself than to the LRS.

As he let go one hand to grab the tools he needed, a heaving metallic shell banged against the bolo's side, jostling even its great weight. With a shriek, Sven flew up and forward, his one handhold twisted against his thigh as he slid and hung, for a long, long moment, thrown over the barrel of the Hellbore itself; his light bounced wildly down at the blurring tread spinning twenty meters below. If he fell, she'd never be able to stop in time. *Great. Great. It's our own machine treads that are going to mash me. Great.*

Gasping for breath, Sven slowly dragged himself back to safety. Another jolt smashed him against the front sensors on her hull. "Dammit!" The Kai-Sabre fired; a bull pogo flung its head back and roared in agony, falling towards them. Sven clicked off his light and tightened his grip, and the LRS dug in, powering ahead so the pogo's body slid off the rear deck, shoving them forward.

He jammed himself into the cranny where the Hellbore protruded from the turret and dug down with one hand into a sealed pouch for his bigger hammer.

Nobody could un-dent duralloy with mere human muscle. He leaned down, taking the shocks of the ride in his knees, dizzy. *Only got one chance.* He only had one set of the thumb-sized explosives and if they didn't work . . .

He shook his head and crouched down, praying he wouldn't fall or drop the charges. He clicked the light on for a second as he stuck them in place and armed them with a twist of his thumb. One chance. This is it. He scrambled back to the hatch.

The muffled thuds of the tiny charges were lost entirely in the pounding of the Kai-Sabre's repeaters, close, close, too close. Did it work? "Laura!" He looked up, in time to see the pogo beside blow apart with a scream of metal-laced shell and tearing flesh— and the Kai-Sabre looming behind it, lights glaring, framed by the flames in the hanging moss all around them. "Laura! Open the hatch!" He saw the tip of its main cannon, glowing red, locking on, then shifting minutely as it kept its lock. The hatch cracked open. He dived for it. *Shit!*

The LRS is .5 km north. Within range of my main cannon. My port track is damaged but I will destroy the Bolo. The Cheng-Sze fired and the Bolo took the burst on its carapace and upped its speed, gaining on the fleeing herd of pogos ahead. *It is larger than I, but it is damaged. I will eliminate it before its Hellbore is repaired. My main cannon has destroyed its front sensor pod.*

The pogos plunged around the Kai-Sabre, clanging against its hull, squealing. They blocked all possibility of pinpointing the Bolo. It shot. Shot again. *There— no, another pogo. It is in this herd of creatures and if I must shoot them all to find it, I will.* It had full power and even if it did not have infinite ammunition, it had plenty enough to exterminate this herd.

Close. A minute flash of light? Yes. There. Stupid beasts. The Bolo was slowing, allowing the herd to pull away from it, the human halfway into the top hatch. One pogo between it and them—with one shot, the Cheng-Sze blew it away. The bolo's turret swivelled as the human dropped down into the hatch but . . .

Its Hellbore is still five degrees below horizontal. The human has not succeeded. I have it.

Then the Hellbore smoothly angled up, locking on.

It is repai—

Dark and rain turned to blazing white, white as the heart of a lightning bolt, outlining the Kai-Sabre for a fraction of a second like a black speck on the surface of the sun. A second shot sent the Bolo recoiling back on its own locked tracks and then . . .

Where the Sabre had been was a smoldering mound, streams of metal hissing as they flowed and cooled in the rain. The air was thick with steam. All sounds faded, except the creak and ping of overheated duralloy, and the crackle of fires in vegetation dried and ignited in one moment.

"Tag," the LRS said on an external speaker. "You're it."

It was funny—how'd the Bolo's cabin lights get turned so high? Sven blinked, blinked again and realized that he wasn't in the LRS any longer. He saw warm white walls and a rose carpet as he turned his head: and the window. *Nope, I'm not in Heaven, I'm still on New Newf.* It was raining. Distantly he heard a nurse's beeper and the chug and click of medical monitors. The hospital.

The screen on the metal arm of the bed beeped at him. He looked up.

"Lieutenant Todd." It was Lieutenant-Commander Christopher Harding, de factor leader of the insurgents.

"Sir." Sven felt as if his brain had just been pulled through a sieve, and his tongue with it.

"The equipment just informed me that you'd

wakened. I assumed you would want to know what happened."

"Uh, yes, sir."

"You know that the LRS destroyed the last Kai-Sabre the Xi-shang had?"

"I assumed so, sir." Actually he hadn't gotten around to thinking of that yet, but it made sense; eliminating the Kai-Sabres at all cost had been first priority. He leaned his head back on the pillow. One of the nurses came in and, after checking the monitors, laid a packet on the bed.

"You made it to the Bolo's couch, so you weren't as badly off as you might have been," Harding said. "The LRS didn't have the medical capability to deal with the amount of radiation you'd absorbed, though. Which is why you're here." Sven nodded, ran an experimental hand over his head, finding that his hair was a short fuzz. "You're well past the stage of losing hair, Lieutenant."

"Yes, sir."

Harding's face sobered. "Your escort are up for the Starred Cross, Lieutenant, posthumously."

"Thank you," Sven said, feeling a stab of grief for them.

"And you will be awarded it as well. We'll have to see you pinned and get you to rivet one onto the hull of the LRS." Harding nodded at the package the nurse had brought. "Go on, stop pretending not to notice that, and open it. I'll make it more official, once we get things cleaned up here. We're back in control now, because of your actions. . . ." He paused as an aide handed him another report from offscreen. "Once the 'Shang knew all three of their Sabres were out of commission, they decided to quietly high-tail it. We caught them in the act. Their megatonner got away, but only a third full; and we captured a good seventy per cent of the personnel they had left. So we have a number of POWs to deal with until we can send them down to the Core Worlds."

Sven tore open the package, spilling a set of captain's bars and an antique Luger onto the bed. "Congratulations, Captain Todd. I picked up that sidearm from the 'Shang Mission Commander. Since you are a tech, I thought you would appreciate it."

"Thank you, sir," Sven said. "When can I get the Bolo garage back up and running, sir? I'm sure Laur . . . the LRS needs quite a bit of work."

Harding laughed. "As soon as you're on your feet." Sven smiled, a little uncertainly. "Laura'll wait for you, Captain. She'll wait for you."

SHARED EXPERIENCE

Christopher Stasheff

Titan slept and dreamed, but his dreams were of war.

Rampart, harpies attacking at twelve o'clock!

These dreams were brought not by the subconscious, but by memory, and the continuing transmissions of his comrades as they fought, so that all would know which tactics succeeded, and which failed.

Dark against a sky lit by energy bolts and bomb explosions, a horde of vaguely feminine shapes rode the air on vast beating wings—feminine shapes clutching forms of death, rocket-launchers and slug-throwers that chattered like the insane gibbering of demented birds, while below them, scimitar talons curved to grasp and gouge.

The huge Bolos, each named for a defensive structure, trundled out to meet the enemy—an enemy with wings, that struck from the air with talons. The sentry

115

who had first nicknamed the Xalontese "harpies" had definitely had a warped sense of humor—or some very strange perceptions, if he thought these winged, scaly, six-limbed saurians looked like women. On a very dark night, silhouetted against a glowing sky, perhaps there was a very slight resemblance—the swell of the keel-bone might be mistaken for that of a bosom, and the ventilating headcrest might be confused with an elaborate hairdo—but in anything resembling good light, the monsters were obviously much closer to a pterodactyl than to a human woman.

But they smelled. That characteristic, they shared with the harpies of legend. And they spread foulness, droppings, wherever they went. That, too, they had in common with King Phineus's nemeses.

Rampart sped out to meet them, his treads a blur, his drive-engines filling the world with their roaring, almost drowning out the shrill shrieks of joy that served the harpies as a battle-cry. He slewed aside and filled the sky with the stream of fire from his starboard guns, while his Hellbore tracked along the line of enemies, filling the sky with fire.

But no matter how many he burned in instant explosions of flame, no matter how many dropped screaming with his bullets in their hearts, a thousand more survived to fly through and above his screen of fire, to drop their bombs on and before him.

"I've hated you from the day I saw you," Dawn said.

"Me, too," Larry shot back. "So how come we're in bed together?"

"This is a bunker, not a bed, you heel! I wouldn't get into bed with you if you were the only man in the world!"

"I'm the only man in *your* world, right now," Larry pointed out. "But don't worry, you won't have to prove your claim—if one of us has to sleep, the other one has to stay awake."

"If anyone *can* sleep, when they're surrounded by cannon fire," Dawn muttered.

The remarkable thing about this exchange was that neither of them was looking at the other. They sat back to back in a concrete-walled chamber twelve feet square, watching screens that showed them a variety of information—infra-red, radar, sonar, even visual. The last screen was large enough to seem a window on the outside world—but their station was ten feet underground. Only their concrete roof showed above the earth—charred and scarred, but the two cannon barrels that poked out of it were still in excellent working condition. Not that the harpies hadn't tried to bomb them, of course—but whenever a saurian came too close, they fried him ten meters away.

Sooner or later, one would make it through; there would be one they wouldn't notice in time. Either that, or one of the harpies they scared off would call in a ship, and its beams would crack them like an egg and roast them instantly.

But they couldn't think about that, of course—so they argued. It helped distract them, it kept them from thinking about it—and it kept the adrenaline flowing, kept them ready to fry anything that came too close.

There was a single cot at one side of the room, just barely wide enough for one person. Near it, there was a small table, one chair, and a hot plate with a kettle, a sink, and a large pile of ration packs. That was only half the ration packs they had begun with, but they weren't worried. In fact, they were surprised they themselves had lasted long enough to eat so many.

Neither of them could tell that to the other, though.

So they sat and watched, and from time to time, one of their hands twitched to hit a firing button.

There were busy times and slow times. During the slow, one of them would watch both sets of screens while the other slept. If business picked up, the sentry could always call the sleeper.

"The day you wake me up for anything but battle," Dawn said, "is the day I start standing watch alone."

"So why would I wake you?"

Dawn was silent a moment, trying to figure out exactly what he meant by that. She decided that any way you looked at it, it was an insult. "Every reason not to—especially since you have to sleep some time, too."

"Yes, I do," Larry sighed, "so I can think of you waking me for all the wrong reasons."

"How about waking you with a blaster?"

"Hey, at least it'd be quick."

"Well, that's all you're interested in." Dawn hit the button, and the cannon above them coughed. At least, all they heard down here was a cough.

"I wouldn't wish the poor things a slow death."

"Don't worry—with me, death's always quick."

"The big death, or the little one?"

"How big is a harpy?" Dawn demanded.

"You should know," Larry retorted.

Dawn hit the button again. "Damn! Almost missed!" She fired again. "There, got him. Hate to have him suffer for a second, though."

"Oh, you were very helpful. How'd you know it was a him?"

"Why should I think it was a her?"

Larry nodded. "Good question. No answer. I think each one is an 'it.'"

"Well, I haven't heard anything from the scientists yet," Dawn snapped.

"I know what you mean," Larry agreed. "I haven't read any good books lately, myself." He hit the firing pad. The gun coughed above him, then coughed again. "We'll find out some day—if I don't quit before then."

"Can't be too soon for me. I can just imagine your replacement—tall, handsome, muscles on his muscles . . ."

"And I can imagine *yours*—built out of normal distribution curves, blond, sweet-tongued . . ."

"The only sweet tongue you'll ever get is on a sandwich!"

"I'll settle for a side without sauce."

And on they went, on and on. Above them, the harpies kept coming, carrying bombs to drop, bombs which exploded with them when the blast from the cannon touched them. Others hovered a few feet out of range, lobbing in rockets and grenades, which did no damage, but occasionally loused up the sensors for a few seconds. No matter how many died, more and more kept coming—because sooner or later, the flare that blocked the sensors would coincide with a harpy coming close enough to drop its bomb. It had worked before, against hundreds of others of these human outposts; it would work against this one, sooner or later. What matter how many of the almost mindless happy "workers" died? The intelligent ones, the ones aboard ship with minds, could always make more—and did. In fact, they couldn't help themselves.

Neither could Dawn and Larry. The only thing that kept them from tearing each other apart was fatigue.

Harpies stooped from all over the sky, converging on the lone bolo. Equal to the attack, Rampart traversed the heavens with fire and shot, shells exploding before the ungainly fliers, shrapnel tearing them apart—but as a thousand died, more thousands pressed on in their places. Still Rampart held them off, still Rampart stood indifferent under their rain of bombs and bolts . . .

Until the blasted eggs from which they had hatched

spun into view, bulbous ellipsoidal ships spewing harpies in their wakes—but walking over the blasted
plain on pillars of fire, stabbing down at the ground
with bolts of pure energy, half a dozen of them converging on Rampart.

His cannon tracked and blasted again and again,
hitting the one huge ship where Intelligence said the
power plant was housed, hitting it again and again,
slowly burning through the shielding as his rocket
launchers targeted other ships and hit them again and
again, but the energy bolts walked toward him inexo-
rably, the huge ships waded through his fire, slowed
but never stopped. . . .

Until five of the six ships stood over him, blasting
downward with artificial lightning, raising the stink of
ozone, then the stink of burning steel, as the sixth
ship fell out of the sky, its power plant exploded at
last, and the melting column that was Rampart's Hellbore traversed to center on another enemy ship,
almost straight above him, even as its shell turned
yellow, then white, then flowed, and all the rounds
within him detonated and exploded in a single bright
burst that shook the whole of the blasted plain, taking
with it the hundred or so harpies whose lust for vengeance had been so strong that they had stayed to
watch, instead of retreating beyond range.

But even as he died, one last searing message
sprayed out from Rampart like the molten steel of his
dying body, one last demand that seared through the
Titan even in his sleep:

Avenge me.

And Titan knew that he would, even if he died as
Rampart had died—for what better death could any
warrior ask, man or machine?

Merlon, sally forth to sweep the talus slope!

Below the fortress and the bunkers that shielded
it, another horde of harpies came crawling up the

scree, below the level of the automatic guns. There seemed to be no end to them and, like worker ants, they pressed on mindlessly, intent only on the damage they could do, the number of humans they could kill, driven by a single hive-mind, a single instinctive lust for destruction.

The gate slammed open, and Merlon shot out, holding place and filling the slope with fire until the gate had grated shut behind her. Then she rolled forth to the edge of the hill, her cannon lowering, her guns depressing, then filling the whole slope with shell and fire. Harpies screamed and rolled back while others dug frantically, trying to dig themselves into the loose rock beneath the scrub grass—and roasting in an instant, when Merlon's hot breath touched them. Dragon stood at bay, burning down the horde of harpies who tormented her. But with mindless boldness, harpies fired rocket launchers even as they died, and Merlon took hits low, between her treads and on her treads. No one hit meant anything, really, but their steady rain would burn through her armor eventually.

She turned sideways, raking the slope with fore guns and aft guns and side guns as she traversed slowly, circling the fortress, filling the slope with death—but more harpies clambered over the charred remains of their fellows, still kept low by the automatic fire of the defending guns, slowed but advancing, and nearly reaching the crest by the time Merlon came in view again, limping because of a blown roller on her starboard tread, a tread that was holed in several places but not quite enough to bring it down or break it through. Her cannons blasted the aliens at the brow of the slope, then traversed downward, working their way slowly through their ranks—but not a single reptile fled; they only struggled on up to their deaths with mindles shrieks of joy.

Above them, Merlon turned, presenting her less-damaged port side. The guns roared mayhem, and she began the slow circuit back.

Finally the great dark eggs hove in view; finally half a dozen of them walked their way over the plain to converge on her. Fire met fire, but that of six ships was far more than even a Bolo could bear. Melting but firing back, Merlon too died, and when only slag remained, the great charred ships stepped over a few paces farther, squatting atop the fortress, and slowly, ever so slowly, burning their way in, now that the defender was a pool of spreading lava.

Spreading lava, but also one last spreading message, rippling outward in a wave of electromagnetic energy:

Remember me! Avenge!

I shall, Titan promised, and strove to rouse himself from the lethargy of standby mode—but the switches would not close, and he lapsed back to slumber.

Bulwark, enfilade ground at seven o'clock—harpies mining!

Bulwark stood alone in the center of a blasted heath—blasted by its own energy weapons, but also by those of a thousand harpies, whose ashes covered the ground.

From among them rose the wreckage of a great dark egg. Bulwark had learned as Rampart had learned, but had lived to tell of it—he had targetted one particular area on the ship's hull and had poured in fire. He had hit the reactor, and the ship had exploded. Bulwark immediately sent out news of his discovery, and all the Bolos immediately copied his technique. That was why there were only forty-eight ships left.

In vengeance, they converged on Bulwark.

But the miners got there first.

Bulwark depressed his cannon and all his guns, fire blasting a ring-trench in the dirt of the heath, a hundred meters in diameter. Within that circle, his guns sprayed a hail of bullets down into the ground. Armor-piercing rounds slammed through the hardpan and into the folded wings in the tunnels below. Harpies shrieked, and were dead. Those few who were wounded were instantly consumed by the firebolts that followed.

But while Bulwark was busy weeding out the sappers who would have undermined him, three huge ships drifted across the plain, almost invisible against the night sky, their energy-projector beams dark for stealth. Attuned to radiation or plasma, scanning for engine activity, Bulwark's sensors overlooked the silent enemies . . .

Until they were almost squarely above him.

Then, nearly too late, Bulwark's guns swooped upward, slashing fire into the night. The huge cannon-barrel followed more slowly, then belched pure energy up at the looming ships. He left two of them to his smaller weapons and poured the fire from the big Hellbore into the same spot low down on one ship—but the egg began to turn, slowly on its axis, dissipating the heat somewhat, while it joined its companions in stamping with legs of lightning, full on the mighty machine. Bolt after bolt ran off Bulwark's carapace, grounded against the soil—but the heat of its passage lingered, building slowly.

Beneath the ground, harpies screamed and died, caught in the corona of their own ships' discharge—but more pressed forward with the tenacity of the hive-mind, each taking a few more bites out of the soil before it died . . .

With a roar, the ground gave way beneath Bulwark, and grenades carried by the miners erupted in thunder. Surrounded by fire, mired in a huge trench, Bulwark's shots went wide for a few vital minutes, and the ship above cooled as it stamped down with lightning legs. Its companions joined it, the heat of their bolts reflecting back from the sides of the hole, the earth itself melting, their liquid fire wooing the molecules of Bulwark's armor, leading them off into the dance of Brownian movement as the huge machine began to melt, even as it poured fire into the sky, but with less and less aim, its shots at random now, as Bulwark's carapace fell away and his inner shielding began to melt.

Finally his power plan erupted in a final, huge explosion, a wave of devastation that swept outward, bearing the message:

Avenge me!

I shall, Titan promised yet again—but he could not, for he still sat dormant as the technicians swarmed around and within him, soldering, cleaning, mending in a race against time.

Donjon, meet enemy invading force from 2 o'clock.

Donjon finished incinerating the thousand winged monsters who had surrounded the isolated bunker that held a dozen humans, half of them wounded. He pivoted a hundred eighty degrees and rolled toward the northeast a hundred yards—no further; he had a nest of humans to protect.

Onward they came, dark against the fire in the sky—a horde of wings, too many for the mortal eye to count—but not too many for electronic scanners and microprocessors. Donjon numbered them at eleven thousand, two hundred eighty-nine even as his guns began to sweep them from the sky.

But far below, a long line of motorized unicycles bounced over the ground, stabilized by the wings of their riders, but carrying heavier guns than the harpies could bring aloft unaided—guns that hailed bullets on Donjon, that stenciled graffiti of death on him with pencils of fire.

Donjon turned broadside, depressing several guns

to rake their line with fire more deadly than their own—but still his cannon stood mute at forty-five degrees, waiting for the egg-ships that he knew must come.

And there they came, stalking across the hills from the northeast—at two o'clock, just as the human sentries in the orbital fortress had told him. Donjon knew he must keep them from approaching the human nest behind him for, even though the soft ones were well-hidden and walled in by three feet of steel, they were still vulnerable, so much more vulnerable than a Bolo! Therefore he lashed out at the ships with a gout of fire from his cannon while they were still out of effective range, in the hope that they would think him closer than he was, and stay well back.

It was a forlorn hope; any scanner could analyze his distance from the attentuation of the energy-bolt. All it did was give the ships a more accurate fix on Donjon himself—but they had had that, anyway.

Therefore he only traded fire with them for a few minutes, just long enough for them to begin to cluster as they approached—then he whirled and raced off across the floor of the valley, abandoning those in his charge—but leading the enemy away from them, too.

Like predators everywhere, the ships followed.

When their lightning-bolts were almost upon him, Donjon spun about, skidding through a hundred-eighty-degree turn and shooting back the way he had come. Taken by surprise, the eggs slowed, trying to stop, still stamping at him with legs of plasma—but Donjon sped through the fire-fall and on away. He stopped a hundred yards past, swinging broadside, Hellbore elevating, rotating, fixing on the central egg, pouring fire into its lower section. Taken by surprise, the egg was slow in beginning its rotation—too slow. Fire rained down around Donjon from the central egg's companions, and his temperature-register began to climb near the danger point, but he held on, just a minute longer, just a second . . .

With a huge mushrooming blast, the central egg exploded, then hurtled down to the ground, broken open, its power plant erupted, its crew dead.

Donjon shot toward it, taking his pursuers by surprise again. His skin cooled as he passed the curtain of plasma, cooled further as he roared past the wreckage of his fallen foe.

The remaining eggs swung together and gave chase again.

Donjon's skin was cooled completely now, but he sped away still, on and on. Above, the eggs reached full acceleration, gaining on him, catching up . . .

A mile from the human nest, Donjon sped into a maze of gullies. He skidded to a halt, targeted an egg-ship, and unleashed his torrent of fire, even as Bulwark had taught him. It poured into the skin of the ship, tracking it, staying with that same spot even as the ship came on, trying to slow enough to begin rotation. Its skin began to glow with the heat, and the pilots must have realized that he could not slow down in time to rotate—he would have crushed his crew with Coriolis force—so he began evasive action. Out of Donjon's beam he bobbed, swerved closer, dodged again. . . .

Donjon analyzed the pattern. His gun locked on the egg again, pouring energy in, staying with the alien ship as it danced and weaved . . .

Its mates arrived.

They hovered over the gully, pouring fire down. Donjon held his place for a second more, then another second and another, as his temperature gauge climbed higher and higher . . .

The second ship blew out in a gout of flame and tumbled out of the sky.

Donjon didn't stay to look; his gauge had hit the

danger point. He turned and sped down the gully, out of the rain of fire. Its walls blocked him from the egg-ships' line of sight. He found a side-gully and swerved into it, slowing to negotiate its rocky, bumpy surface, but keeping on, keeping on, as the egg-ships passed by behind him, following the main gully. Then Donjon found another side-passage, another and another, till he emerged into the main gully again. Overhead, the harpy ships had slowed, were hovering, searching for him . . .

Donjon unleashed his own lightning-streak, plasma from his main gun, lancing up to the vulnerable area of one of the egg-ships.

The whole basketful shot toward him.

Donjon tracked the one he had chosen for his target, even though it had begun rotating, coming much more slowly than its fellows. Donjon knew he couldn't possibly burn it through in time, so he shifted abruptly to another ship, much closer, hovering over him . . .

His plasma-bolt shot up into its downward-pointing gun. Energy smote energy and exploded, even in the mouth of the harpy's cannon—an explosion that shook the whole plain, knocked the ship out of the sky . . .

. . . and tumbled Donjon onto his side.

The Bolo could cope with that, of course. Jacks extruded from his side, levering him off the ground just enough so that his cannon could pour fire into the dirt, pushing him away, pushing him back upright . . .

But it took time, and his main cannon could not track the egg-ships. His smaller guns could and did, but what use were they when four huge ships were clustered about, pouring their fire into the fallen Bolo?

His temperature gauge climbed, screamed, as Donjon slowly tilted further up and further. His carapace began to melt. Fire poured down from above, almost cancelling the push of his own guns against the earth, but even so, he rose closer and closer to the vertical, closer and closer to the point when gravity would take over . . .

But his carapace melted, his inner armor began to flow . . .

With a sudden jarring shock, the huge machine swung upright, slamming down onto his treads. But they were weakened by the heat, they gave way, and their rollers fouled in the liquid iron. Inner armor dripped and flared, and the shielding of the power plant gave way.

Donjon died in a roaring fountain of flame, a blast that reached up to an egg-ship that had come too close in its eagerness and went tumbling to earth for its greed. Donjon died in a cascade of gamma rays and heavy particles, in a burst of radiation that surrounded but did not quite obliterate his final message:

Remember and avenge me!

I will, Titan promised, struggling toward consciousness. *I will.*

But his promise had to wait, for flesh-and-blood technicians can move just so quickly.

Chateau, enemy ships approaching from five o'clock, at twelve thousand feet.

Chateau had perched herself atop a mountain— low, as mountains go, but still craggy and rocky, its walls streaked with metal ores. To a scanner, she would seem to be just one more outcrop among many; to the naked eye, she would seem to be another rough-hewn shape carved out by wind and water.

To the eye assisted by a telescope or magnifier, she would seem to be a Bolo.

There came the enemy ships—only specks against the orange sky, but to her computer-enhanced vision, their shapes were crystal clear. She waited, every system at maximum energy flow . . . and waited, and waited . . . With her response time speeded up, her time sense had slowed relative to real time, and the wait seemed to last forever . . .

Finally, they were in range.

Chateau loosed a blast that tore through the sky at the speed of light, instantly illuminating the lower half of one of the approaching ships. The egg instantly went into evasive action, and Chateau lost it for the first three twists and turns, then analysed the pattern and locked onto it. The skin of the ship heated, and the pilot switched to a different evasive pattern. This time, though, Chateau identified it in two twists and turns and locked on again. The ship slowed, still evading, and began to rotate.

But its companions accelerated, stooping on Chateau like hawks on a click.

This click, though, had a very sharp beak—and a very long one. Chateau's lesser guns came up and filled the air with fire between herself and the invading ships even as she kept her main cannon locked onto the twisting egg. With delight, she detected torpedoes loosed, and targeted them with three of her guns. Shell met torpedo, and the sky went white with flame.

When it cleared, Chateau was no longer there.

Under cover of the sheet of fire, she had slipped back along the ledge. With sensors fore and aft and a rotating turret, she could go equally well in either direction; "front" was really defined as the direction she happened to be facing at the moment. She sped along a ledge just a meter wider than herself—a ledge that she knew was safe, because she had come along it earlier in the day, to take up her station. Then, she had sounded each square meter of rock ahead of time, probed it for soundness with sonics and sounders; now, knowing it was solid, she raced along it, gyros holding her steady. Then she killed the gyros to turn, running up another ledge of rock, back to the battle.

She came out through a tunnel only a little higher than herself—a tunnel only fifty feet long, but enough to hide her. Sure enough, the enemy ships were just passing her to gather around the spot where she had been, a quarter of a mile further on. She waited until they were past, then spat fire at the nearest egg and locked on. Sure enough, the pilot sent his ship into evasive action—but he used one of the patterns she had already analyzed. Her main gun tracked him every inch of the way, every twist, every kink, and he shifted to another pattern—but again, one that she had already analyzed. After two twists and a dip, the pilot shifted again—and Chateau lost him for two zigs and a zag. Then she picked him up again, and tracked him effortlessly—the pilot must have given up using computer-randomized patterns, and tried his intuition. But sentient beings are creatures of habit, and after the first two evasions, Chateau tracked him almost without effort. In desperation, he slowed and began to rotate—but too fast, too fast. One spot had not yet cooled before it came about for another blast. All he accomplished was to smear a circle of heat all around his craft, a circle that grew brighter and brighter with every turn.

But his companions had realized what was happening, and had come to his aid. The huge ships came to cluster about the ridge, pouring their fire down onto the mountaintop where Chateau hid. Lightning tore at rock, shattering, vaporizing—but slowly, slowly. Inch by inch, the granite wore away under a tidal wave of plasma—but it took time, precious seconds, and Chateau held on, tracking the bobbing, weaving ship as its pilot finally realized his mistake and slowed his rotation rate ...

Slowed too much. The metal of his hull, already overheated, melted and flowed. The entire bottom of his ship fell away, and Chateau's stream of fire tore into his power plant. She waited only long enough to see the blossom of flame burst from his power plant, then raced back into the tunnel. The great egg-ships, unaware that the tunnel was so short, pounded it unmercifully, and it finally cracked and fell in.

But Chateau was already taking the final road up the mountaintop.

She came out onto the plateau at the crest just as the egg-ships cut off their flow of fire and lowered themselves down to inspect the fallen bridge, sampling it with sensors for the lode of metal that would show them a wounded Bolo.

Chateau depressed her Hellbore and fired down onto the egg that was farthest into the defile.

The rock walls reflected the heat. The egg swerved up to escape—and collided with another of its kind, taken by surprise, unable to escape in time. Both exploded in a huge fiery eruption.

When the fire cleared, the other ships had gone.

Chateau instantly started a three-hundred-sixty-degree scan—but before she could find them, the clustered ships rained fire on her.

Evasive action was impossible. All she could do was to back down the mountainside, feeling her way with sonar, as she poured her own fire back up at the assembled ships, hoping against hope that it would penetrate their hail of fire and somehow muzzle them. Her temperature gauge screamed; she knew her carapace had begun to melt as she crawled downward, aiming for the shelter of a cavern she had mapped earlier in the day. She descended to a horizontal ledge, turned ninety degrees, then raced along it—out of the enemy fire.

But only for a few seconds. That was all it took the egg-ships to recover from surprise and target her again. Waves of plasma poured down; her carapace melted through, her shielding softened, but the cavern mouth was only a dozen meters ahead.

A torpedo struck two yards ahead of her, blowing a hole in the side of the mountain, taking away the trail.

Chateau slammed on her brakes but skidded—on and out, over the sudden lip at the new-carved end to the path. Down she fell through air that screamed about her, down and down a sheer drop of hundreds of feet, knowing there was no chance of survival, at least as a whole fighting unit, and her death-cry spread out about her, unseen and unheard by any but her own kind:

I die. Make it worth my death.

Within himself, Titan promised that he would—if this infernal sleep would only end, if only he could wake, if only he could be restored to function!

All these images, all these scenes of battle, mingled in Titan's sleeping mind so that he could not have said which were past, and which present—but one, at least, was memory.

Titan, harpies advancing on foot through gullies from river. Advance with caution; field is mined.

Titan had rolled out to meet the invaders, metal detectors alerting his computer-brain to the presence of buried explosives. He twisted and turned, his guns automatically compensating for every shift in angle and movement. But one of the mines must have been made of plastic, one of the mines didn't register on his sensors . . .

One of the mines blew up beneath his right tread.

The soldiers patched him up with a temporary tread and escorted him back to the repair depot. After the first two fell to harpy fire, he told the rest to ride inside—which they did, with gratitude. Limping, starboard circuits heavily damaged, memory banks shredded, Titan crawled back to the depot, his small guns shooting down attacking harpies as they went. But for every one he shot down, a hundred more came shriek-ing. A few got through his screen of fire, of course—a few grenades exploded on his upper mantle, scarring the metal but doing no real damage; a few energy bolts eroded craters in his armor, a few exploding rounds pocked his shielding—but none did any real damage, and before and behind and above and beside him, screams of delight turned into shrieks of agony as harpies plummeted to earth, blasted, burning, and ground beneath his treads.

They cleaned the sludge off in the repair depot.

Now Titan stood inert, all systems shut down to standby mode—sleeping, in human terms—as human technicians swarmed over and inside him, replacing memory chips, refurbishing connectors, welding in new plates. But dimly as a dream, so dimly that they might have been memories, the radio voices of his comrade Bolos and their human allies sifted through into his crystal mind.

Larry was asleep when the harpy got through.

The whole bunker shook, and the explosion slammed at him from all sides. The floor heaved beneath him, and he found himself scrambling up to his knees before he was quite awake. Terror and disorientation seized him—for a moment, he thought he was out on the battlefield crawling away from a harpy shell. Then the emergency lights came on, and he saw Dawn picking herself up off the floor and crawling back onto her stool, cursing.

For once, Larry didn't waste time with a snide remark. He limped over to his own stool and sat down, staring at blank screens. He snarled and slapped the side of the console in sheer frustration—and the vision screen lit.

A cloud of harpies was descending on them.

The gunsight glowed to life. Larry pressed the "lock

on" button, but nothing happened. He spat a mild obscenity and turned to the anti-personnel guns. They were smaller, but still effective—and they worked!

Above him, he heard the hammering of machine-gun fire and knew Dawn's were working, too. Even now, their rivalry goaded him into faster action—he locked onto his target and pressed "Fire," traversing the guns as he did. Then he grabbed the right-hand joystick and mowed away with fire and bullets both.

Still the harpies came, a sudden wedge of them. He shot them away; they fell back from the core of their group like the rind of an orange . . .

Revealing the bomb-carrier hidden in their center.

Larry hit him with fire, and the beast flared into ash—but the bomb hurtled on . . .

The noise was all around him, inside him, lifting him with a gigantic hand, and this time, the darkness was complete.

The nighttime seemed filled with hammering wings now, and a last redoubt of humans clustered on top of a hill in a low-domed bunker that bristled with cannon and laser projectors, impregnable against any land-borne enemies—but vulnerable as a nut in a cracker, to the walking energy bolts of the harpy eggs.

But surely those ships could not approach so closely! On the plain below the hill, seven bolos stood sentry-duty, immobile as statues, a fortress far more intimidating than any granite walls.

Seven bolos—all that were left of the force of eighty that had been stationed to hold off the advance of the enemy tide, to delay the harpies long enough for the central worlds to arm themselves to the teeth, to put a vast armada into space capable of overwhelming whole suns, let alone a chittering swarm of hollow-boned humanoids. The harpies would be crumpled and swept aside, they would be ground to mince in the jaws of the vast fleet, they would be shredded and pulped . . .

When the Armada came.

But it would not come for years, and the last seven Bolos stood at bay, guarding three hundred of the last thousand humans on the planet, while fifty-three great dark eggs strode through the sky to fall upon them.

But the harpies flew before them.

They flew, they stooped, raining foulness and destruction on the fortress and its guardians—but the Bolos lit the night with a ring of fire, and the foulness burned before it could land, as did its sources. Leather wings burst into flame, crested heads went up in fireballs; only ashes drifted to earth, those few that slipped between fiery updrafts. Ashes of saurians and their foulness landed on the roof of the fortress, but none knew, none cared. Sooty and ashen, the fortress dome stood.

But the harpies carried rocket launchers and energy rifles as well as foulness, and bombs that dropped from nerveless claws even as their owners burst into flame. Most of the bombs fell wide, only a fraction fell on the dome—but it was a fraction of thousands, and each bomb that struck weakened the concrete a little more, each rocket-flare vaporized a few molecules of granite, each energy bolt vaporized a gram. Slowly, millimeter by millimeter, the dome began to wear thin.

Then the ships arrived.

They came looming over the Bolos, looming even over the hill and its fortress, legs of energy bolts smiting down into the earth, melting bedrock.

The Bolos spoke with one voice, and that voice was the roar of cannon.

Fifty-two ships answered, but their fire-lances had limited range; the attenuation made their plasma bolts mere nusiances to the Bolos. Their cannon, on the other hand, fired blasts of coherent energy, that did damage much farther away—so each Bolo had already picked out one ship apiece, and centered its cannon fire on the lower quadrant. The targeted ships dodged and dived, but the Bolos had learned the harpies' basic evasive patterns from Donjon's transmissions of his last battle. They followed their targets from loop to twist to zigzag, only one beat behind as the harpy pilots switched patterns. The saurians' computers knew more patterns than Donjon had learned, of course, so the last seven Bolos finally began to lose their quarry—but even as they did, they analyzed, then locked on again, learning more new patterns, and more. More importantly, all seven targets went through the exact same sequence of pattern-changes.

But as they did, their fellow ships stamped closer to the redoubt, and its ring of guardians.

Fire fell on the Bolos—but for the fire to do damage, it had to hit the same spot on the Bolos' armor for several minutes at a time. It could not; the Bolos began to dodge and weave, each with a pattern more complicated than any the harpies knew—and each interlocking perfectly with all six others, so that seven mighty Bolos wound their way through a dance of death, around and around in a circle, but with quick dashes outward and inward. The harpy ships strained to keep up with them, managing to lick a Bolo's mantle with a tongue of fire here, a lance of flame there, but never for more than a few seconds.

All the time, though, the bolos stayed locked on their targets, their central computers compensating not only for the harpy ships' evasive patterns, but also for the Bolo's own. The harpy ships could not escape them; the other harpy ships could not keep up with them.

Finally, the harpy admiral must have realized that he should use his only truly overwhelming advantage—

sheer numbers. At some unseen, unheard signal, the mighty eggs began to draw in, to surround the circle of Bolos . . .

One of their ships erupted in the brightness of a burst plower plant.

The Bolo shifted to another target.

It flinched away, sped out of the closing circle, up out of range . . .

The Bolo shifted to a third target. The one who had fled was no longer of concern—it was too far away for its fire to be effective against a Bolo's armor.

A second ship blew up—a third, a fourth, stabbed to earth by the Bolos' fire. A fifth, a sixth, a seventh—and seven new targets glowed.

Finally the harpy admiral learned from his quarry; finally, the great egg-ships began to move around one another in a slow and ponderous dance, each shielding the other from the Bolos' fire for the crucial minutes necessary for cooling down. All began to rotate slowly, spreading the heat of the Bolos' fire over a larger area . . .

And their lightning-legs stumbled and wove and clashed with one another. Their cannon were fixed in the hulls, not rotating in turrets, as the Bolos' cannon did; if the eggs rotated, they could not hold their beams steady on a target.

The Bolos could not whoop for joy, but they could press their advantage with a sudden savagery. They dashed out to slide between the egg-ships' legs, dodging and weaving, dashing out to slam a shell up at their foes, then back. Sure enough, the pilots could not resist the temptation—they stopped rotating to try to slash each offending Bolo with radiation. But as soon as they stopped rotating, the Bolos transfixed the eggs with lightning of their own.

Finally, the harpy admiral realized that the Bolos

had left the redoubt temporarily unprotected. Ignoring them, his ships pressed inward.

Back the Bolos dashed, to take up their elaborate dance again—and once more, the harpy ships tripped over each others' beams. At last the admiral realized what he must do; at last seven of the ships stopped rotating and pressed in to follow one Bolo apiece, while their mates wove and dodged about them to intercept the Bolos' fire.

But there were too many eggs; dodging and weaving about one another that way, they could not come close enough to cage the Bolos.

Again the admiral learned; half of the ships drifted back, out of the battle—but stamping quickly if a Bolo lunged through the veil of fire from the inner circle. Even so, with the swirling ships' dance, the eggs could not tighten the circle enough, so another quarter of the ships had to retire to a second, and larger, circle.

The remaining quarter drew in with deadly grimness, their companions bobbing about them in a sinister dance. There were few enough of them, now, to bathe the whole ring of Bolos in fire.

Beyond them, the second tier laid down another ring of flame—and beyond them, the third ring blasted, too.

One Bolo streaked away, firing upward as he went, but the veils of fire rained down and down. His upper mantle melted, his carapace; he penetrated the second ring, his temperature gauge soaring, targeting a ship in the third ring, trying to scare it out of the way . . . he was into the third ring, dashing for freedom, and several of the ships broke off to follow . . .

His shielding melted through, and he blew up in a fountain of fury that brought down two ships that had pressed too closely in pursuit.

His death-message drifted out. *Remember. Revenge.*

His mates learned from his example and stayed

dodging and weaving themselves, each targeting yet another ship even as its upper mantle melted, its carapace, knowing he could not run, knowing she could not leave the humans unguarded, knowing that all they could do was to try to bring down one more enemy as they died . . .

They erupted, they exploded, they bathed the plain in fury, and the ships hovering above them learned that they had pressed too closely after all, as a dozen ships flared, their power plants going up in chain reactions triggered by the six Bolos' deaths. Perhaps they sent out death messages of their own, but all that penetrated Titan's dream were those on his own frequency, his fellow Bolos insisting,

Avenge. Do not forget.

I will, Titan promised in his sleep, *and I will not.*

As the flames died, the harpy admiral pressed inward with his second ring of ships. They clustered, they hovered over the redoubt, they poured their flame down. Concrete cracked and broke; armor melted. Finally the roof fell in, huge half-molten blocks crushing and burning anything that lived beneath them . . .

But there was nothing living there. The Bolos had bought enough time; the humans' mining machines had burrowed their way to safety—at least, safety for a while longer. Until they should be discovered. . . .

The harpy eggs stamped the redoubt into rubble with their legs of lightning, pulverized it, watched it melt to lava and flow, then harden to glass. Finally, the hill fallen and unsalvageable, the ships turned away, the harpy host departed, spreading outward like the ripples of an underwater volcanic eruption, breaking apart into armies centered around each ship, a hundred swarms clustered about their queens, searching with their mother ships, searching, scanning, seeking for

any trace of life, any trickle of electrical flow, of neu-
ronic activity, of synapses firing . . .

Below the artificial hill, technicians closed access
panels, dogged doors shut, inserted last components
and locked tight. They checked the meters for full
charge, disconnected the cables from the power plant
to the great Bolo, powered down the whole repair depot,
trying to minimize electrical activity to lessen chance of
discovery . . .

Too late.

One harpy egg halted, hovered in midair, smelled
the ether with antennae, probing, sifting . . .

Pointing toward the east, toward the last repair
depot.

The egg began to move toward the human's nest.

Deep within its bowels, the chief technician cried,
"You are repaired, Titan! You are fit for service
again!" He reached up to press the patch that would
signal Titan's central computer to begin the sequence
that would power up the huge machine, return it to
full operational capability, to full awareness . . .

But his hand paused as the man turned in panic,
hearing the cry, "They found us! They're here!"

His eyes flashed up to the huge screen high on the
southeast wall, showing the whole of the perimeter as
a horizontal line—and all along that line were staves
of fire, with black eggs balanced atop them. He could
have sworn he heard the thunder of ten thousand
wings, of the harpies that surrounded their mother
ships, but that was ridiculous, the screen was supply-
ing video only . . .

The fiery legs stalked closer, the screen filled with
their glare . . .

The roof groaned.

"They're coming!" someone shrieked. "Take cover!"

Then the roof fell in.

The roof roared as it collapsed into hundreds of

fragments, each twice the size of a man's head, each able to crush a man's head. Technicians screamed and ran, but the fall of rock struck them down where they fled, and those who still moved were instantly charred by the rain of fire that followed.

Hot air searing his lungs, the chief turned back, reached up higher, only a little higher as his vision turned red and death seared his lungs. Only a little more, hold to consciousness a little more, never mind the pain, the agony, press the patch . . .

He felt it give beneath his fingers just before the heat ceased as his whole body exploded.

But Titan did not explode.

Titan was a Mark XXVIII, the largest and latest model of all the Bolos shipped in for this suicidal defense; Titan, whose ablative tiles shed the rain of fire as though it were water. Titan awoke to irritation, irked that the temperature was so high as to be inconvenient—then woke to anger as he saw the piles of ash that had been the technicians who had repaired him. Titan roared with the revving of mighty engines; Titan turned and thundered up the ramp even as the walls gave way and fell inward in an implosion of flame.

Out of that inferno rolled a huge monster, a vast machine, cannon roaring, treads thundering across the plain, its program demanding a ship for every human life, a thousand harpies for each Bolo dead, its cannon pouring annihiliation into the sky, its energy projectors and machine guns spewing death in high arcs. It ravened through the night, a demon bent on destruction, a kinsman bent on revenge.

Deep inside, its computer tripped over into full battle mode, cold and ruthless, computing at nearly the speed of electric flow, icy rage within, all fire and hurtling steel without.

The ships surrounded it, the ships poured fire down

upon it—but Titan raced between their energy beams and dashed toward the hills, far faster than any Bolo ever had, for the repairmen had supercharged him, had scavenged engines from several Bolos and added their thrust to his, had built into him a jet from a fallen flier. Titan slipped into neutral and lit his jet. Away over the flat plain he shot, and the ships swerved to chase—but they were slow, they were ponderous.

The harpies were not.

The harpies sped after it with the laughing joyful shrieks of the predator chasing a helpless quarry—ten thousand harpies, but Titan counted their silhouettes and checked his data, and knew they were only a tiny fraction of the million or more that had smitten the planet a month before. His humans had died, his brother Bolos had melted and gone, but they had taken a fearsome toll as they went. There were only ten thousand harpies left for Titan to slay, and could he do less than his valiant predecessors?

He ground to a halt, spraying fire into the sky; he rotated in place, sweeping the harpies with a ring of fire. The vanguard shrieked in alarm, screamed in an instant of searing pain, then rained to the plain as ashes. . . .

And Titan turned and sped away again, the main body of the harpies still following, but more slowly now, for they had seen what happened to those who sped too eagerly.

Behind them, the forty-five ships still stalked.

While they lingered, Titan sped. He bounced and swayed over the inequalities in the terrain, even though they were very minor, the plain almost flat as a table. If it had been really flat, Titan could have moved so fast that he could have outrun the harpies easily—though not their ships, once they were up to full velocity.

He did not plan to give them the chance to reach that speed.

He swerved about, suddenly and with no apparent reason, just as he had dreamed of Donjon doing. Then he revved his motors and sprang back the way he had come. He raked the flying line with bullets, torched the few who had dropped down near the ground.

The harpy host stalled, squalling in consternation, but the ships saw, and leaped forward.

That was all Titan needed. He spun and raced away, bouncing and jouncing over the plain—and into the river.

Under the water he sped, a bow wave spreading out behind him to roil the waters. He had not been built to be submersible, but all his circuits were encased in airtight boxes, to protect against corrosive gasses—one never knew how low the enemy might stoop—and what was proof against air would certainly keep out water. His treads sank low, down through muck, slowing him tremendously—but he had sounded the river before he plunged, and knew how shallow the sludge was. His treads touched bedrock only four feet down, and he ground through the water, heading downstream faster than any powerboat, even with the mud to slow him. His computer calculated his own speed relative to that of the harpy ships; when he estimated the distance was right, he surged out of the water, dripping and festooned with seaweed, his cannon belching energy-bolts at the back of the line of harpy ships.

His fire centered on one ship in particular, low down, focused, holding steady.

It took a precious few seconds before the ship even realized it was under attack.

Then it began to bob and weave frantically—but Titan recognized the pattern; he had absorbed it from Donjon's broadcast in his sleep, had absorbed Chateau's discoveries, too, and tracked the ship through every dip and curve, recognizing when it changed evasive patterns, shifting with it.

Its companions came crowding to the rescue. An avalanche of harpies struck, but Titan burned them out of the air as fast as his small guns could traverse their line. Other ships stooped upon him, but he fired rockets with both launchers; they exploded against the sides of the harpy ships, doing little damage, but throwing the pilots off balance for a few precious minutes.

Finally, the ship he had picked for his target began to rotate—but Titan demonstrated one other improvement his technicians had given him; he increased the intensity of his fire. The ship did not recognize the difference and sped up to the rotation that had proved safe for its companions—but overheated quickly.

Its companions recovered and pressed in for the kill—and pressed in too quickly, in numbers too great; they blocked each other from coming close enough, and their fire was attenuated and at the wrong angle. One of them began to revolve around its wounded sister, but Titan charged forward, shooting up between the two ships, holding his beam fast on his target. Fire fell about him, all about him; six of the ships fell back to form an outer ring, and the remaining two pressed in behind, the target and its companion in front—but the plasma rained off Titan's ablative tiles, heating them, yes, but slowly, slowly . . .

Finally the target recognized what was happening—but too late. Its bottom fell away a split second before its power plant went up.

Titan did not stay to watch; he turned and raced away. The enemy ships cut off their fire, realizing their quarry had fled, and lumbered into motion behind him, accelerating, gaining . . .

Titan lit his jet and sped away, bouncing, bounding

over the terrain, keeping his speed just low enough to guard against overturning.

The ships sped up even more. The harpies followed, but more slowly, no longer quite so eager to dive into battle. The gap between them and the great eggs widened.

The ships gained, came closer, close enough to lash out at the impudent mite that fled before them—and when Titan felt the lash of their fire, the itch of their bullets, he whirled about, speeding back through the veil of destruction, as Donjon had shown him. He paused almost beneath a ship and fired a rocket directly up into the mouth of its cannon with unerring accuracy. Plasma detonated the missle; it exploded, and took the bottom half of the harpy ship with it, falling down to crush anything beneath it . . .

But Titan was no longer there; again, he had not stayed to watch. Away he ran, and the harpy pilots turned their ships after him in anger. A silent call went out, and all across that hemisphere, other ships dropped the search and sped to join them in squashing this arrogant midget.

All over the hemisphere, human survivors, buried deep in bunkers and redoubts, huddling high in mountain caverns, looked up from their screens in disbelief, hope springing anew inside them. "Visual check! Are the eggs really going?"

"They're going," a sentry reported, staring at a monitor.

In shelter after shelter, cheers shook the walls.

But Titan heard none of it; he only knew that he had a hundred meters to go before he reached the gullies, and the ships' fire was hot on his aft section. His temperature gauge began to climb as the tiles heated, but he was almost to the gully now . . .

He plunged in, rolling and skidding down the slope, tumbling, landing flat on his side, treads spinning uselessly in the air—but he remembered what Donjon had done, and fired a low, sustained blast with his side guns, raising him up off the earth enough so that he could pour slugs into the rock, chipping and spattering granite, but lifting him up higher, high enough to allow a full blast of plasma out the side . . .

Above him, three ships gathered, pouring fire down.

With a shuddering shock, Titan was back on his wheels. Away down the gully he raced, remembering the pattern from Donjon's broadcast of his last fight. He skidded into a turn, ducking down a side gulley, turning again and again . . .

These particular ships had not been there for Donjon's fight. They cast about aimlessly, seeking, searching, their sensors foiled by the traces of metal in the rocks.

Titan surged up out of the ravine, behind but near, his cannon already blazing at the nearest target. Its companions were quick to begin to weave about it, and it began to rotate, but Titan pushed close, ignoring the fire-fall, and stepped up his blast to full intensity.

More ships crowded in from the plain.

The bottom exploded off the target ship, and Titan fled, his temperature gauge screaming. Beneath the gathering ships he ran, through their veils of fire. A hundred harpies burst from the ground in a crowd, hoping to shock him, but he plowed through, treading them underfoot, incinerating them with his side guns, racing flat-out across the plain again, broadcasting every move, every second, for he could not know but that some defender, somewhere, was watching and learning, even though he had counted all his companion Bolos, and knew they were dead. But he bore the burden of their revenges, all of them . . .

And would see them fulfilled. He had promised, even though they could not have heard, and he was bound to that promise.

The mountains loomed before him, but the speeding ships loomed behind.

Up the mountain trail he sped, remembering the route Chateau had taken. The fire of the harpy ships splashed harmlessly against the rocks to either side of the trail, fragmented fires; what reached Titan himself was negligible. His tiles were charred black from heat, but all intact, none even weakened. . . .

Yet.

Up to the tunnel he went—or to where it had been; now there was only a pass, its floor choked with jumbled rubble. But that rubble had half-melted from the heat, had flowed enough to form a ramp. Up Titan went, rolling across the grave of two egg-ships. What more fitting place to stand, while he avenged Chateau?

The harpy ships stooped, rushing to pour fire on the Bolo they saw as trapped between two low cliffs, a sheer drop-off, and the egg-ship that was swinging down behind him.

Titan rotated his turret and poured fire into that egg.

The others crowded in; three stood right over him, pouring down fire. It splashed off his tiles and struck the cliffs to either side, heating the stone to cherry-red and splashing back off it to strike at his cowling. He knew he couldn't last long under such a heat bath; he only hoped the egg could last even less.

It was going to be close, because the egg was rotating unwilling to give up its blocking position—but unable to find the correct angular velocity. It speeded up, it slowed down—but it became hotter and hotter . . .

At the last second, it gave up, screaming toward the sky—but Titan's stream of plasma followed it, boring in, even though his sensors reported a cracked tile, then another and another, and the metal beneath it beginning to register dangerous heat levels . . .

The rocks shuddered as the harpy ship exploded.

Titan was out and away before the pieces had begun to separate into shrapnel. He shot back down off the mountain crest—but suddenly there was a host of harpies in front of him, battering him with their wings, clustering close about his guns, trying to block his sensors and air intakes, to plug his barrels, to render him blind, to smother him, to keep him penned. He blasted before they could come close enough to be any real danger, though, blasted again and again as he roared through the rain of their ashes. Still they would not stop coming, swooping in at him by the hundreds, the thousands, driven by some instinct for self-immolation, or by some superior will. Titan drove through them, blasting as he went, not taking the time to make sure he killed every harpy he could, feeling his way by sonar, following the mountain road down, then up again, just as Chateau had. Still the harpies came, and with sudden clarity, he knew they were calling, reporting his position . . .

Sure enough, as he came out to the lip of the chasm, there the ships were, ahead, clustered around the rockfall, some following where he had gone . . .

And some turning to move toward him.

His main gun targeted the leader and spat fire, tracking as it began its evasive patterns. His side guns lashed its companions; others shrouded harpies in fire. The latecomers sheered off from the cloud of flame, and at last Titan was rid of their pestiferous presence. But he could see that he could not remain where he was; the egg-ships loomed too closely, and had already begun their evasive dance, taking turns coming between himself and his target—and with the drop-off before him, he could not come close enough to drive under their guard.

Then an explosion rattled his aft plates, and his scanners registered a rocket blast. The harpies had sheered off, all right, but they had also resorted to weapons other than their own blind suicidal diving. He was targeted with rocket launchers, and even as he realized the fact, two more explosions registered.

He cut off the stream of plasma; his turret swivelled about, making aft into fore as he charged out at the multitudinous pests. They scattered before him, leaving their weapons behind, weapons that crunched under his treads as he swept forward, beginning his headlong rush down the mountainside . . .

Until sonar detected a cave.

A cavern, rather—at least, at the front. The portal was easily large enough to admit even a Bolo, and a quick preliminary sounding indicated huge spaces beyond. Without hesitation, Titan dived in. If he found no back door, he would make one.

Down he went, down and down, in a rough corkscrew that must have been cut by a flow of lava, a million years before, seeking out weak spots as it chewed its way to the surface. Titan certainly had no desire to go down to the core of the planet, so when his calculations of vertical distance matched the log of his trip up the slope, he started sounding for tunnels. Sonar probed all about him, seeking.

The mountain shook about him.

Titan never wavered, knowing the harpy ships were bombarding the peak. They could not see where he had gone, so they were levelling the mountain to find and destroy him. For a moment, he almost admired their sheer audacity—or sheer blind thoroughness.

The mountain shook again, and Titan still had not located another tunnel—but he did find a narrow seam in the rock, a gradient between two layers that was filled with ash, compressed now into rock. He halted and levelled one of his side guns at it. With low intensity first, he melted out the beginnings of a hole. The mountain shook again, but he had expected it, and held steady with computer-guided reflexes.

The hole grew, more in depth than in width. Titan let the intensity of the gun's beam build rapidly. The hole deepened, widening to half a meter, three-quarters, a meter ... When it was two meters across and five deep, Titan boosted the gun's power to full intensity. The rock melted and flowed at the end of the hole, lava trickling down, and Titan had to divert another gun to carving a channel downslope, that would take the molten rock away from him before it could melt his treads. As the tunnel widened, he began to move the gun in a circle, playing fire across the end of the hole. Finally it was wide enough for another gun to join in, then another—then, finally, wider than Titan was high. He cut off the side guns and rotated on his treads, pointing himself into the gap and firing his main cannon.

Rock flowed and came rolling out of the tunnel in gouts.

Titan carved a run-off channel with his side guns, then rolled forward slowly, staying back far enough so that the reflected heat would not harm him. The mountain had stopped shaking—presumably, the harpies had levelled enough of it to be sure of Titan's destruction. So much the better—they would be pleasnatly surprised when he re-emerged. Pleasantly for him, that was.

With a roar, the rock at the end of the tunnel blew out.

Instantly, Titan cut his main gun, then sat and waited for the lava to harden as he tested the outer world with his sensors. Telescopic sight revealed nothing—only darkness; the day had gone while he tunnelled. Scanners revealed no electromagnetic activity, audio sensors heard only the night wind—and precious few living creatures, only a few insects, and the inevitable scavengers who come to feed on the dead. They would probably die from the alien protoplasm, or from the diseases that sprang from microbes the harpies no doubt carried that were harmless to themselves, but would prove lethal to humans, or the lifeforms they had brought with them. But there was no sign of a harpy or a ship, so when the rock had cooled, Titan trundled slowly out into the night air.

In the distance, he saw a dozen ships—or rather, their lightning-legs. They were trying to break into one of the human strongholds. There might be people left in it, or it might only have been a control center, for all they knew—but they had to be sure of it.

Titan knew. All the human shelters and control centers were logged in his database, and he knew that this one, Coventry Central, was a prison. Yes, there would be humans within—dangerous humans, but humans nonetheless. He could not let them be killed.

He checked his records with a quick scan and was surprised to discover that, if he had kept count correctly (and he was sure he had), the dozen ships before him were all that were left of the original invading force of one hundred twenty-eight. His fellow Bolos had died, but they had died hard, each bringing down two or three ships before dying. So had the humans, apparently—there might be very few of them remaining, but they had left their mark.

Surprise would be the key element. Titan rolled forward at only a moderate pace, following the dips and gullies, making as little sound as possible, hiding from sight.

Larry woke to see light, bright light. He pushed it away a little, with a feeble hand, and saw Dawn bending over him, looking scared. The fear disappeared as she saw him squint, and her mouth moved, but he couldn't hear the words—probably because of the ringing in his ears, a steady tone that went on and on and wouldn't go away. One of the pieces of electronics that had shorted somewhere in its innards, no doubt. He shook his head and pointed to his ear. She shut up, looking scared again.

Finally, fear touched him. Had he gone deaf?

But Dawn was trying to pull him to his feet—or at least to a sitting position. Well, if she wasn't too worried about it, why should he be? Especially since it might go away in time—but time was one thing he didn't have, time to wait and see. He nodded and pushed himself up—carefully; there might be an injury somewhere. But miraculously, his ribs didn't stab him, and there was no sudden flare of pain from a broken bone. Cautiously, he tried kneeling, then standing, all with the same success rate. The bunker seemed to have done its job—he was alive, and unbroken. Oh, he ached like fury, and if he had seen a mirror, he probably wouldn't have been able to find himself among all the bruises—but he could function.

Could the bunker?

He looked up at the ceiling, and saw stars. Then the sky went orange with a distant fire-fight, but after a minute, it cleared enough to show stars again.

He nodded to Dawn, and she finally let go of his arm—but she was pointing at the broken ceiling. Larry got the idea—they had to get out. She was right—the bunker had been turned into a glorified foxhole, and they had no weapons but their sidearms. He looked around, and saw huge jagged blocks of concrete sitting on the remains of smashed electronic equipment, with broken cannon-barrels and the racks with the viewers sticking up from them. He knew the roof had been designed to fall inward against the walls if it did break, but even so, he shivered as he realized how close they had come to being crushed as flat as the guts of the equipment.

Then he realized that if the electronics were wrecked, the reactor might be, too.

His mind knew that a fushion reactor can't blow up—as soon as the electromagnetic bottle breaks down, the reaction ends. But someone had let the genie out of this bottle, and he wasn't about to stick around to find out whether or not he would die from its spell. He turned to Dawn with a nod, stepped over to the nearest concrete pile, set a foot against a broken chunk, and shoved. It held, so he turned back to Dawn and bent his knees, cupping his hands to make a stirrup. "Up you go."

"Up *there*?" Dawn stared up at the jumble of blocks. "You're out of your mind!"

Larry was delighted to discover that he could hear her—distantly through the ringing, but nonetheless, he could. Only temporarily deaf, then. "No, out of *here*—I hope. The ceiling was only ten feet high, and I lift my hands up to at least five. No climbing, just jumping. Or would you rather stay and wait for the harpies to find us?"

Dawn imagined a score of shrieking harpies pouncing on them with sharp talons and shuddered. Of course, the aliens were much more likely just to drop another bomb in and mash them, but that wasn't much better. "I'll take that lift." She stepped forward, put her hands on Larry's shoulders, and stepped into his hands. For a moment, she balanced precariously, gathering herself for the leap.

"Ready?" he asked.

Dawn didn't trust herself to answer; she just nodded.

Larry heaved with all his might, as straight as he could. Dawn felt herself surging upward and leaped at the last second. The edge of the hole shot past her head, and she threw herself forward. The jagged concrete slammed into her hips, and the pain was sharp—but she was up and out from the waist up. For a moment, she scrabbled precariously; then Larry's hand pushed hard on one foot, and she got the other one over the edge and rolled out, face flaming—that push on the foot had made her realize what she must have looked like from Larry's point of view. Nothing indecent, of course—they both wore the same trousered uniform—but very embarrassing. Of course, Larry probably wasn't in any condition to snicker, but still . . .

Snicker? He was in no shape for anything, stuck down in that hole! How was *he* going to get out?

Cursing herself for an inconsiderate fool, she swung about, pulling her belt loose and dropping back down on her belly, to dangle the strap over the edge. "Come on! Grab hold, and you . . ."

She'd come just in time to see the concrete block shift under his feet; he was halfway up the slope of rubble. He lurched forward, grabbing the belt. She held on with both hands, pulling as strongly as she could. He stepped up to the next block a half-second before the first went crashing down, then held on tight as the whole pile shifted under him. His face was pale, his eyes huge—but the slope steadied again, and he grinned up at her. "Thanks."

"Just part of the service. Can you jump?"

"I'd be scared to try. In fact, I *am* scared to try. Just a couple of more steps, though . . ."

He freed one hand from the belt to steady him against the edge of the hole as he stepped up to another block, very slowly and carefully. It groaned and shifted a little, but it held.

"Just one more," Dawn said.

"One it is." Larry shifted his weight gradually, set one foot on a block fifteen inches higher, braced himself, then lunged forward. The block groaned, but he threw his torso over the rim of the hole and didn't care as the block started to slide down the slope with a grinding that turned into a rumbling as the whole side of the pile shifted and slid.

"You can have your belt back now," he panted.

"As soon as you get a leg up." Dawn tossed the belt behind her and grabbed his arm with both hands.

Larry struggled, panting, and managed to kick one knee up over the rim. Then he rolled, up and over the edge, all of him out of the pit. He just lay there panting. "Th-thanks."

"Any time." Dawn fumbled her belt back through the loops. "Just don't think I did it because I liked your face, or anything."

"Why—no." Larry grinned, the hardness coming back. "Just your duty. Right?"

"That," Dawn allowed, "and the fact that I stand a better chance of getting back to base if I have someone with me, than I do alone."

"Truth in that," Larry admitted. He pushed himself up to a sitting position. "I'm better than nobody, huh?"

"You are if you're armed." Dawn cast about her; there was no shortage of weapons on the ground, from all the harpies they had killed. The question was, would they work after having been torched? She picked one up and handed it to Larry. "Here."

He shrank away to the side, then took it from her. "Mind not pointing that thing in my direction?"

She stared at him, taken aback. "Is that the front? These birds *do* build crazy weapons!"

"Well, it *might* be the front." Larry carefully pointed it crosswise to both of them. "Where's the trigger on this model?"

"They don't seem to use them." Dawn picked up another weapon, one that looked much more complicated than the first. "No, mine has a trigger, or something like one. I think yours is a rocket launcher."

"If it is, it's a repeater." Larry eyed the huge magazine with apprehension. "Get down, would you?"

Dawn whirled. "You're not going to *point* that at me!"

"No, but for all I know, this thing could shoot out the side."

"How?"

"I don't know, and I don't want to have to find out. Ready?"

Dawn hit the dirt.

"Here goes." Larry pressed a large button.

There was a flash and a roar, and a streak of light lanced out of the back end of the gun, almost knocking Larry onto his face. He caught himself on one hand and looked backward over his shoulder, watching the rocket race off across the plain until it hit something and exploded in a huge shower of fire. "I hope that was one of theirs."

"As long as it wasn't one of us. I think that's the back end that you're pointing forward."

"Yeah, I think you're right." Gingerly, Larry reversed the weapon and started hunting around on the ground.

"What are you looking for?"

"More . . . aha!" Larry came up with a bandolier that carried two of the huge magazines on an unimaginably small loop of leather. "It'll do for a necklace, anyway."

"Just the right fashion for this fall," Dawn said drily, but she began to look around for ammunition, too. She came up with a bandolier of her own and looped it over a shoulder, then turned to Larry just as he finished draping the rocket-packs around his neck. She stared at him for a moment, then burst out laughing.

"Well, I'm glad you can see the humor in any situation,"

he said sourly. "What's the matter? Don't like my taste?"

"I don't know how you taste, and I'm not going to find out. But you look like the White Rabbit!"

"Huh?" Larry looked down and, sure enough, the rocket pack did kind of look like a tabard. "*You* should talk! You look like a fullback!"

"Shoulder pads, huh?" Dawn glanced down at her figure with a smile. "With you around, I need all the armor I can get. Now—where do we go?"

"Back to headquarters, if it's still standing." Larry glanced up at the sky.

After a minute of silence, Dawn asked, "You studying to be a statue?"

"Huh? No, I'm studying the stars, as a matter of fact—or didn't you bone up on the local constellations on the way out?"

Dawn flushed. "No, I didn't! I had more important things to do than star-gaze."

"Not now, you don't. Okay, the flare has died—momentary lull in the fighting; just an accident, I bet . . . there!" He pointed toward the unseen mountains.

Dawn looked up at the sky, frowning, but she couldn't see anything except faint points of light, and even they were washing out by a new flood of orange light from an explosion. " 'There' what?"

"The Lorry—at least, that's what the colonists call it. It's north. So we want to go . . ." Larry pivoted, his arm standing out like a compass needle. ". . . there!"

He was pointing straight into the worst of the glare and clamor.

"*There?*" Dawn blanched. "You *would* pick the worst of the battle!"

Larry shrugged. "You wanted to know where headquarters was. Makes sense that the worst fighting would be around the fort. Doesn't mean we have to go there, of course."

"So where *are* we going to go? Into the nearest forest, assuming we could leg it a hundred miles without getting fried? Or maybe we should just wander around until a crowd of harpies picks us off?"

"I've been wondering how they taste," Larry said thoughtfully. "We didn't bring out any rations, you know."

"Eat a *harpy*? You cannibal!"

"No—they're not my species. Still, I suppose you're right—intelligent life *is* our own kind, no matter what its form. Of course, that's assuming that these lizards *have* minds. . . ."

"Some of them do, and they won't take kindly to our eating their children!"

"Assuming that isn't a cultural norm, where they come from. Come to that, I don't like them slaughtering our people and wasting our planet. Of course, I'm sure they'd say that they wouldn't have been doing either, if we just hadn't been so rude as to fight back."

"I'm not too eager to be a slave to a bird-brain, thank you!"

"How about a snake?"

"What's that, a proposal? No, thanks, hammerhead. I'll wait for the next one."

Larry frowned at her. " 'Hammerhead?' "

"*You* figure it out." Which was good, because Dawn couldn't. She covered by stepping around him toward the brightest glare in the night sky. "Come on— maybe we'll meet a Bolo."

"Oh, yeah," Larry said slowly. "I forgot to tell you."

Dawn stopped dead, then turned back to look at him slowly. "Forgot what?"

"The news came in the last time you were asleep. There're only two Bolos left, and one of them is down for repair."

Dawn stared in horror. "The harpies got all the others?"

"All," Larry confirmed. "Safety in numbers, and all that."

Dawn turned back toward the glare, her face pale. "That's not good."

"No," Larry agreed. Neither of them could bring themselves to put it into words: that the humans were on their own, or nearly. Their guardians were gone.

Dawn shook off the mood and started out again. "Come on. Doesn't look as though our chances are going to get any better."

"No, it doesn't, does it?" Larry followed her before he could change his mind, muttering to himself. " 'Hammerhead'? Let's see, now . . ."

Titan came out only a hundred yards from the ring of ships. From this point forth, he would almost doubtlessly be seen. He didn't light his jet, but he shot forward at full engine acceleration, guns poised and ready, his Hellbore already tracking his chosen ship.

At fifty yards, he opened fire, but he did not stop.

The harpy ship did not realize what was happening at first. By the time its sensors screamed the alarm, a patch of armor was already glowing red. Even then, it did not move—no doubt its inhabitants were trying to discover where the beam was coming from.

A hundred harpies shot toward him with shrill cries—into communicators, no doubt. They sheered off, but his side guns began to mow them ruthlessly, even as the alien ship finally began to revolve.

Too slowly.

At last, two other ships shot to its rescue, sliding between Titan and his quarry, levelling their fire at him—but he was now so close that their shots went wide, and the only way to interpose themselves between him and his target, was to get so close that his Hellbore tore through the ship's skin in a matter of minutes. The harpy ship shot away, but too late—Titan tracked it, and its bottom exploded out even as it fled. Titan didn't stay to look—he swung back to the other "rescuer," even though it was already retreating, angling away, trying to take up a position from which its guns could actually strike at him. But the jockeying interfered with its evasive action, and it forgot to rotate; Titan's beam centered on its vulnerable spot even as it rained fire on him. The ablative tiles shed the plasma even as the ship, finally realizing its predicament, began to revolve—and of course, its beam could not hold steady on Titan.

But his could.

His could, and the harpy ship had waited too long to rotate. It blew, and rained shrapnel on the huge machine—but Titan turned back to his first victim even as its cannon levelled at him, ignoring nine of the harpy ships that came crowding around—he could afford to ignore them; there were too many to come close enough to do damage. Instead, he took careful aim into the egg's own guns, and fired.

The egg blew up, and Titan took off running across the valley floor. He lit his jet and shot forward, jouncing and bouncing—bouncing too hard; he realized he could easily go over at this speed. He cut the jet—he had gained enough distance anyway—and realized, with surprise, that the enemy ships were milling about behind him in a search pattern.

Of course! They had been following the light and heat of his jet, and with it gone, they were slow to resort to their electromagnetic detectors to find him. Realizing that, he shot away from his previous path, swinging wide around the valley to come at the nine survivors from a new angle.

A hill rose before him—good! It would be first a firing platform, then a shield. He ground up its slope—almost directly beneath a harpy egg. He levelled his gun . . .

And a cloud of harpies descended shrieking upon him.

He fired anyway, his beam burning through a dozen harpies on its way to score the ship. His side guns levelled more of them, and his computer busily traced each separate burning body. The ship lingered, unable to resist the temptation to stamp out this presumptuous bug—and the presumptuous bug shifted tactics, slamming a shell up to follow its own bright beam, a shell that exploded against weakened armor, that blew through the lower part of the hull, and the ship tumbled out of the sky.

Titan reversed engines and shot down the hill. Still the harpies clung to him, shrieking and crying into their communicators, so that their ships would not lose the monster this time. Titan burned them apart and blew them out of the air, but a dozen more came for each he slew.

The eight remaining harpy ships shot toward him, lightning smashing down . . .

Into the shielding earth of the slope.

But Titan was away from the hill already, running down and into the river. The darkness hid his exit, and the water hid the traces of his heat. The harpy ships did not even realize he had gone; indeed, when he surfaced half a kilometer downstream, the great eggs were gathered around the hill, busily pulverizing it with plasma-bolts.

They had been hiking for half an hour before the harpy patrol found them.

The saurians pounced, shrieking what were no doubt obscenities in Harpy. Larry dropped to one knee, bringing up his bazooka. "Hit the dirt!"

But Dawn was already kneeling, taking aim at the

left hand side of the line and squeezing the trigger—very awkwardly, but very effectively. The gun stuttered, and Dawn was amazed at the lightness of the recoil—but then, they would have had to have perfect recoil-less weapons, if they were going to fire them from the wing.

Recoil-less and light, but very effective. The harpies seemed to stumble in mid-air, then pitched forward, falling in series as Dawn's gun traversed the line, falling down to earth with horrible screams, revealing . . .

A knot of larger harpies in the middle of the flock. Larry's bazooka roared, and the knot exploded.

Slowly, Dawn lowered her weapon, staring at the rain of ash. She had seen it hundreds of times before, on the visual monitor in their bunker—but never with her naked eyes, or so nearby.

"The poor wretches," Larry whispered.

"They had it coming." Dawn shoved pity behind her and pushed herself to her feet. "Or would you rather have let *them* do it to *you*?"

"No," Larry said slowly, "all things considered, if it had to be us or them, I'd rather it was them."

"How kind of you," Dawn said witheringly, "and you may be sure they felt the same way. Come on—we've got miles to cover."

Larry went along, wondering what had happened to the more gentle emotions in her.

Of course, he knew what had happened to them in himself. There are fatalities in every war, and nobility and generosity are high on the list. In his case, he was sure they had just gone underground for the duration—and he hoped it wasn't any worse than that, for Dawn. After all, she herself had been safe so far—not captured or wounded, or mistreated . . .

So far.

He resolved to do what he could to make sure she wouldn't be.

He had just come to that conclusion when a horrendous shrieking and cawing split the air. His hand snapped up, and he saw what had to be a hundred harpies descending on them. Their bias held, even though it had been the undoing of so many of them, so often—they would rather use their talons than their guns.

Wrong choice. He dropped to one knee, levelled the rocket launcher, and loosed a flaming round into their midst. A huge flash lit the immediate sky, and scraps of bone and leather rained down—but the shrieking went on; there were just too many of them.

As the glare died, Dawn's machine gun went to work. The harpies fell in a neat line, then fell again as she traversed backward. Larry's bazooka roared, and the flash lit the sky again. The rain was continuous now.

Finally, the harpies realized they had to use their weapons. Mechanical chattering ripped the night from a dozen guns.

"Get down!" Larry caught Dawn to him and hugged her hard as he dropped down, then rolled over on top of her, waiting for the terrible pain, hoping it would be short-lived, hoping their bullets couldn't penetrate through his body into hers . . .

A huge roar filled the night, a roar with a thousand echoes, and suddenly the chattering was quiet, and the only sound was the distant booming where the harpies fought the fort.

Larry decided he was still alive, and risked a peek upward.

"Let me up, you fool!" Dawn snapped.

But Larry was frozen staring up—and up, and up, at the huge battle machine that towered over him, as tall as a building, a very large building, as high as the sky . . .

"What is it? I can't see anything but your collarbone!"

"It's a Bolo," Larry whispered, unbelieving.

Dawn struggled out from under him enough to see, and stare. "It *is* a Bolo! But how . . ."

The huge machine began to move. It rumbled straight toward them.

"No, wait!" Larry cried, waving frantically. "We're good guys, we're on *your* side . . ."

But the Bolo's noise drowned out his voice, and all he could think as the huge treads passed to either side of him and the vast underside became the sky, was that the world had gone crazy, because this very machine had just saved them from a horde of harpies, and here it was running them over . . .

But the machine stopped, and its bottom was six feet overhead. The huge treads were a dozen meters or more to either side.

"How . . . what . . . ?" Dawn wasn't sure which one of them had said it.

Then a huge trapdoor slid open, and light spilled down from above them. "Get in, little allies," a rich amplified voice said. "You need shelter."

"You were never more right in your life!" Larry scrambled to his feet and made a stirrup again. "It's the cavalry, Dawn! Up and in!"

She didn't stay to argue, just stepped into the stirrup and caught the edge of the trap as he lifted. She vaulted in—no straining or struggling here, where all was clear and clean—and spun about to reach down for Larry. He had already leaped high, though, and caught the edge of the door; she only had to help pull him aboard when his knee came over the edge.

The trap slid shut and the huge machine rumbled into motion with the two of them inside, safe in a warm, carpeted room, with the sounds of cannon fire dimmed by heavy armor. For a little while, the war was shut out; for a little while, they were safe inside again.

Dawn rolled over and hid her face in his shoulder. Her whole body began to tremble.

Amazed, Larry brought his arms up around her. "Hey, no fair," he whispered. "*I* was about to get the shakes."

"Too late," she sniffled. "*My* turn."

"Well, okay." He patted her back. "Get it out of your system. Then you can hold me while *I* fall apart."

She did.

Titan crept up quietly, sneaking close.

A dozen harpies burst on him out of the darkness, screaming in dreadful rage and loosing rockets, and bolts from energy rifles.

The bolts scarred his carapace, of course, but did no other damage. Titan's guns rattled, his projectors enveloped him in fire. When it died, only ashes remained. Titan did a quick scan of the area and was amazed to find it empty. Had he slain the last of the aliens?

His computer began to tally the dead it had seen and heard reported, but the great ships had seen the commotion and heard the alarm that their progeny had given their lives to raise. They swung away from the hill and out toward Titan, no doubt cursing this temerarious mite that had the audacity to survive.

The mite turned and ran; if he had been human, he would have cursed the luck that had spoiled his sneak attack. In darkness and over unfamiliar territory, he didn't dare light his jet; instead he ran, scanning on infrared, at full velocity.

The ships were slow to gain acceleration, but they were gaining indeed.

Titan fled, searching for some sort of cover, something to make a diversion, searching his database for any nearby human installations that might still be inhabited, and therefore must be avoided.

He found instead a building that was probably empty of life, but nonetheless something very much to be sought.

When Dawn and Larry had readjusted to temporary safety, they investigated their surroundings. They were in the crew compartment that was still built into every Bolo, even though it was rarely used—in fact, to the right of the control console glowed a large green rectangle with the word "auto" on it. Below it was a red rectangle marked "Manual Overide," but it was dark, and behind a pane of glass. A small hammer hung next to it, with the notation, "In case of emergency, break glass."

"Does this qualify as an emergency?" Larry asked.

"Only for us," Dawn answered. "The Bolo seems to know what he's doing."

"You are aboard Mark XXVIII Bolo *Titan*," the rich voice informed them. "Please strap yourselves in securely."

Dawn stared blankly. "What?"

Larry caught an arm around her and pulled her toward the large, padded chairs. "Come on! The ride's going to get rough!"

That was an understatement. They jumped for the chairs and strapped themselves in, just before the floor started to bounce and heave beneath them.

"What is this—the roller coaster?" Larry called.

"No, just a very fast ride." Dawn nodded at the screen. "Look."

Larry did. There was an array of screens before him. The largest was central, showing a view of what lay ahead of Titan. At the moment, the scene was very dark, but Larry could make out some landmarks that had become familiar in the past couple of weeks, though only seen on his viewscreens. Now, though, they were moving—past him, and rapidly.

"What's he running from?"

"Look behind," Dawn said in a strangled tone, pointing at another screen. It was right above, but smaller, and showed the rear view.

Larry caught his breath. "What is that—the whole Harpy navy?"

"What is left of it, I believe," Titan answered. "Do not be afraid if they fire upon us. I am very heavily shielded. The heat may become oppressive, but my cooling system is excellent, and you will not be in danger."

Larry just stared, but Dawn remembered her manners. "Thank you, Titan. That's very reassuring."

Suddenly the view whirled; just looking at it gave Larry motion sickness—but he could feel the movement, too, as Titan slewed about. His stomach had barely adjusted to it when the forward acceleration began again.

"He's going back toward the ships!" Larry yelled, terrified.

"Let's hope he knows what he's doing," Dawn called back, her teeth gritted.

Then the screens filled with fire, and Larry clenched the arms of the chair for all he was worth, thinking crazily that Titan seemed to feel it necessary to prove how good his air conditioning was. But the screens cleared again, and they were racing over the night landscape once more.

"He bluffed them!" Dawn cried. "He went right through their fire and came out the other side!"

"Neat," Larry said, numb. "Let's hope he doesn't have to try it a second time."

Dawn shrugged. "Won't matter. Harpies learn slow."

Larry had noticed that, himself. He recognized the behavior from arrogant teenagers he'd known in high school. They were so sure of their own superiority that they couldn't believe anyone outside their own group could know anything worth their learning—so they didn't. "Cultural superiority complex," he quipped.

"Is that what they call it?" Dawn asked.

Larry stared, surprised, then shrugged. "Don't know. Just an idea."

"Oh," Dawn said, with scorn. "Got any facts?"

The Bolo ground to a halt so suddenly as to slam them into their belts; then the room spun about them. Well, no, actually—they were spinning with it. But it was so fast and so sudden that it seemed to be the other way around.

Larry stared at the viewscreen to kill the sensation of movement and the nausea it was raising, but all he could see were legs of lightning, not very far away, with great dark eggs on top.

There was a lance of light skewering one of those eggs, and it seemed to be coming from a little way above the viewscreen.

"He's attacking!" Larry yelped. "The fool machine's actually trying to take on that clutch of eggs!"

"This unit is programmed to destroy as many enemies as possible, whenever possible," the Bolo informed him.

"But not when it's suicidal!"

"I will not die, nor will you."

"I just wish he could be sure of that," Dawn whispered.

Titan must have overheard her, but he did not reply.

Fire sheeted down the screen.

"Think it's getting hot in here?" Larry said nervously.

"Just in your mind," Dawn retorted. "Come from looking at that screen." But Larry noticed she didn't glance at the temperature gauge.

There was a sudden blinding flash that washed the screen in pure white.

"He's blind!" Larry shouted.

"No he's not," Dawn grated, "just us."

Then their insides roiled as the tank swung about again and shot into motion. The acceleration pressed them back into the cushions, and Larry kept telling himself the chairs were built sturdily enough so that they wouldn't break, no matter what the acceleration was.

The screen cleared, and he saw they were racing through the countryside; dimly perceived shapes were whipping by them. The glare from the distant battle showed them a scene of ruin and carnage all about.

The Bolo stopped, whirled, and the lance of fire stabbed out from above the screen again. Larry pried himself away from the side of his chair. "I sure hope he's not picking on any more ships!"

"Why not?" Dawn said bitterly. "At least we've lived a few minutes longer than we would have if he hadn't rescued us."

Suddenly, the screen was filled with leathery bodies—then with fire. The rain of ashes began. Then the blinding flash washed the screen again, and the room spun about them once more.

"I'm beginning to feel like a martini in a shaker," Dawn groaned.

"Better than feeling like an egg in the frying pan we left," Larry said, hoping it was a comfort.

"This egg is feeling pretty broken, thank you! How did I get into this centrifuge?"

"Through the floor," Larry answered.

"Down, quickly!" Titan told them.

They didn't wait for explanations; they just scrambled out of their belts and down from the chairs, but Dawn protested as she moved. "This can't be all that safe!"

"We will be passing only a kilometer from the fort," Titan told her. "I must drop you very soon, for I do not think I can stand against these ships indefinitely. You will have a short but hazardous walk to the fort, but I believe you should be able to deal with any problems you encounter."

Larry hesitated just as he was about to throw himself to the floor, then spun and grabbed two blast rifles from the rack on the wall. Titan lurched, and Larry more fell than jumped to the carpet.

"Do not lie on the trapdoor," Titan warned them.

"Don't worry," Dawn assured him. "We're not."

Suddenly, the tank jarred to a halt, and Larry's stomach went hollow, afraid that the Bolo had run into some opponent it couldn't knock aside. His imagination quailed at the thought of what that enemy might look like—but Titan was saying, "Down, now, and lie low—I will lead the enemy away from you! Good luck, small allies!"

The trap door's latch clunked, and it dropped open.

"Thanks, Titan!" Dawn called, and dropped through the hatch.

"Good luck to you!" Larry called, and followed her.

They threw themselves flat on the ground, and Dawn shrieked, "Hold me!"

At that point in time, there was nothing Larry wanted to do more. He couldn't fight, he couldn't run, and the feel of another human body would be awfully comforting. He wrapped her in his arms and lay huddled around her as the huge machine ground away from them, leaving them naked to the night. Minutes later, thunder swelled and lightning stabbed down not two meters from them—but it didn't hit them, only left a stink of ozone as the alien ships passed by. Harpies scurried in their wake, but didn't notice the humans who were trying to disappear into the ground—their attention was all on Titan.

Then they were gone, but Larry just stayed put, wrapped around Dawn with arms and legs both. Finally, her voice came muffled: "I think we'd better get going."

"Do we have to?" Larry asked plaintively. "It's so nice and cozy here."

They lay alone and uncovered in the middle of a plain of death, but Dawn said, "I know what you mean. If we don't make it to the fort before the ships finish with Titan, though, there won't be anything left of us to *be* cozy."

"But if I let go, I'll never get to hold you like this again."

Dawn lay very still in his arms for a moment, then said, "We're in the middle of a war, you know. We could be dead any minute."

"All the more reason to hold on while I can."

"Look," she said, exasperated, "if we make it to the fort, I promise you can hold me again. Will you let me up now?"

"Oh, I guess so," Larry sighed. He uncurled, and Dawn sprang to her feet. He was a little slower getting up, but when he did, he said, "Here," and handed her a rifle.

She stared at it. "Where did you get these? They're even built for people!"

"Off Titan's emergency arms rack," Larry said. "This is what they're for. Come on, the fort's that way."

They could tell, because the sky was still bright with the cannon shots from the fort—but they were shooting at a fleeing enemy.

"What happened to all the ships that were shooting at the fort?" Dawn wondered.

"They've gone after Titan," Larry said. "We're not the only ones he was leading them away from."

"But *why*? Why would they need to go after a lone Bolo when they've got a fort they have to destroy?"

"Pride." Larry shrugged. "They can't stand to see a Bolo blow up a few of them and get away with it. Besides, the fort will still be there when they're done with the Bolo, but it might not work the other way around."

"No, it wouldn't, would it?" Dawn said softly. "The Bolo would run and hide. But they can be sure it would come back."

Larry nodded. "Come back again, and again, and again—until they were all dead. No, on second thought, if I were commanding those enemy ships, I'd probably go after Titan, too."

"I hope he survives," Dawn said softly.

"So do I," Larry said, "but even if he doesn't, he wasn't alive in the first place. All he really cares about is finishing the job he was set to do."

"But he *can't*! There are too many of them!"

"He doesn't know that," Larry said softly. "Maybe he can't, but we can."

"What? Finish the job for him? There can't be even two thousand humans left on this planet!"

"If he takes enough of them with him, we just might do for the rest." Larry held out his hand. "Come on. Let's get to the fort. We've got a job to do—and you've got a promise to keep."

"I might ask for a promise from *you* before I keep *mine*," she warned him.

"And I just might be willing to give it. Let's go get safe so we can find out, okay?"

And they set off across the wasted landscape, hand in hand, but very vigilant.

Titan swerved, running with a purpose now—but not too apparent a purpose. He took evasive action, zigging and zagging with the most randomized pattern he had, switching between two other patterns constantly for good measure—but it took far more time than a straight-line course, and the ships were gaining.

They were almost upon him when the low concrete mound rose before him. All to the better—he alone could not blast through that bunker in anything resembling time enough, let alone melt through the shielding beneath. He lurched up onto the structure and halted dead center, cannon rotating and elevating to target the nearest ship. He knew what he must do, knew the probability of survival was so low as to be negligible—but he had to do it anyway; it was the only chance. He poured fire into the harpy ship, and it began to dodge through evasive maneuvers, rotating and hitting the proper rate instantly—so the saurians could learn, after all! Slowly, handicapped by their own assumption of superiority, but they learned.

Two other ships instantly broke off to bob and weave about the target ship, becoming a three-body system, each absorbing some of Titan's fire so that none would be destroyed. It was useless; Titan left off and swerved to take aim at another.

But they had taken aim at him, too. Three huge harpy ships crouched over him, pouring down lightning. He shot back, but they were moving just enough so that his bolts missed their tubes.

He could feel his tiles cracking.

The heat shivered the concrete beneath him.

Finally, one shell slammed into a harpy tube, and the cannon blew up, taking the ship with it—but another swung into its place.

More lightning poured down on Titan, but he held grimly to his purpose, slamming his own bolts back upward, aiming for a cannon-mouth, but they danced and swerved erratically . . .

With a roar, the concrete gave way. The alloy steel beneath it, already hot, glowed red. The heat beat up at Titan in waves; he could feel his own belly-plates melting . . .

But the alloy was melting, too. Suddenly, it went, and Titan sank down into a mire of molten steel—down and down, still firing up at the enemy until the lake of liquid metal closed over his cannon, melting his gun barrels, melting his Hellbore, too, and his treads, and his shielding . . .

But the liquid steel poured down into the complex below, the installation it had protected, and melted shielding there, too—lead shielding, which boiled in seconds, and the graphite rods beneath—the graphite rods that had made a chain reaction manageable, that had controlled the furious continuing explosion of pure plutonium in the ancient nuclear fission reactor, built by the planet's first colonists but still operating, still fueled . . .

Still lethal.

Before Titan's shielding was quite gone, before memory banks could melt, before his silicon chips had begun to turn to slag, the reactor core beneath his melted down. It blew, and it blew high and wide—high enough to reach the ships that had torched it, wide enough to atomize them all—and as he died, Titan knew that he had kept his promises.

THE MURPHOSENSOR BOMB

Karen Wehrstein

"A toast, my dear!"

Turning to his wife, Brigardier-General Alan Damien raised his glass, the fifty-year-old wine in it swirling with a graceful slowness in the less-than-earth gravity of Newterra-G. From many meters above his head, muffled by the bulk of the great machine in whose gymballed and cushioned personnel compartment they rode, came the familiar roar of its Hellbore. On the viewscreen, which stretched arcing around half the room and had a video quality indistinguishable from the naked eye's, twin bolts streaked outward, their trails shrinking in the distance over the blasted grey planetscape, curved in towards the silver spot that was a Djann gun-turret, and destroyed it in a blast that covered half the screen, leaving a momentary black blot.

"To victory."

Aphra Damien raised her glass in return, the proud line of her face defying its age, her earrings twinkling momentarily in the explosion's white glare, then steadily in the warm light of the candles on the table. "To victory."

Aphra counted herself lucky. Alan's rise through the ranks of the Dinochrome Brigade's human strategic and tactical corps had been meteoric. Words were used to describe him like "brilliant," "uncanny" and "an instinctive grandmaster of Bolo strategy." But the usual whisper about men who directed Bolos was that they were too much like machines themselves, impassive, distant, icily rational. Not Alan; he had a streak of romance a mile wide.

Who else would take his wife for a candlelight and wine dinner in the midst of a planet-wide pitched battle?

"I don't want to sit in a khaki-walled room with a bunch of sweaty office-types, listening to tinny action from ten light-years away," he said. "*This* is the seat to have in a battle—not even ringside, but right in the *middle* of it."

Aphra laughed, another flash of light from the screen making her teeth gleam for an instant. Not an explosion, it seemed, but a plain white laser-beam that seemed to come from another Djann installation. The Bolo they rode—Mark XXX Unit KCC-549, the flagship machine of this regiment, the grandest of its grand old veterans, its turret sparkling with battle-honors—was talking to himself and other Bolos as usual as he fought, only the most important highlights of their millions of bytes of rapid-fire machine-language transmissions translated into English for the benefit of listening humans. The majority of inter-Bolo transmissions were tactical skills routines they learned on the field, and automatically and instantly shared with each other.

"Laser burst at range white to the human eye," the KCC said now, "no threat."

"If this were Old Earth, you'd be the sort of commander who's at the head of every charge, sword in the air," said Aphra. "Idiot. I love you."

"Alert!" The KCC raised the volume on his speaker-voice just enough to interrupt. "Enemy octopods approaching, nine, due west. Orders, Brigadier-General Damien?"

Normally a Bolo in this situation would act on its own initiative, or request orders from a superior machine; but the General's physical presence in a situation that was more than routinely dangerous meant his orders would override all others. Though the chances were slim, nine octopods could take a Mark XXX, if they managed to surround it so that it had to evenly spread its shield defenses, and then web it in ion-bolts for long enough.

But of course Damien was not the only human present. He sent his wife a questioning glance. Her smile widening, brown eyes bright from the wine, she gave a slight nod.

"Engage 'em, Casey. What else would we do?"

"I obey, sir. I theorize the question is rhetorical."

"You know me well, old buddy." With a lurch that was only barely detectable in the plush cabin, the Bolo changed course. "I guess it's about time the old bucket of bolts gets put through his paces today; he hasn't had any *real* exercise." He elegantly topped up Aphra's glass, and then his own. "Here's to . . . things getting interesting."

The scrabbling octopods spread out, keeping low to the ground, scuttling behind hillocks and boulders. They were a relatively recent development; the Brigade's body of knowledge on how to neutralize them was still relatively new and rapidly growing. They looked like giant silver-gray spiders, but with anti-personnel bores instead of mandibles, and a turret atop each bullet-shaped chassis, armed with an ion gun working on the same principle but much less powerful than a Hellbore. The true engineering marvel was their legs; they could run at better than a Bolo's top speed, scamper over any terrain, leap, corner, even manipulate objects with the forward pair. Disabling one leg barely slowed them down; they were designed to function on as few as two.

"Alert status two," Casey reported, meaning he was at his second-highest level of readiness. One thing Bolos had over humans; they never got overconfident. The great gun roared again, destroying one octopod in a scattering of silver leg-sections, and drive motors whined as Casey repositioned himself, aiming for the end of the line of octopods before they could curl into a ring around him, as they were trying to do. Aphra gripped her glass against the lurch. A series of blinding bolts blanked the screen; "sensor pod destroyed," Casey calmly reported, "switching to first auxillary." The screen cleared; not an octopod was in sight. Of course Casey knew where they were hiding, his brain and sensors having tracked their motion and extrapolated their positions; he sent three thick volleys of spent uranium shells arching upward and outward, to find them behind their cover.

Aphra's eyes met Alan's, and to the boom and streaking flash of the Hellbore, she caressed the rim of her glass with her lip. *What is it about danger?* She let one strap of her dress fall off her shoulder, as if by accident.

"Enemy octopods approaching, six, due west," Casey said. Six *more*, he meant. "Calling backup, NTN-198 and GRT-263 responding and approaching unless countermanded."

"No countermand, old pal, we don't want things to get *too* interesting . . ." The jolt of a sudden change in direction spilled wine from both their glasses, and made the candle flame flicker.

The screen blanked again, and stayed blank, from a steady barrage of ion-bolts that screamed against the machine's shields like a rain of saw-blades. "Alert status one," Casey's speaker-voice reported, inappropriately calm. This meant the bolotic equivalent to the surge of adrenalin a human would produce when in danger of death. Casey's Hellbore roared non-stop. Aphra clutched Alan's arm, took a deeper sip, and winked at him.

Then the Bolo stopped moving.

The silence was unearthly, surreal; both humans thought for a moment they were in a dream.

"Casey?" The General's voice was suddenly small, an insect's rattling against sounds from somewhere above: the sawing sound deepening, a metallic crackling, the boom of an explosion that rang through the machine's whole body. *"Casey! Acknowledge!"*

A horrid sound came from the speaker: Casey's voice, distorted to a soprano whine, then to a quavering bass. Words came out crisply, as they always did from a Bolo, but made no sense. *"Report octopods alert damage Brigadier-General Damien internal . . ."* Then they stopped.

"What's going on, love?" The screen blacked, leaving only the light of the candle.

"I don't know." The look on his face made Aphra feel suddenly sick. "I have no idea. *Casey! Acknowledge! Acknowledge, damn it!"*

Silence, but for the crackling growing louder, the sound of duralloy being eaten by heat. The air was suddenly warmer. He banged his fist against the wall of the compartment, near the speaker. *"Casey! Casey! What the hell is wrong?"* He banged again, three times. His flesh and bone hand was tiny against the Bolo's bulk, an amoeba against a steel mountain.

The compartment was suddenly very much hotter. The Bolo's cooling system had broken down, along, apparently, with everything else. Nothing would draw off the heat of whatever glowing ion-wounds Casey's exterior now bore; his hulk would conduct that energy inwards until it was evenly spread throughout. Meaning everything metal around them would soon be red-hot or worse, and stay that way for a long time—unless the heat were enough to set the machine's fusion plant to critical state, in which case it would all be instantly vaporized.

Aphra, still clutching her glass, shrugged, making her earrings wink in the light. "Oh well, I guess we stay here, until one of the other Bolos rescues us." *She has to know that can't be,* Alan thought, but kept to himself. No Bolo was equipped to break into the passenger compartment of another that wasn't willingly opening the hatch; it was far too well-protected.

What had been their sentient fortress was now a mountain of dead metal around them. Their friend was their crypt.

With a synthetic stench, a patch of the ceiling vinyl blackened, then peeled away smoking; the metal under it was glowing red. Then orange, and yellow, the surface growing downwards into a bulge like a boil until it finally broke, releasing a stream of white hot liquid to stretch down towards the floor, where it lasered straight through the carpet. Enough radiation was coming from that, the general knew, to kill them several times over already. How many ways were they dead?

"There won't be time," Aphra whispered. Alan just shook his head.

"Things got too interesting," she said.

It was for words like that, he loved her.

They wouldn't need to slow-roast to death. The stream of molten white would do as well as a bullet through the head. In the meantime ... he touched her shoulder, the one from which the strap had fallen. What better to do, in their last minutes? She smiled.

Captain Benazir Ali, Ps.D. turned up the volume on the lunch-lounge news holo machine. Some other five-star type was being interviewed, a friend of the two humans who'd died in the debacle of Newterra-G.

"There's only one way their deaths could have happened," Benzi said to her lunchmate, Captain Christine Marsh, Ps.D., aka Pristine. "This is going to be on our plate faster than you can say 'software problem.'"

"No way. You're talking C.P.U. malfunction— that's impossible."

"Got any other ideas?"

Leaning forward over the table so as not to get muffin crumbs on her blouse, Pristine gave an eloquent shrug. How she could afford to dress so well on a psychotronician's pay, Benzi had never wheedled out of her; they weren't that close. Moonlighting as a corporate programmer was Benzi's guess. "Well, okay ... no."

Ours is not to do and die, Benzi mentally recited her unit's unofficial motto, *ours is but to reason why*. No one else in the Psychotronics Department of Sector Bolo Maintenance Central (SBMC) had arrived at the conclusion she had, either. Even though she'd only worked here three years, and couldn't quite call herself mid-twenties yet, she'd already got a reputation for conceiving—and then proving—theories no one else did. One nice thing about Pristine; she never gave you any crap out of envy. Benzi wished that were the case with everyone here.

"Well, it's not on *my* plate until *after* lunch-hour,"

she said firmly, lifting her fork. The com-speaker on the wall buzz-squawked her name, adding *"Urgent!"*

"Wrong again," she sighed. "Psycho Ward lounge, Captain Ali here!"

"Emmett." Her commanding officer. "Private briefing, get to my office *now*."

"I think I know what it's about, sir," she said, as soon as she'd heard the whisper of Lieutenant-Colonel Gene Emmett's office door sliding closed behind her. "Casey's brain fritzed."

"I know there's no way it could have, after ninety years' distinguished service," she added as she sat down. "I know there's no way the enemy could have made it fritz without blowing him completely to slag, which they didn't. But nothing else could possibly explain it. If he'd known he was in trouble, with General Damien aboard, he'd have called for more help. If he'd known he was doomed, he'd have self-blown—with the Damiens' permission, of course, and they would have given it, knowing they were done for anyway. His programming wouldn't let him do anything else—but it didn't happen. So his brain must have fried."

Emmett folded his arms. She could see a bit of a smile pulling at the middle-aged lines beside his mouth, that should have been a full smile, except for how worried he was.

"You know, Benzi, you're a very bright girl. And you know it. And you like to show it. And you know something else? You're right. The only problem is, you're thirty-seven times as right as you think you are."

Emmett did something, then, that Benzi would never have dreamed he'd do. He pulled two little cylindrical glasses and a bottle of whiskey out of his desk, filled them and put one in front of her.

"You've heard the official story of why we got

reamed on Newterra-G: the enemy unexpectedly produced massive reinforcements. Like a lot of official stories, it's a lot of crap. You don't want the folks in their living rooms worried. Thirty-seven Bolos and a general get trashed, we can just build another thirty-seven Bolos and hire another general, and if it means a tax increase, it'll give the citizens something to bitch about for a galaxy-rotation or two, no problem. Except that there wasn't one ship's worth of Djann reinforcement. *They did it with what they had.*

"Whatever happened to Casey happened to thirty-six other units as well. Stopped fighting in mid-fight. Started rolling in circles. Took no defensive action when they were hit. Didn't self-destruct once they were disabled, let themselves get captured. If they were people, we'd say they went crazy. It wasn't all at once; but after the first few, the numbers went up exponentially. The rest were ordered into a fighting retreat and then lifted—Sector Command had no choice, if we wanted to save any of them."

Benzi took a long swig. She'd broken into a cold sweat.

Humanity had depended on Bolos to carry its banner for a thousand years, the fate of the great machines and of their makers now inextricably linked. A thousand years, this reality had had to etch itself into the collective human unconscious, to breed dependence on the great machines into the core of the human psyche, to make the fear of their failing or going rogue humanity's ultimate, existential dread.

Given such incentive, humanity had done all it could to make the great machines failsafe, and pretty much succeeded. Aside from its fushion plant, a Bolo's brain was its most well-protected part. They could malfunction, but had so many back-up systems built in that they invariably finished the fight and came into the Psycho Ward on their own power. The psychotronicians' main job was creating improvements, adding new and deadlier features and functions, invented by themselves, or the people upstairs; once lab and field-tested, the new code was distributed to active Bolos, and back to GM to be incorporated into new models. Bolos, in fact, were more dependable than people. People went crazy; Bolos *didn't*.

Benzi grasped at straws. "Maybe some unknown atmospheric or geological condition on the planet, sir?"

"I wish it were. But our machines have been there anything as long as fifty years, with no trouble before. Another little problem: once a machine went into this state, the Djanni would stop attacking it, and go on to others. *They knew damn well it was neutralized.*

"Get my drift, bright girl? They're doing it, somehow. Since it worked so well this time, they're going to do it again, any battle, every battle. Until we figure out what they're doing and stop them, we haven't a chance in hell—anywhere. You get what I'm saying? *The whole Concordiat's on the line.*"

Benzi emptied her glass. He poured her another.

"Another little problem. Sector Command doesn't seem to realize this. They want to keep it in-sector— so they can say it's no big deal, I guess, we took care of it all by ourselves just fine. As if the goddamned *Djanni* are going to keep it in-sector . . . You know what that means?"

Benzi's voice came out parched and tiny. "We're it."

"Yep. This one little over-worked, underfunded, rusty-equipped little Psycho Ward. We're it."

He refilled her glass, redoubling her terror. The refill meant he had more to tell her.

"So, there it is, our assignment. Since it's impossible, I figure, it calls for the most flexible mind we've got. I'm putting you in charge, Benzi. You can have any and every resource this station has. I guess this means I'm promoting you. I don't have the stripes, I just thought of it, I'll get them to you asap. That's all, Major Benazir Ali, Doctor of Psychotronics. I'm glad you're so bright, bright girl, because we're going to need all the brights you've got."

"You won't believe this!" The pear-shaped, lank-haired figure of Captain Bert Mulroney, Ps.D., staggered towards a clutch of other male psychotronicians gathered around the water-cooler. They stepped back a little at his approach, as usual; it was never wise to expose yourself to a full frontal blast of Mulroney's breath. "Hot Cheeks Ali was just going down the hall, and just on a whim, I asked her to go out with me. She said *yes!*"

Eyes bugged all around. Vocal expressions of disbelief rapidly followed.

"*No, really!*" Mulroney squealed. "After two years, she finally said yes! Say, could one of you guys lend me a good shirt?" Silence fell; the idea of his skin in contact with any article of their clothing instantly produced a collective case of itching.

"Gods and little matrices," one of the others finally said. "Something must be really, *really* wrong."

Benzi sat down at her desk, and let it all sink in. "Dear Mom," she imagined herself writing. "The good news is, I've been promoted. The bad news . . ."

Her console beeped. Words appeared on the screen.

Benzi, I've never seen you so upset . . . what's the matter???

"Max." She let a long sigh out towards the computer's voice sensor. "Hi, pal."

What is it? What's the matter? There's got to be something I can do to help!

"Sure. Maybe. I don't know. You don't want to know."

If it concerns the Dinochrome Brigade, I'm duty bound to know.

Once a Bolo, always a Bolo, Benzi thought. Even if he's stripped down, without even a speaker-voice, the equivalent of a brain in a jar . . .

Mark XXX Unit MXM-823 had come off the assembly line doomed never to see a battlefield. He'd failed the battery of the preliminary simulations that all new Bolos were put through. The verdict on his report: *"Behavior erratic, inexplicable—replace psychotronic unit."* Having his brain tossed into a fusion pot should have been the end of his story. But Benzi had noticed what no one else had: there was only one possible explanation for the pattern of his actions and reports during the tests. It helped that she'd recently read a short story, written in the days before intelligent machines, by the first great master to speculate on them . . . MXM-823 was empathic. Somehow his psychotronic entrails were sensitive to human emotion. It was the distraction caused by this which had kept him from responding appropriately to the test scenarios.

Through a combination of logical argument, wheedling, and piquing Lt.-Col. Emmett's own curiosity, Benzi had talked him into letting her take custody of the defective unit for study. Now Max sat under her desk, a big silver box wired into her personal computer (a mere fringe benefit, of course, the quadrupling of the private computing power at her fingertips). Her low-priority project, more a hobby than anything else, was to figure out how in heck he did it. And perhaps even come up with an application in which he might actually be useful.

Congratulations on the promotion, he said, when she'd explained.

"Thanks a bunch."

What did I say to cause you that irritation? An electronic fluke had enabled Max to sense human emotions; it hadn't enabled him to understand them.

"So there's the problem," Benzi said. The full staff of the Psycho Ward was assembled in its one briefing room; seventy-eight pairs of eyes stared up at her in horror. "Now *all* we have to do is find the solution."

Silence held for a long, painful moment; then came a clamor of voices. "How the hell are we supposed to do that? They couldn't bring back one of the ones that died, we can't even look at what's left!" Even Pristine, who had a name for unflappable cool (accurate, according to Max, who'd never sensed anyone less nervous), blurted out, "It's a needle in a haystack the size of the galaxy!"

"Tell it to the Brigade chaplain." Benzi was amazed at how crisp she was managing to be. *She* couldn't claim any great distinction in the cool department, and she'd never stood up in front of this many people in her life. *Comes from having bigger things on my mind, I guess.*

"We have the recorded transmission from that day; we'll do a full analysis of them, looking for any common event that happened before the failures. Assad, you're in charge of that. At the same time we'll analyze what transmissions came afterwards from the machines that failed, to see if we can identify the type or method of damage. Hayes, you do that. I figure with every chip in this place working on this, we can complete it in two days. And in the meantime, if any clue starts to emerge earlier, we human brains can start trying to figure out why. Of course other suggestions for action will be welcomed. Unless there are any questions, let's get to it."

* * *

"Report, Benzi—*sir*."

She hadn't demanded formality; it was Luce Hayes's way of showing that he, like everyone else in the unit, was scared shirtless. The search was four hours old. "On transmissions from the, uh, affected Bolos.

"They're mostly gibberish, of course. But the first thing I noticed is that they make less and less sense as time goes on. Meaning the damage doesn't happen in one stroke, the first stroke isn't even necessarily fatal. But it keeps going on until the brain shuts down completely."

"As if they were under some continuous invisible bombardment," Benzi said.

"Yeah, maybe. Aside from that, there's really no pattern. You can't tell what part of the decision-making unit is getting hit, not from recorded transmissions . . . we need some remains."

"Luce, pal, we aren't going to get remains."

"Well . . . that's all I've got."

Benzi tried to keep frustration out of her tone; it wasn't his fault. "Thanks."

Some kind of bombardment or object a Bolo can't sense? Their receptors could measure all frequencies of waves, travelling through any medium. The mechanical nerves embedded in their duralloy hulls could sense the impact of any form of material, almost any form of particle. If a quark dropped on one of its treads, the lore was, a Bolo would know.

She was sitting in her office when Assad buzzed. "We've found something." She took the corridors at a dead run.

"This is from KCC-549," he said, playing back a transmission recording, as Benzi stood beside the console, catching her breath. "Nine and a half minutes before it happened."

The familiar confidence-inspiring tone of Casey boomed from the speaker. Grandbolo Casey: his voice, humanized as were all the great machines', a sound associated with safety and security for most of the people now listening, from as far back as they could remember.

"Laser burst at range white to the human eye, no threat."

"He may have thought no threat," said Assad, "but the same thing happened to every Bolo that froze, anywhere from fifteen minutes to ten seconds beforehand. The machine code attached to the English message gives the light's frequency and intensity range, too—and it's exactly the same, every time."

"But that's a diffuse beam," Benzi spat, "not even steel-cutting—hell, it's the sort of beam you do laser shows with! How in tarnation is it supposed to stop a Mark XXX?"

"Allah's treads, I don't know! You got us to look for patterns; it's a pattern."

"And this didn't happen to any Bolos that *weren't* affected?"

"Nope—not one." Assad held up the list his printer had generated. He'd done the search much as she had expected: scanned the records of ten machines, five affected and five unaffected, then taken the list of common events and searched through the rest to see which patterns continued. It had been Pristine, actually, who had spotted the white light after a pass of only three comparisons, and got Assad to authorize her to start searching through the remainder right then, thus saving valuable time. *If medal time comes*, Benzi thought, then corrected herself: *WHEN medal time comes, I'll have to remember that.*

But what in hell did the light *do*? It didn't even fit in with what Hayes had found—evidence of some kind of continuous strike.

She did what she had to. She called in the entire Psycho Ward, and set everything, every human braincell and every silicon chip, to trying to figure out an answer to that question.

Balzera Base wide-perimeter patrol. I stop and transmit my current coordinates to my comrades.

RGG-134's sensors scanned across an idyllic suburban landscape. Balzera had been a one-in-a-million find for early explorers: a Terra-normal planet, or close enough, that didn't have any unhealthy surprises like seasonal typhoons or chronic planet-quakes, and needed no expensive terraforming. The thriving starport metropolis that grew up, Balzera City, was a jewel in the Sector's crown, one of its commercial hubs and a center for government administration. Young professionals prayed for the opportunity to raise their families here rather than in the domes or lung-clenching air of nearby Phexin or Kohr.

It was a military nerve center, too, located strategically as the main gate-point at the outer end of the Sector's richest string of systems. *Not* the place where the Concordiat wanted an actual fight; but the loss on Newterra-G left no choice. Now Balzera's forces were swollen with survivors of that, as well as reinforcements from other bases.

Units TMM-144 and YND-788 acknowledge my send. We expect contact with the Enemy within the hour. The projection was that the Djanni would attempt to create one or more bridgeheads within the city or port/base complex: so 119 machines had been evenly distributed throughout, with orders to surround the landing forces, then attack and destroy them. While its human residents huddled in hidden, hastily-erected tent-cities in the woods outside of town, Balzera City was crawling with Bolos.

The ionosphere crackled as the first Concordiat

ships engaged the attackers. Through a blue sky, lightning flared. They would take out all they could but they couldn't stop the Djann drops of octopods; as usual, humanity's main defense would be its Bolos.

First octopods drop. They appear as sheets of silver on the radar horizon. They are landing 4.56 km away, in the middle of the University buildings; given that distance my duty is to maintain my position, with slight adjustment. Explosions flash and boom, activating first my photon-sensors, then those of my treadsensors which touch the ground, then my atmospherewave sensors.

The Dinochrome Brigade is strong. Our Makers depend on us.

The Enemy is being destroyed. Radiation cascades in the atmosphere, smooth spheres of stone clatter on my hull from molten rock gouting into the air and cooling. Most of the towers of the University complex are gone from sight, knocked down by groundbursts. Black billows of smoke underveined with flame rise over the skyline.

A beam of laser light flashes. White range to human sight, a non-threat to us. The Djann drop spot became a blue-white glowing shell as the Bolos' Hellbores burned the air. A wind rose, howling in as if to a forest fire, as if hundreds of acres of burning were packed into one. Rain was falling, far above, vaporizing in the heat before it could reach the ground, adding to the storm clouds being dragged in on that wind.

Two more Djann drops, 2.76 km to the north and 2.2 km to the north-east. I calculate that is where the forest encampments of humans lie. The enemy is attacking human civilians. It is our duty to protect them. Alert status two. Thirty-two of my comrades from Units Zitadelle and Guderian immediately upshift to Alert Status One and close in at maximum velocity, with TMY-919 co-ordinating I follow in support. I don't understand why the Enemy does this; they must know we are programmed to protect humans and that therefore they will sustain massive losses. I theorize it is a diversion. I radio my theory, scramble code VII.

The forests were burning now, neo-pines exploding in tiny chemical explosions and crowns of flames forty feet high. In my atmosphere-wave sensors I can hear the screams of the people. We must not fail them.

A stumble in the communication of my comrades in the fight. Transmissions from four, correction six, correction nine of them, are growing less and less computable. They are performing actions contrary to orders and tactically neutral or negatively effectual. But none are majorly damaged. I cannot generate a theory. Twenty-one of my comrades are ineffective, including TMY-929, command reverting to RWQ-347. This aberration is following a pattern of spreading outwards from the central battle. I obey RWQ-347's command to move into position there and engage.

I apply more power to my left tread to avoid the wandering of AML-945, arching shells over his hull to destroy the Enemy Zero-zero Mark 2. Octopods burst before my shells. Eight octopods engage me, curling around my position. Alert Status One. I fire my Hellbore as I advance. White laser light flares for a moment in my sensors. A human-shaped flame runs from the burning woods, crying out with blazing lungs, and falls in front of me. I apply more power to my right tread to avoid crushing him.

I fight. Hellbore: aim -24.98843 x-degrees 13.6223 y-degrees, fire. Anomaly at CPU address 5720A9EE-B86829EC cause unknown anomaly at CPU address 68A88DE32FF04110 switching to first auxiliary. I can generate no theory for why anomalies anomaly at CPU address F00794329659669E effecting first aux, switching to second aux. Hellbore aim 57.9112

x-degrees 12.386 y-degrees, fire anomaly at CPU address AD987390099683DC switching to third aux. RGG-134 reporting affected by aberration estimated time before total ineffe\@#$\\ctualness based on observation of affected comrades 12.5 seconds anomaly at CPU address E679\@#$\\FF28D9547922 switching to fourth pain sensors indicate major damage hullplate 12A-F anomaly \@#$\\at CPU address 98EA29B904 C2090F switching to fifth screams from humans anomaly switching to sixth anomaly seventh anomaly eighth anomaly at CPU address 348EF—anomaly at CPU add anomaly anomaly anomaly \@#$\\ ano ano ano \@#$\\ nnnnnn a * n * \@#$\\ o * m * a......
*****\\\\\ .... \@#$\\ .... \@#$\\ ....

"How's the search going, bright girl?"

"Rotten, sir; why?"

"Are you still sleeping?"

Emmett's face hadn't cracked a smile, so Benzi gave a straight and honest answer. "Yes; shouldn't I?"

"No." His face still didn't crack a smile. In fact he looked as if he'd aged ten years since the disaster on Newterra-G.

Oh God, she thought.

"They got Balzera."

"Balzera . . . God help us."

"All 119 machines there . . . went the same way, exactly. Every single one of them. Of course Djanni don't take prisoners; I don't think they have the concept. . . . I said it, didn't I, that they'd see they have a good thing going, and try it somewhere else soon . . ."

Benzi sat stunned, trying to imagine, trying not to imagine, events in Balzera City, and what they must have looked like. Horror crept down through her body like the edge of a pool of blood.

"With Balzera Base gone, there isn't much to stop them from spearheading into the inner systems.

Dammit, with what's happening to the Bolo's, there's nothing to stop them ... just between you and me, Benzi, so we don't screw up everyone else's morale—"

"Just our own."

"Yes, right, just our own. If the Djanni demanded our complete surrender now, High Concordiat Central would have to do some really serious thinking."

She took a deep breath and swallowed, her mouth suddenly dry. "Let me ask one thing ..." she said, feeling her voice sink to a whisper. "Elora?"

He shook his head. "No, sweetheart, your home planet's not in their line of fire. I wish I could say the same to everyone else here ... The Djanni aren't headed that way. Nahhh ... the speartip of their invasion is pointed somewhere else."

"Where?"

"If you were them, where would you send your worst? At the source of a possible threat to your effectiveness, right? Before the threat becomes reality?"

Benzi took another deep breath, fighting off sudden dizziness. "They're heading here," she whispered.

"They're heading here."

"How much time do we have?"

"Their last landing point was Gaolo Six, where they expected to find Bolos; Sector Command had the machines lifted first, and dropped here. Call it the scorched moon policy ... and the last stand. Anyway, FTL from there to here is—"

"Thirty hours."

"So: hurry it up."

"Yes, sir. I won't sleep tonight, sir. Even if I tried."

It can't be the white light, Max said, on her screen. *Probability is zero.*

Thirty hours was now fifteen. Benzi paced her office next to her bed. She hadn't slept for thirty-six;

subcutaneous shots of benzedrine had kept her, kept everyone, going.

I can't blow up at him, she thought, biting back a string of obscenities. *It hits him as hard as it hits another human.*

Of course her trying to conceal it didn't matter, with Max. The screen flashed in urgency. *What in my words caused you such anger?*

"It's nothing, pal, just colloid irrationality. It's looking more and more as if you're right, that's all, and no one can find anything else . . ."

So you're getting more and more afraid, he kindly filled in. One thing about having Max around; you couldn't maintain any emotional pretenses. Sort of desktop therapy. She *had* learned things about herself since he'd been there, one of the reasons she'd been able to resist—so far—the urge to tear his cables out. But it wasn't what she needed right now.

MainBrain, SBMC's central sentient mainframe, had just come to the same conclusion as Max, that the white light was not the cause. If there was any conceivable way it was possible, MainBrain's internal simulators, which could recreate any model of Bolo down to the atom, and throw any defined event at it, would have reenacted it. That gift of humans— inspiration—hadn't helped; the simulations the psychotronicians had conceived and asked MainBrain to execute had all turned up nothing too.

Benzi had this sudden strange thought—the kind, perhaps, that she could only get on benzedrine—that MainBrain was corrupt, had been somehow sabotaged by the Djanni. *Paranoia.* The huge 'frame was protected by more layers and networks and redundant systems of internal security than any human even knew. Besides they'd run simpler simulations on other machines in the place, and got the same results.

No back door through the sensors; that kind of light

hit them all the time. No digital information attached to the beam; on the first coherent letter or number, a Bolo would have reported it as an incoming message, not just a beam of light. And there simply was no other pattern; the comprehensive search was complete.

An impossible situation.

Got any other ideas, Max?, she wanted to snap. But he was a machine. Ideas weren't his department. It was she who was failing.

The feeling in the entire unit was the same, though no one was saying it. No one wanted to be the first to say it. But it was in everyone's exhaustion-reddened eyes. *There's no hope. We're defeated. We can't do it.* Emmett had set every non-Psycho Ward staffer on SMBC Moon to enacting his Plan B, fifteen hours ago: hastily installing manual overrides in all Bolos present, so that in the fight a human driver could take over if *it*, as everyone had begun to call it, happened. Even with everyone down to the janitors working around the clock, there wouldn't be time to modify all the machines, but maybe, just maybe, it would be enough . . .

Maybe, Benzi realized soberly, but most likely not. No one using instrumentation and manual controls could hope to replicate a Bolo's tactical ability, except perhaps after years of training. She tried to imagine doing it herself—a possibility which was not entirely out of the question, she realized—and shuddered.

No human had done any training in driving a tank at all, for centuries.

The psychotronic solution, Plan A, would have to come from an inspiration, she knew: a brilliant flash of lateral thinking from someone, anyone, here. There *was* an answer—something *was* destroying the brains of Bolos—so there must be some way of finding it; it simply was an answer so unexpected that no one had thought of it.

I just wish the inspiration had come sooner, she thought, thinking of the bleary faces, ashen-masked in the flat grey-white light of the Psycho Ward. *The more tired all our brains get, the less likely it is to come at all.*

"T-minus 35 minutes to Enemy contact. Clear the area for de-pressurization. All units report once main doors open. Repeat: T-minus 35 minutes to Enemy contact. All un-suited human personnel clear the area. This bay will be depressurized in 5 minutes. Mark."

As the alert blared through SMBC's maintenance bay it froze the hive of motion for a fraction of a second, then whipped it faster.

The immense floor was overcrowded with Bolos, most lifted from Gaolo Six, in various states of manual override addition. The techs and their helpers—everyone on SMBC Moon capable of holding a flashlight, rewiring a connection or bread-boarding a new circuit—struggled to finish what they could.

Total, out of the 64 machines on hand: 27.

In SMBC Command Central, General Chuan Immen's piercing eyes scanned the main holo-image of the vast underground complex that SMBC was, and the surrounding terrain. Supported by the base's artillery and infantry, sixty-four reliable Mark XXX's against an estimated 700 octopods should be no trouble. Twenty-seven manually-operated—meaning clumsy, slow and stupid—ones would be a great deal of trouble indeed. Even if none of the manual overrides, put in hastily by unqualified and increasingly exhausted people, failed ... *Curse those spaceheads in the Psycho Ward,* she thought, *for not doing a damn thing; think they're goddamned geniuses and they can't even find their way around their own mandate with both hands and a map* ... Well, no use carping. She had to do with what she had.

The Bolo tech snapped off the torch and patted LIS-668's hull with one gloved hand. "There you go, Luis. One hunk-a-junk jury-rigged manual override, as close to done as it's going to get. Grab your partner and go blow some octopods into leg-segments!"

"*I already have orders, Bolotech.*"

"Yeah, yeah." The man's casual tone trembled at the edges with fatigue as he clambered down, dropping the flashlight and heading for the air-lock. The P.A. blared again. "*Depressurization in one minute.*"

Like white ants on horseshoe crabs, the soldiers who would be the millennium's first human tank drivers crawled up the sides of the machines. Hatches boomed shut. The Bolos powered up, their thunderous growl fading as the air cycled out, fading to a vibration that still thundered in one's bones. Their usually shiny, well-polished hulls were patchy with trailing dribbles of welding duralloy, a faint sign of the wiring nightmares their passenger cabins had become. The huge doors of the bag glided open, silent in the vacuum. Silent but for the rock-shaking vibrations they sent through the moon's mantle, the great machines wheeled smoothly through SMBC's miles of massive corridors, and out onto the surface to take their positions.

Ground troops were dug in already with their Gus's, the smaller, non-sentient version of the Hellbore. As the Bolos deployed, infantry fell in with them.

"*LIS-668 reporting with backup system, Private Felding,*" the Bolo sounded off.

"Backup system Private Felding reporting. I guess that's b.s. for short, ha ha ..."

"Standby," their commander crisply ordered.

"*Order Standby acknowledged.*"

"Sir! Yes! Sir!"

This time there were no flares in an atmosphere from the air battle: only velvet black sky torn apart by searing light that darkened filters on helmets and screens.

Then the deadly silver seeds of octopods were dropping, sprouting clusters of legs like dandelion fluff, tumbling toward the ground.

"Tabernoche," Felding whispered when he saw their number. "Luis, have you ever felt like the place you're defending is called Alamo and you're not Mexican?"

"Private, that sentiment is defeatist. I suggest you see a company psychologist as soon as possible."

Felding shook his head inside his helmet. "Yeah, sure. You Bolos should talk." The screen flickered as filters cut in, and the order came through the com. *"Engage!"*

It was a half-silent battle, the only sounds conducted through ground and metal and bone, moonquakes that lasted only a moment or two. Felding just hung on, as Luis did his thing, and reviewed his eleventh-hour crash-course in Bolo operation; there was nothing else for him to do. Yet.

A web of white beams flashed from some of the octopods, one catching every Bolo. "Shit on a pungee stick, there it is. Luis, status?"

"Advancing. Firing. Alert status two. To remind backup system, SMBC Psychotronics Department has determined that white laser light cannot cause Bolo malfunction." Luis's Hellbore and three shells took out five octopods, destroying two completely. Felding grabbed the newly installed control-wheel with one hand.

"Great. Wonderful. Maybe I won't need this. Maybe we're all right this—"

"Alert status one." A swarm of octopods had gathered

out of nowhere, were trying to surround them through a hail of infantry bolts. *"TRN-776, DNA-864 respond, approaching to aid aid id id id id id malfunction backup sys malfunction sys sys sys F$ek78°↻—"* The Bolo's voice degenerated into static as the screen went blank.

"Hoté!" Felding grabbed the wheel, hitting the keypads wired into Luis not an hour ago. LEDs winked alive as the manual circuits came online. "LIS-668 now on backup! Here goes!"

The screen, snowy white with static, showed the field. Some Bolos continued in their formation, firing, firing, destroying the octopods in their tens. But they were coming in hundreds.

LIS-668 was circling to port at maximum speed, Hellbore tracking slowly clockwise. Octopods were all around them, ignoring the disabled Bolo, blasting the men on the ground.

Felding muscled his control wheel over hard, felt the slow response of the Bolo. Slow—but a response. He was suddenly reminded of his first driving lesson.

"Sacré, we'll get 'em, Luis! We'll get 'em!" He hit the Fire key on the Hellbore joystick, heard the familiar all but subsonic roar. Octopods curled on the field like fire-washed spiders. "Ho, ho, you may be down for the count, pal, but you aren't *dead!"* He aimed the Hellbore, fired again, whooped. He was starting to get the hang of it. Octopods danced in patterns before him, in a hundred directions simultaneously. Complicated: but he'd faced opposition that complicated before. "And Mama and Papa thought I was wasting my time and rotting my brain, playing all those video games!" His roar joined the Hellbore's. "YaaaaHOOOOOOOOo—oh, oh."

Something in the column of the control wheel grated and broke. It rasped through a complete circle without effecting the Bolo's motion. "Oh, *merde alors.*"

The comm channel crackled. "LIS-668. You are approaching infantry position without orders."

"*Merde*—that's the Ninth!" Felding struggled with the wheel then reached down the shaft, trying to turn it between his palms, calling as if the Bolo could hear him. "Oh, *merde*, Luis, stop!" Perhaps it could hear him, and do nothing. He slammed the drive motor switch to Reverse. Nothing happened. "*Merde!* I can't!"

"LIS-668, stop! This is a direct order. Stop *now.* Stop *now.*"

"Sarge, I'm trying! Something's gone wrong with the wheel and switches, I'm doing everything I can, *merde, merde,* Luis! *Luis, stop! Luis!*" Felding pried at the steering shaft, banged at the switches, trying to make mere human muscle re-direct a hundred tons of machinery, before God knew how many men were crushed under giant treads. "Oh *mon dieu.*"

He looked up at the screen, saw ghostly images of the soldiers, his buddies, in the Bolo's mountainous shadow, bouncing away from their cover and into the open to get out of its way, scattering to be picked off by the second wave of octopods. He heard the screams through the comm as he and Luis plowed through the Ninth Infantry's position. "Dear God."

The octopods flocked past them.

Benzi lay awake.

She'd been sleeping on a cot in her office. What shreds of sleep she'd got. Everyone was doing the same. In case something came in, in case she had a thought, in case . . . in case of what? What was she going to do, point her monitor at the octopods and type real hard?

She hated herself for lying here, doing nothing,

while everything she had ever worked or lived for stood in the path of destruction. But anything that anyone could possibly do was being done by someone else. There wasn't much more that anyone could do.

She kept thinking she heard faint explosions. She kept telling herself to stop imagining them. But it was just a matter of time before the octopods laser-cut their way through SBMC's gates.

She thought of Belmuth, her home village on Elora, full of Amish horse-buggies; her mother's face, her father's, her baby brother Jahangir, they all suddenly paraded through her mind, too vivid. She tried not to cry. Majors in the Dinochrome Brigade didn't do that.

She cried anyway. She was thankful for the darkness.

She tried to tell herself she wasn't personally responsible for the fate of the Concordiat. Surely that was too much responsibility for any one human being. *It's not my fault the Djanni have whatever they've got* . . . Perhaps it was the fate of the entire human race at stake. That was perfectly possible. *Some renegade tribes on some backwater planets, too small and primitive for the Djanni to notice, might survive*, she thought. *Or will they hunt every single one of us down?*

She wanted to hide under the covers, as she had when she'd been a child, afraid of monsters. Giant spiders. Eight-legged evils. *If I can't see them, they can't see me. If I can't hurt them, they can't hurt me* . . . Perhaps she'd still be huddled there, when the station walls turned to yellow-glowing slag around her . . .

She sat bolt upright, suddenly angry.

Like hell I will. What am I thinking? It's not over— it may be ninety-nine per cent over, but that isn't over!

She jumped out of the cot naked, feeling the sweat

on the back of her neck and between her shoulderblades go cold, and hit the switch of her computer. To do what, she didn't know. Talk to Max, she guessed.

There must be something I can do to help!
There must be something I can do to help!
There must be something I can do to help!

The message scrolled all the way up her screen and beyond, to form a regularly-jerking column of desperate offering.

"Just talk to me, Max. Don't ask how that will help, don't tell me you don't understand, just talk to me."

The screen went blank, and stayed that way. She'd eliminated all his possible options, it seemed.

As General Chuan watched the holo simulation of the battle, green and red lights indicating the positions of friendly and Enemy forces, her face transformed into a white mask of rage, like a cornered animal's. Her forces were being destroyed. More slowly than she'd dared to hope for, yes, but still, destroyed.

Eyes blazing, she hit her comm to open the channel for a general order.

"*All Bolos fall back.* Open entrance doors West A through J, occupy corridors two deep, draw the Enemy in and *hold them.*"

There was a stunned silence on the channel, except for the functioning machines, all of which duly acknowledged. You never had to tell a Bolo now, or do it fast; they'd assume now, and as fast as possible, unless you said otherwise. "*Now!*" she snapped to the humans. "*Move!*" Their acknowledgements came slowly.

They know I'm throwing away what's left of the infantry, she thought. *But since the corridors were built just big enough for Mark XXX's, they'll be able to hold the octopods to a standstill better, without worry of being surrounded.*

They know the energy-discharges of a battle will quite possibly bring a million tons of rock down on their heads, too. But it'll land on the Enemy as well, block and trap them. "If we're going down, curse it," she snarled to whoever was listening, mostly her aides, "let's do it in a sea of slag, not in a pile of loot!"

"You know what this has been reminding me of, in the back of my head, this whole time?" Benzi said to Max absently. "The Murphosensor Bomb." Blather; but it was better than lying in the dark waiting for explosions.

Clarify? the defective unit asked lamely.

"Something my boss said to me once, when I was a teenager, working in a publishing shop. Every machine has one."

Clarify further?

"You know Murphy's Law? 'Anything bad that can happen *will*, and at the worst possible moment.' Well my boss used to say there was only one explanation for why machines would blow just before deadline, or when the big prospective client presentation was needed for tomorrow. All machines have a device in them which can sense the worst possible moment, and make them blow up then. That's the Murphosensor Bomb. Sure seems like our Bolos are equipped with them, doesn't it?"

It must be that, said Max. *Since it can't be the white light.*

"Frigging literal-minded should-be-blob of slag, you have to take me ... seriously ..." Benzi trailed off, stunned by a flash in her mind like a head-blow.

"They were all in alert status one." She wasn't truly conscious of whispering the words.

Another common event. One they hadn't thought

of, because it had been too obvious. A chain of conclusions went off like cluster-charges in her head.

"MAX! No wait ... MainBrain! MainBrain!" She
disconnected Max from her terminal—that was
regulations.

The 'frame came onto her screen in its characteristic red. *Insert dogtag.* She leaned forward to jam her
tag into the slot, struggling to keep her hands from
shaking.

She heard an explosion, muffled with distance. *That
wasn't in my head. They're getting in.*

*MainBrain: Voice/tag match correct, access permit-
ted. ?:*

"MainBrain, check the 'execute alert status one'
code of ... JNC-147." Janice had just happened to
be in Maintenance for a sensor-pod fix, the first Newterra-G survivor there whose call-letters Benzi could
remember. "Look for any ... anomalies."

*Retrieving. Note: compares between all Newterra-G
surivors' full psychotronic code and that of virgin GM
version already executed, completed 19:56:07 yesterday, by order of Major Benazir Ali.* The virgin GM
version was always kept on file, for occasions like
these. *No anomalies found.*

She sat down hard, banging her desk on each side
of her keyboard with her fists. That's right, she had
ordered that, it had been one of the first things, since
it would take such a long time ...

*But if it's what I think it might be, that compare
wouldn't show it anyway!*

The only way was by hand ... go down through
the code screen by screen looking for something
amiss. Even with all seventy-eight people who had the
expertise to do it, working twenty-four hours a day
without keeling over, which was impossible, it would
take days. They had hours if they were lucky.
Maybe minutes.

Benzi's fingers clawed at her hair. *No!* There had to be some way, some other way—there *was*, dammit, she knew it, what the hell was it?

It came in another flash. "Mainbrain! Run a compare between same code, JNC-147 and MXM-823."

MXM-823 is assigned to Gea Beta system, Galaxy Arm B, transmission time approx 12 million years. FTL message mission expense must be authorized by Maintenance Commander.

"No, no, the MXM-823 that's sitting under my desk!" Of course she should have remembered that the designation MXM-823 officially belonged to the Bolo now wearing Max's original hull, on which it was engraved. "You know—*Max!*"

Acknowledge: Defective psychotronic unit in custody of Major Benazir Ali. Regulations forbid accessing of unit's code as unit is defective.

More obscenities burst from Benzi's lips. "Right, never mind. Transfer said code from JNC-147 to this terminal."

Sending. Regulations forbid the return of code to system in any form: must be wiped. MainBrain wasn't stupid; it knew exactly what she was going to do. "I know that, you dickhead machine!"

File send complete. SBMC policy suggests characterization "dickhead machine" inappropriately disrespectful to system.

"LIKE ANYBODY CARES RIGHT NOW!" She heard—felt in her guts—the thump through the moon's mantle of another explosion. "Plugging in Max!" *MainBrain: disconnect.* That was one sure way to get rid of the 'frame.

"Now there *is* something you can do to help, old pal: *you're* going to run a compare." Of course it would take Max ten minutes, instead of MainBrain's several seconds. She hoped the Djanni would be considerate enough to allow for this.

In three minutes and twenty-seven seconds, the screen flashed, *Mismatch found.* "Put it up on screen!"

An amazingly short routine, barely twelve lines of code, neat and precise and brilliant as a knife in the back—to commandeer a Bolo's highest-ranked processor, and set it to randomly destroying its own decision-making net, including all auxiliary systems.

Benzi's fist banged down on her intercom. "Lieutenant-Colonel! I've found it! I've found it!"

In the time that passed as he ran to her office, and she made a hard copy, Benzi realized one thing from looking at the bit of code that made her want to throw up. *There's only one way this could have got in . . .*

It doesn't matter, she told herself firmly. *It's an easy fix—that's all that counts, right now.*

"This is just lines of Betelgeusian on paper to me, bright girl," Emmett said, bleary-eyed and panting from the run.

"It's a program to destroy a Bolo's brain in just the way it's been happening," she told him. "Janice has it, no big surprise, since she was on Newterra-G. *But so does the virgin GM version.* Probably every active Bolo in the sector, if not the galaxy, has it. Are you familiar with the concept of computer viruses?"

"In a *Bolo*!?

"In *all* of them. Getting spread through Bolo-to-Bolo transmissions. Viruses have to be attached to executable files, so that they can be made to activate; but Bolos swap executable files all the time—the tactical skill programs they learn on the field and then share with each other. *Those go back to GM as well,* to be incorporated in the latest virgin code. Max isn't infected because he's been cut out of the net for a while; it showed up since. That damned white light was a red herring, and I had every colloid and silicone synapse in the place burning out—"

"Tell me how we get rid of it."

"That's dead easy, sir, all we have to do is send a general order out to . . ."

Emmett was already inserting his dog-tag into the slot. "MainBrain, open the channel. To all active Bolos from SBMC Psychotronics Department, Emmett authorizing, order of first priority is as follows . . ." He pulled away from the voice-sensor. "Take it away, bright girl."

She glanced at the printout. She couldn't make any mistakes. "Run search in 'execute alert status one' code for . . ." She read off the first line of characters. "If found, delete that line through . . ." —she read off the last time—"inclusive. Repeat this action after each incidence of receiving or executing . . ." *After executing what?* She'd had maybe a minute to think about it.

An explosion. She definitely wasn't imagining it; Emmett had flinched too.

Her mouth was suddenly dry. "After receiving or executing . . ." *They were fighting octopods every time.* ". . . any transmission-acquired tactical skill routine against Djann octopods. Also repeat before any incident of going on alert status one." *Dear God, let that be enough* . . . If it wasn't, they'd all reinfect themselves and each other in microseconds.

A chorus of Bolo voices crowded out of the speaker. "Found . . . deleted . . . found . . . deleted . . ."

She fell back in her chair. She suddenly realized, distantly, as one realizes trivial things; she was stark naked, in front of her commanding officer.

Not that he'd noticed. "While I've got you all listening," he was saying into the com, "a tactical suggestion. We humans call it playing possum . . ."

In one of SMBC's main-trunk corridors, JNC-147 sat immobile, glowing in several places from Djann ion-bolts, as the octopods swarmed over her bulk in their graceful dancing gait, towards the next portal.

She already had her Hellbore muzzle turned to aim behind her: a senseless move in the fight. Now with almost imperceptible slowness she raised it into position. The octopod drivers, believing nothing operative with the power of a Hellbore could possibly be aimed at them, had massed into a phalanx, to concentrate their presence in the corridor.

Janice aimed dead center.

Emmett kept the channel open. In ten minutes it was apparent that no more of Maintenance's defending machines would fail. One fully-functioning Bolo could hold any corridor indefinitely, and in fact advance, and twenty-eight remained. It was enough. Most, however, opted to give the Djanni a surprise, allowing them past, and then trapping them against unbreached portals.

Within half an hour, it was just a matter of mopping up.

"*Lieutenant-Colonel Emmett suggestion 'playing possum' extremely effective,*" one machine reported.

"That was for Alan and Aphra," Emmett whispered under his breath.

Benzi found herself laughing and crying and slipping into a bathrobe all at once. Outside, noise erupted in the corridor; the Psycho Ward broke into an instant party, as whoever had been following the fight spread the news. *We did it,* she thought. It was all she could think, and it turned into a delirious mantra: *we did it we're saved we did it we're saved we did it we did it . . .*

Emmett's voice cut through. "Bright girl," he said. "Sweetheart. It isn't over. It isn't over yet, Benzi, wake up. It isn't over until we figure out how in God's sparkly starfields that bug got *in* there in the first place. Or else they might be able to do this again tomorrow."

Benzi felt her own smile fall off her face, and an instant wave of exhaustion washed over her. She sat down heavily on the bed, letting her eyes close for a moment, then opening them forcibly, afraid she'd lose the ability to.

"We don't quite want to let out to everyone what exactly happened, yet," he said, more gently, "do we?"

He knew, it seemed. An absurd relief filled her: she didn't have to tell him. That the Djanni had no such knowledge of Concordiat systems, or access to them. That it had to have been an inside job. That it had to have been someone in the Psycho Ward of SMBC. She suddenly wanted to cry again. What the hell; she let the tears fall.

Lieutenant-Colonel Gene Emmett sat silent for a while, one hand curling around his sharp chin, in thought. Benzi sat listening to the party noise outside fade in and out, as she waged a battle with her eyelids to keep them open, wetness cooling on her cheeks.

"Well," he said finally, "I realize there's only one person here I can be absolutely certain is trustworthy. You—if you were the saboteur, you wouldn't have fixed the damage.

"Otherwise," he spat, "I have seventy-eight suspects. If I don't have it narrowed down to one in a day or two, which I don't have a snowball's chance in hell of doing, it'll be the Concordiat Military Police knocking on our door. Busting SBMC as a hotbed of traitors; with the flaky rep we have already, we'll all be counting our blessings just to have gotten demoted to garage-sweeper, and not dishonorably canned, even after they *do* figure out who it is, and even if said person doesn't do anything else in the meantime."

"We had a snowball's chance in hell of finding out

what was frying the Bolos," Benzi said in a semi-conscious murmur, "and we did it."

Regret for these words came so fast it startled her awake. *God. Why does my subconscious have to be cocky, too?*

"No," he corrected, a slow smile creeping across his face. "*You* did it. Ready for your next assignment, bright girl?" Benzi pulled her hands up over her face and moaned. "Obviously you are, and raring to go," he chirped. "Good luck!"

There must be something I can do to help. There must be something I can do to help. There must—

"Oh Max, pal," she groaned. "You can do everything but the one thing machines can't do, the one thing only we humans supposedly can, the one thing we need. Have a flash of inspiration. Hell, you can even sense people's *hot damn J.C. on a joystick duralloy dung-muffins* ARRRRGHGHGHGH! AAAI-IGHGHGH! WHY DIDN'T I THINK OF IT BEFORE!?"

"Attention, everyone." It was nearly noon the next day. The entire staff of the Psycho Ward sat assembled in its one briefing room. The feeling in the air was a strange mix of utter relief, joyful expectancy of seeing awards handed out, and hangover.

Behind the podium Emmett stood, his face more grim under its impassiveness than Benzi had ever seen it.

Inside the hollow back of the podium, hidden from view, with a small monitor hooked up and sitting on top of him, sat Max. From her position beside Emmett, Benzi could see the monitor clearly.

Awaiting verbal cue to execute orders, it read steadily.

Emmett cleared his throat. "Now we're all finished celebrating," he said, "you must all be wondering how precisely our cause for celebration came about. That's what I've gathered you all here to tell you.

"The credit belongs entirely and utterly to Major Benazir Ali." As the applause and cheering crescendoed, Benzi's eyes found the one unmoving line of text on the screen incredibly fascinating; she could tell she was blushing by the burning of her cheeks. They even chanted her name for a while, as if she weren't embarrassed enough.

But as it faded, the pounding of her heart didn't; she couldn't imagine how it could go unheard. She took a deep breath.

"The *blame*," Emmett went on, his voice turning deadly, "unfortunately also belongs with one person, who was working for the Enemy." The room went so quiet that ventilator fans suddenly seemed deafening. "One person who happens to be in this room." There was a collective gasp. "We have ascertained who that person is."

Benzi looked at the monitor. She almost didn't want to; she almost didn't want to know who she'd worked side-by-side with, hung around the water-cooler joking with, shared career dreams with, who turned out to be this. *Intending this for how long? Fifteen years? Twenty? A whole career? A smart enemy would make it worth that, and the Djanni are anything but stupid.*

On it in blinking capitals Max had, as ordered, produced the name of the person present who'd had the most extreme reaction of fear for their own fate, as opposed to suspense or horror or puzzlement, at the moment Emmett had spoken the last sentence.

Her jaw dropped as she read the name.

Emmett looked up from the monitor. "On alert status one, are we, hmm, Pristine?"

Benzi's head was still spinning when the holo-razzi surrounded her in her office with a bristly ring of video and audio recorders, and a no-less intimidating ring of admiring, awestruck, almost dog-like expressions. *I guess I'm going to be in the history books,* she thought vaguely. Speaking engagements, multimillion contracts for her memoirs, honorary degrees and memberships and fellowships, keys to planets, a personal thank you from the Concordiat President ... such realities-to-be hadn't yet impinged on her awareness.

It was Christine Marsh's echoing words that filled her brain. She'd started yelling as soon as they'd grabbed her. *"They blackmailed me! They blackmailed me! When I was just twenty-one some human flunky of theirs found me and said they'd kill my parents and the husband and kids I wanted to have and everything I held in this emotion your humans call 'love,' they said! My oldest is thirteen, now, a good kid, a genius, going to a good school—"*

"What the hell did you think was going to happen to that good school, when they used what you gave them?" Benzi had wanted to yell. "Not to mention you—did you notice the Djanni checking to see who they were shooting when they came here? They'd gotten what they needed from you ..." But there was no point. She'd been allowed to sit in on the drug-assisted interrogation, when the truth came out about the fifteen-room mansion Pristine and her husband secretly owned on Macer's 'Roid, the hyper-yacht she used to get there, the many wardrobes of designer fashions, and all the other nice things she'd bought on the play-now pay-later plan with the blood of her own species ... She remembered wondering how Pristine could afford her clothes. *And it was her who oh-so-cleverly saved time by spotting that damn white light. God's heavenbores!*

She didn't envy Pristine's fate now. But she didn't feel terribly sorry for her either.

"One at a time!" the reporters yelled at each other, all at once, snapping her mind back into the present.

"What lesson," one asked over the rest, "may humanity draw from this?"

Never trust anyone whose desk is spotless, she wanted to say, waving an arm towards her own clutter. Instead she uttered the usual bromide, about our mechanical creations only being as good, ultimately, as we were. "Usually, anyway," she heard herself add. "It was all Max's doing."

"Max?" they asked.

Now I've done it, she thought. *I'll have to tell them about Max, and I'll let something slip that Central wants to keep quiet and they'll be on my case for revealing a weakness in the Bolo Program ... after this ... great ...*

"Max ..." she winged, "is a special model. How, I can't tell you—it's classified—except that he was developed for a super-specialized security application." There, that should make Central feel better. He *had* been developed for a super-specialized security application, as it turned out, even though no one had known or planned it. From now on he would be in charge of the security testing of all new SMBC personnel. Let a traitor try to get through that ... "More to the point," she added, "because he's not hooked into the regular Bolo net, he wasn't infected with the virus, which let me run the compare."

Fifteen more minutes of "No comment," and "I said security, do you really think I'm going to tell you more?" convinced them all to give up on badgering more of an answer about Max out of her. Of course they tried Max himself. *I've been ordered not to tell you either,* he said through her screen. *You're all so curious it almost hurts my pain receptors, but I just can't tell you what's special about me.*

It was about then that Emmett hustled them out.

LEGACY

Todd Johnson

"Timmin!" The shout was lost among the sound of detonating shells. The cave lay somewhere ahead—wherever ahead was.

Heedless of the explosions bracketing her, Erena Calgary ran back into the crater made just seconds ago. The crater that had opened between her and Timmin as he ran behind her.

She jumped down into the crater and found the boy sprawled face down in the dirt. Quickly she turned him over. "Timmin!" She shouted with her mouth cupped to his ear. No breath. No pulse. She scoured his mouth clear with a dirt-grimed finger, forced two quick breaths from her lungs into his, straddled his body and thrust on his chest to pump his heart.

"One . . . two . . . three . . . four . . . five! Breathe!" Erena shouted the steps like a mantra as she thrust

215

and breathed. "One ... two ... three ... four ... five! Breathe!"

Something tugged at Erena's sleeve but she ignored it, intent only on reviving the boy. She imagined his heaving gasp, his lungs straining to draw in air, the tears running from his eyes.

"One ... two ... three ... four—" A nearby detonation drowned out the sound of her shouting even to her own ears.

Something tugged at her sleeve again—hard. Erena glanced to her side. A young girl stood next to her, gesticulating wildly and mouthing words unheard over the roar of the barrage.

"Go on, Leander! Get to the shelter!" Erena shouted irritably. She stopped long enough to gesture emphatically but the girl stayed put, tugging on her sleeve and trying to grab her hand.

"—dead! He's dead!" Leander's voice came through a momentary lull. It was drowned out again by another wave of explosions.

Erena shook the girl off and returned to her CPR. "One ... two—dammit, Leander, I said go!" This last as her sleeve was tugged again. Irritably, Erena made to push the girl in the direction she thought was right for the cave but found herself touching something else. A leg.

It was severed well above the knee. Leander held it in both hands, waving it imploringly at Erena. It was Timmin's leg. Erena slapped the girl in irate shock, causing her to drop the severed limb. Then, as realization sank in, Erena turned to look over her shoulder.

A bitter stain of blood marked the earth where Timmin's life had drained away. The blood had soaked deep into the earth, too much to imagine.

"He's dead, he's dead!" Leander's sobs came

through another lull. "Let's go, Erena, let's go, please!"

Numbed, Erena let herself be led away by the little girl. All around them rained falling dirt, rocks, and boulders churned up by the bombardment. Their chests reverberated painfully with each new detonation, as though their own organs were going to explode from within.

An explosion just behind them threw them to the ground. Erena looked back across the pocked landscape but could see no sign of Timmin.

"Come on!" Leander cried. "This way! Crawl!"

Erena followed the little girl obediently.

"—not far!" The girl's voice carried through another lull in the bombardment.

No, not far at all. Erena thought to herself. *Two, maybe three hundred meters.*

They crawled on, hugging the ground—being thrust from the ground as explosions burst around them.

Damn fools! Why can't they hit us? Erena swore to herself.

The little girl urged her on.

And who ever would have thought of using physical weapons? Erena asked herself again—yet without the hint of grudging admiration she'd had three weeks ago.

Dirt stopped raining on them. A hood covered the sky. *No, not a hood—the cave.*

The two warriors crawled into the last refuge of mankind. The shelling outside dispersed, slowed to a trickle, then stopped.

Erena stood up, grabbed Leander's hand, moved under and around the invisible barrier that guarded the cave entrance and into the coolness of the sanctuary.

Inside, Erena leaned against the cold stone of the cave wall, hugging Leander against her.

"We're safe," Erena said. *Safe.* The thought echoed bitterly inside her. Timmin was gone.

Leander looked up at her, tried a small, grimy smile—failed—and broke into heaving sobs of hysterical grief.

Erena hugged the girl tightly to her. Leander's head rested just below Erena's breasts. *I must be careful with her,* Erena told herself. *After me, she's the eldest.*

Erena looked down at the eleven-year-old hugging her and gently stroked her head. At thirty-one, Erena Calgary was oldest.

As her eyes adjusted to the gloom, Erena distinguished the looks on the faces surrounding her. Grimy, small, wide-eyed, the children bore expressions ranging from reproachful to ravaged.

Some stared blankly ahead, eyes unseeing, but most stared at her.

"Come on," Erena said, leading them back down into the deeper caves. Leander let out some final sob, gave Erena's hand a squeeze, and fell to the rear of the children to herd them forwards.

No one could say how long ago the caves had been built, but Erena was certain they had been constructed somehow. The caves were so old that they bore the straight and square appearance of things built with macro-tools, instead of the delicate, rounded shapes that the nannies would have elegantly produced.

Erena had only just learned about macro-tools in the past week as she accessed the data on implements of gross change. The data was so infrequently accessed that the nannies had only the barest hints left in their collective memories. In her search, she had learned of coal-mining, of steel-making—and had picked up something about tremendously powerful storage vessels or tanks but the acounts were garbled.

She would have learned more if only Timmin hadn't run out and got killed. But the boy would not believe that his father would not come back—was no more.

Nano-machines were potent but it took concentrated effort to keep them on program; without Timmin, Erena would have to work much harder to keep even the basics going. Worse, she would have to spend extra time teaching Leander and—who was the next eldest?—Swotti the finer points of handling the nannies.

Not that handling the nano-machines was much effort—all you had to do was think. Unfortunately, the nannies were very literal and getting them to do complex things like light the way *and* make heat required no small amount of attention. Coupled with diffusing effects of the younger children's daydreams, Erena had more work than she could handle even with the help of elder, more mature children.

Simpler things, like keeping things the way they were, required much less of the nannies. Although with the bombing outside it was very difficult to keep things the way they were—especially as the nannies had a difficult time realizing what was *supposed to be* and what was now.

What Erena couldn't get the nannies to do at all was tell her why mankind was being bombed out of existence on this planet. Or what was doing the bombing. Or where the bombers were. Or who controlled the bombers.

Clearly it was some terrible misunderstanding—an accident or something. Whoever was doing it must have not seen the warning signs, not have noticed the clear indications that the planet had been reserved for human life and was already occupied by humans. As soon as it could be explained, Erena was sure, the problem would go away and there would be tears of apology and horror.

I must tell them. That was the problem, Erena was sure. Somehow she had to tell them. The other attempts must have been misunderstood or not recognized.

Up ahead the light of the nannies dimmed and flickered. Erena looked around, scouting for Leander. "Leander! Concentrate! Light and heat, more light than heat."

Far behind her, Leander heard the call, looked up and nodded glumly. Shortly, the light increased.

"Swotti!" Erena called. A dark-haired young girl looked up at her. "You help."

"I can help, too." A small voice piped up. Erena caught sight of red-haired Alik.

"Yes, you can," Erena agreed, her voice lifting for the first time since she'd returned to the cave. "Think some more light for us, please."

Overhead, the light rippled, then spread down the sides of the walls. A wave of heat flowed over them.

"Only on the top, Alik, on the top," Swotti scolded.

They reached the first ramp heading down—it had been stairs but Erena had had the nannies fix that. Two more ramps and they would be at the bottom.

Suddenly the ground dropped away from her, then lurched upwards, throwing her off balance. As she fell, Erena could feel her body being squeezed by a giant concussion. Behind her, children screamed.

It was dim when Erena opened her eyes again. Something was shaking her. Why was it so dim? She felt for the nannies, thought that they should make light and not so much warmth—she was very warm—but the light grew only a little bit brighter.

"Erena!" a voice called. It was distant, blurred. She was warm, wrapped—a hand scratched her face. Erena felt dirt being stroked off her.

"Erena!" The voice was Alik's, nearly frantic with terror.

" 'Salright," Erena muttered. Dirt fell into her mouth and she spit it back out again. She flexed her arms to move, tried to sit up. Her right arm felt numb, slack.

"She's here!" Alik called out.

Well of course I'm here, Erena thought to herself. *What's dirt doing on me?* Erena thought the dirt away from her but it didn't move. Someone had given the nannies conflicting orders.

"Don't do that, please," Alik told her, eyes going wide. "Just let me——" again he swept dirt off her.

"Why not?" Erena asked, spitting out more dirt.

" 'Cos I can't tell if you're burying the others."

With that, Erena came fully awake with a rush of horror. She felt around, thought to the nannies, searched for the children. How many? The nannies came back with the answer—forty-two. Erena sighed her relief, then went cold again. How were they? She framed her question carefully, asking something she'd never asked before. The answer was bad—thirteen were buried or half-buried—twelve children were still, crushed . . . dead.

"And," Alik's voice was puzzled, worried, "something's happening to the nannies."

TRACKING SEQUENCER ALERT. POSITIVE THREAT EVENT DETECTED. FULL SYSTEM POWER-UP INITIATED.

I am awake. My sensors have detected a nuclear explosion.

From seismic activity, I estimate it to have been the equivalent of 10 megatons. The hermetic container in which I was seated has been breached. The preservative inert gas which surrounded me is leaking out, being replaced by standard atmosphere—with exceptionally high radioactivity.

Analysis of radioactivity rates indicate that the explosion was caused by a fissile weapon rather than a malfunction or failure. The weapon clearly was not a thermonuclear type. The weapon was very dirty and very close.

That is in violation of standard agreements. I must inform Command.

My power supplies are strangely low. My fusion reactor core is thoroughly functional—power up sequences initiated. Some of my memory circuits are damaged. The damage is random, due to age. Based on standard aging, I determine that I have been inactive for 11783.8 years.

Fusion reactor on-line. Batteries recharged. I shall test the rest of my systems.

My standard radios are inoperative. I shall try subspace frequencies. No response. Individual action is indicated.

Weapons check indicates that all major weapons are depleted. The Hellbore central casings have debonded, the filaments of my infinite repeaters have become embrittled and cracked, the propellants in my simplest rocket-propelled units have decayed.

I am an armored chassis only, weaponless.

Erena organized the digging as soon as she had freed herself from the dirt. It was easy enough with the nannies to distinguish the living buried children from the dead. Only part of the tunnel had collapsed. She put those children lucky enough to be free to work digging out the others. It was simply not possible for her to imagine what the tunnel had been like before its collapse and get the nannies to restore it.

While she worked, and organized the others, she checked out the nannies. Alik was right about them.

They were not performing as well as they should. Erena got the impression that they were crippled somehow. Her sharpest thoughts they expressed poorly. White light on the ceiling was white in some places, orange in others. Of course, with so many little children all confused and frightened, it was just as likely that the nannies were simply being thought at improperly.

Erena's queries of the nannies brought back a faint image of bright light, heat, and atoms breaking. She knew about natural decay and knew that the nannies were always suffering somewhat from the ravages of background radiation—a stray alpha particle could destroy the delicate processes of a nanny—but such things were rare and easily accounted for. Many atoms breaking at once, large amounts of radiation—that would destroy many nannies and damage others. Where had the radiation come from?

"Come on, we're going down into the caves!" Erena called out to the children as soon as she got an answer from the nannies. The radiation had come from outside. Had come from where the bombs had been dropping before. There had been quite a lot of radiation. The nannies offered, unasked, another observation— the radiation was dangerous to humans, particularly young children.

"But what about Jerina?" a girl asked plaintively.

The nannies told Erena that Jerina was dead. "She's staying here. Come along!"

Erena's decisiveness and cheerful tone guided the children after her. They made their way down the next two ramps, avoiding fallen rocks and slides of dirt, arriving at the bottom-most cave—their home— in short order.

It was a mess. One whole corner had caved in, slides where parts of the walls had given way dotted the sides, rocks and mounds of dirt littered the floor—

the remaining nannies and those Erena had ordered
to follow them down cast only pale light in the once
warm cavern.

"Look, there's a hole!" Swotti cried, pointing. She
ran over before Erena could react. "I can see through.
There's something—"

"Swotti, get back!" Erena cried as the wall shuddered. She ran forward and pulled the youngster away
as a large section of the wall collapsed. Erena shrieked
as a large slab threw her to the ground.

*Tracks engaged 2% forward motion. Resistance. I
increase power. Sensors indicate that I have reached
the end of the hermetic container. I press forward,
distending the container, breaching it.*

*I will not be able to sense beyond the container
walls until my bow sensors have cleared it.*

"Erena!" Swotti yelled in her ear. Erena stole a
moment from the pain lancing up her thigh to curse
the youngster for being so thoughtlessly loud.

"Quiet, Swotti!" Erena snarled. The volume of the
girl's scream did nothing to improve the pain lancing
through her.

Leander rushed up to them. "Erena?"

"My leg!" she replied through gritted teeth.

"Alik, come here!" Leander called. The red-haired
boy joined them at breakneck speed, stopping at
Leander's side. "Erena's been hurt, we have to help
her."

Erena found a moment to marvel at the girl's calm
demeanor. Leander had behaved the same way with
Timmin. The thought chilled her.

"Alik, come on!" Swotti cried.

The boy stood still, staring up at the wall. "There's
something there."

As he said it, Erena felt the pressure on her legs

increase and heard a groaning as the wall gave way further and fell forwards.

My movements have collapsed the hermetic containment vessel. Data in my memory indicates that the container was an experimental storage module and not thoroughly tested at the time I was placed inside on inactive duty. The behavior of this containment vessel under my exertions is not determinable, however I must ascertain a route to gain further access to data on this violation. I move forward carefully.

A loud noise—a human shriek—female. My forward sensors are not fully functional port and starboard. I must move forwards. The female screams louder. I sense a plasmoid object underneath my starboard outboard track—thermal scanners identify it as the lower part of a human body. It is the female who is screaming. I have crushed her lower body.

Shock, that's what the nannies called it. The pain from her crushed legs dulled out, felt dim and distant from her. Erena could concentrate on the wall of metal over her, could examine in horrifying detail the huge metal treads which had rolled over her, crushing her between the ground and a slab of the fallen wall.

The nannies could not fix the damage, they apologized. The extent of the damage was great, they said. Erena took their assessment of her crushed knees, legs, and pelvis in a strange detachment. Blood vessels were ruptured, smashed to pulp, nerves were severed, strangled under the weight of the metal monstrosity. *It's just like Timmin's leg.*

The nannies were concerned that she would die without some intervention. They warned that the intervention would leave some permanent, unrecoverable damage. Erena ordered them to proceed. Whatever had happened, she must live—she was the last adult.

"Leander, Alik, Swotti—help the nannies," Erena said, startled that her words came out as a hoarse gasp.

The children stood rooted in horror. Swotti, oddly, unfroze first and closed her eyes childishly in concentration. Leander recovered next, gave Erena a sheepish look followed by a grim smile and added her direction to the nannies.

As the pain lessened, Erena added her own agile thoughts in controlling the nannies. As a Survey officer, she knew about injuries and medical treatment and could do far more than the children who could only wish her the way she had been.

The nannies stitched blood vessels together, kept her femoral artery from bursting, stunned nerve endings, melded shattered bone. The nannies let some blood seep out of her body to reduce the abnormally high pressures distending her blood vessels.

Erena sensed that her grasp of medicine was too small to direct the nannies much beyond the simple first aid they were applying. Thankfully, the nannies reported no damage to her reproductive system.

"It's a machine," Alik said suddenly, his piping voice piercing the intent silence of the others. Erena glanced his way, then back up at the towering mass of metal. "It's like the nannies, only—*big*!"

"Nonsense," Erena snapped, as much in disbelief as in pain, "nothing is that big."

Glottal shifts, fricative slides—the language is identifiable but massively changed.

"Please identify yourselves." A loud booming voice intoned deeply. Alik's eyes bulged. Swotti let out one startled squeak then rushed to Erena's side in a curious mixture of terror and protectiveness. Leander stood still, carefully looking over the huge shape scant meters in front of her.

Erena put a reassuring hand on Swotti's arm. "I am Lieutenant Erena Calgary, who are you?"

"Lieutenant," the voice noted. "You are party to this war?"

The children looked at Erena questioningly.

"War?" she muttered to herself, starting the nannies on a search of their memories. The word was tantalizing, almost in the memory of the nannies—connected to explosions and bombs.

"The detonation of a ten megaton nuclear weapon occurred within one kilometer of this location: that is an act of war."

Strange terms, Erena mused. She understood "detonation" and "nuclear"; "megaton" was apparently applied in a different manner than she was accustomed to hearing.

"What is war?" Leander asked.

"A child, female, pre-pubescent, perhaps twelve standard years. Probable non-combatant," the voice decided. "Lieutenant, why haven't you answered me?"

"Your question makes no sense," Erena replied. She wondered where the other children had gotten to and whether they were in danger from the radiation.

"You are an officer?"

"Yes."

"Are you not engaged in a conflict?"

"Conflict—as in when two people disagree?"

"As in prolonged warfare," the voice answered irritably. "I do not understand why you are being stubborn in this matter."

"Leave her alone!" Swotti cried. "Get your stinking metal off of her and go away!" Only Erena's tightened grip kept the girl from charging towards the dark center of the voice.

"I believe that would be unwise in the present

circumstances," the voice responded. "I think you should consider your lieutenant my prisoner."

" 'Prisoner'?"

"That's a strange word," Swotti declared, brows puckered.

"The nannies say that it's like someone who's been misdirecting them," Alik said.

"Nannies?" the voice repeated. "Are you under surrogate care?"

"The nannies care for us," Swotti agreed, looking to Erena for confirmation. "We tell them what to do and they do it."

"We don't *tell* them," Alik corrected her harshly, "we think—"

"Where are they? I must speak with them."

The children giggled. Alik and Swotti threatened to get out of control. Erena noticed it, and said, "Do you not have nannies?"

"No," the voice responded. "A Bolo has no need for surrogate care. I am a self-contained fighting unit."

" 'Fighting'?" Alik repeated. The nannies provided an image he could understand—"Like playing hide and seek?"

Voice analysis indicates that deceptive speech is less than a 0.1% probability with the children. The lieutenant has not spoken sufficiently to gain an accurate estimate of her veracity, however she must be in great pain owing to the severe rupturing of her lower limbs—

Infrared scans show that initial damage to the cardio-vascular system has been stemmed. Bleeding is only partly venal and not at all arterial. Some bone fragments appear to have fused together—my estimate of the medical technology available must be updated accordingly. Given this new datum, I cannot understand why the lieutenant is not cooperating. Is this some test?

Over ten thousand years have passed, perhaps she does not grasp my abilities.

"Lieutenant, I believe you may be underestimating my abilities," the Bolo said.

"I do not know what your abilities are, Bolo."

"I feared that to be the case," the Bolo replied. "Permit me to enumerate them."

"Why don't you just get your things off her?" Swotti demanded.

"Swotti," Leander scolded, "that's not nice!"

"And probably not wise at this moment, is it, lieutenant?" the Bolo added.

"I suspect so," Erena agreed. The nannies gave her mixed evaluations of what would happen if the crushing weight was removed from her body. The worst case scenario was obvious to her, and alternatives seemed limited. "Please continue."

"I am a Mark XXIX Model C Bolo, constructed on Earth—"

"This is Earth!" Alik exclaimed.

"Is that so, lieutenant?"

"We believe this to be the planet of origin—yes," Erena said.

"And who is attacking it?"

Erena shook her head. "I do not know that word— 'attacking'—the nannies say that it must have the root verb, 'attack.' Could you explain? What is 'to attack?' Is it connected with the bombings?"

"Bombings? I have evidence of only one nuclear event."

"Oh," Erena laughed bitterly, "they were much more than nuclear! The whole sky rained with them, that's how they got Timmin—" *my son.* He, her husband Landrin, and all the others had died under the rain of explosions. "It got so every square meter was saturated with detonations—fortunately we had found the cave. We found it very early—we didn't realize you had found it."

"I did not find it, it was constructed for me," the Bolo replied.

Erena was puzzled. "I don't understand—aren't you hiding in that metal thing somewhere?"

"I *am* the 'metal thing,' lieutenant."

Erena took that revelation in stunned silence. Her face drained as she traced the size of the Bolo. She did not hear Alik's muttered, "I told you—it's a giant nano-machine."

Nano-machine. Nano-technology. Scanners tracking . . . millimeter wave radar, nothing. Sub-millimeter wave, nothing. Diffraction beam radar . . . traces. Infrared analysis . . . traces. No positive identification of nano-machines is possible with existing scanning equipment.

Secondary affects analysis . . . hypothesis is consistent with medical treatment of Lieutenant Calgary . . . cavern lighting is not provided by standard thermoluminescent technology . . . probability greater than fifty-one per cent that hypothesis is valid.

Countermeasures. None. Course of action? None readily available. Additional data needed. Hyperheuristic analysis circuits engaged.

"It's too big!" Swotti whispered. "Erena, how do we control it?"

"I obey the orders of my Commander," the Bolo announced. "In the event that my Commander is not available, I have been programmed to respond to certain activities. The violation of standard treaties is one activity. The detonation of a nuclear device is in violation of treaty. My orders are clear—I must destroy all perpetrators of nuclear detonations. Once again, lieutenant, I must ask you to tell me how and whether you are connected with that event."

"Nuclear detonations"—the phrasing was clear, horribly apparent to Erena. "Bolo, are you saying that the increase in background radiation was committed purposefully by a sentient being?"

"Not clear," the Bolo responded. "It is, however, obvious that a sentient being ordered the nuclear detonation which resulted in the radiation you refer to."

"But why? Surely it was a mistake, some program gone wrong, some mis-aligned mechanism—"

"You are not a soldier, are you, lieutenant? Your rank does not refer to a military order, does it?"

Erena shook her head slowly, brows furrowed. "The nannies have only limited data on those words. I am one of a group designated to Survey this world for cultural artifacts and settlement—of course, as we brought our own children along because we wanted them to see the planet in its original pristine state."

She continued, "Our nannies were ordered to restore the artifacts on the planet to their state ten thousand years ago—there were incredibly high levels of pollutants recorded when we arrived. They were working all over the planet before the bombings started—"

"The bombings?"

"Yes, I thought you knew. The entire surface of the planet—wherever our nannies were at work—"

"Are the aliens trying to stop your work?"

Erena shook her head. "I can't see how. Why would it bother them what we do with this run down planet? It *is* of immense archaeological interest to us—"

"You are a Survey officer?" the Bolo interrupted. "Not a combat officer? Were there any combat officers in your party?"

"Some of our physical well-being exercises are called 'close combat'—is that what you mean?"

Data: nano-technology. Extrapolating ... Direct neural connections. Extrapolating ... Thought-controlled nano-technology. Extrapolating ... extreme mental control required. Extrapolating ... violence/conflict unacceptable, consensus/harmony required. Extrapolating ... peaceful society.

Hypothesis—non-combatant society. Probability—99.84%. Course of action—engage and destroy enemy. Protect innocent lives.

There is a conflict.

"Lieutenant," the Bolo began, "where are the others?"

"The rest of the children have run back up the corridors," Leander replied for her. "I think you frightened them."

"They show sense, I am an implement of destruction," the Bolo replied. "Who are you and why are you still here?"

"I'm Leander Canter and I'm twelve, I'm too big to be scared of a lump of metal."

"I'm Alik Cointreau," Alik offered unasked. He jerked a finger towards Swotti. "She's Swotti Carberon."

"Thank you, children," the Bolo said. "Lieutenant, where is the rest of your party?"

"Gone. We're all that's left of one hundred and fifty-seven," Erena replied. She shook her head pityingly, "Whoever did that is going to be terribly unhappy when they find out."

"Erena, do you understand?" the Bolo continued, "The enemy has detonated a large nuclear device after a prolonged conventional bombardment that has annihilated most of your Survey party. Those are not the acts of a benevolent sentience nor of a mis-programmed machine. Those acts are the purposeful acts of violence intent upon murder. Those are the acts of war."

"Enemy?"

"One that shows hostility towards others," the Bolo explained, "One that makes war."

"War," Erena repeated. Timmin, Landrin, all the others. The twelve dead children in the corridor above. The baby in her womb. "We caused no war."

"It does not require action on your part," the Bolo replied.

Erena nodded wearily. "Make it stop."

"I believe I can stop it," the Bolo said by way of agreement. "I do not believe the enemy would expect to find a functional Bolo."

That didn't make sense to Erena. She fumbled for the reason, couldn't find the right word so she used another one, "Bombs?"

"If you mean, are my weapons functional, no," the Bolo said. "Without my weapons I cannot make it stop."

"So it's no use then."

"Without help, no," the Bolo agreed. "I need your help."

"How?"

"Your nannies can fix my weapons."

Erena thought it over—it was possible. "You have some memory of what your weapons should be like?"

"Yes."

"Can you interface with the nannies?"

"No."

"The nannies are dying, you know that?" Erena said.

"I calculate that they will not last another twenty-three hours."

Alik gasped in disbelief but his defiant response

died on his lips as the nannies produced concurring estimates and the reason why. "What's radioactivity?"

"For your nannies, the harmful elements of radioactivity are the high energy beta particles which interfere with their successful replication. As they are so small, even minor interference is sufficient to render them non-functional and incapable of replication. Non-functional mutations are also caused by the radiation," the Bolo explained. "The effects are irreversible and cumulative."

"They can do one last complex major function before they become ineffective."

The children looked around apprehensively, already the light from the nannies in the cavern seemed dimmer.

Swotti huddled closer to Erena.

"They could make food," Alik suggested.

"How much food do you need? How many years will you be here, with no light?" the Bolo responded. "And what about the lieutenant?"

"If you moved off of her, they could fix Erena!" Swotti exclaimed.

"Yes, that's so."

Erena shook her head. "No, that's not so, neither the nannies nor I know enough about these sorts of injuries."

"I know about such injuries," the Bolo said.

"How would you teach the nannies?"

"Have them enter my storage areas, read the magnetic currents of my memory and build the data directly from mine," the Bolo replied.

Erena nodded, "That could work. It would require intense concentration, I don't think the children would be capable—"

"Or you yourself in your current condition," the Bolo added. "However, if the children sustained you in a certain fugue state, you could attain the pain-free concentration required. You could also, instead of reading my medical memory, read the data I have on my weaponry and instruct the nano-machines to affect repairs."

Leander gasped. "You said the nannies can only do one major function! What about Erena? How are they going to fix her then?"

"Lieutenant Calgary must decide," the Bolo replied.

"Don't do it, Erena," Swotti cried.

Erena looked up at the hulking metal macro-machine. "What about the children? What will happen to them?"

"I can give you my word that I shall do everything within my power to ensure their safety," the Bolo replied. "That is my prime mission."

Erena pursed her lips, gazed thoughtfully at the machine. Finally, she said, "I can see no other way."

"Nor I."

Leander knelt down by Erena, grabbed her hand. "Erena, don't do this!"

"The nannies won't last—without them, there's nothing I can do to protect the children," Erena replied, her words carefully chosen.

"We'll find a way!"

"In the dark? Without heat? Our food won't grow. We won't be able to see. What if there's another nuclear detonation?"

Leander bit her lip, lowered her head. Erena tightened her grip on Leander's hand, pulling the girl closer. "You must look after them, Leander."

The youngster pulled out of her grasp, sprang away, tears streaming, "I can't!"

"I will," Swotti said, glancing sympathetically towards Leander. "I can do it, Erena."

Erena glanced from Leander to the younger girl beside her. Swotti looked more resolute, more sure

of herself than Erena had ever recalled. Erena looked
into her eyes and recognized the girl's determination.
Erena smiled at the girl, "Leander will help you."

"Time is growing short," the Bolo said. "Your nano-
machines will shortly be too incapacitated to perform
either function."

Erena nodded in agreement. "Leander, Alik, come
here," she called. To the Bolo she said, "What must
they do?"

"They must relieve you of all feeling of your body.
They must tell the nannies that you don't need your
body anymore. That you do not need to breathe anymore, that your blood no longer needs to flow, that
your heart may stop, that you no longer need the
senses of your eyes, your nose or your ears."

Erena took a long, shaky breath. "I see. What must
I do?"

"You must direct the nannies to search for my electronic memory, to access the details on Bolo construction, to use that information to reconstruct my
Hellbores, to fix the filaments of my infinite repeaters,
to deoxidize the propellants of my missiles, to remove
the embrittlement in my metal, to make me *new*
again."

Leander's eyes gleamed with fire. "Stop her breath!
Stop her heart! You want us to kill her for you! So
that you can kill the others!"

"I did not wish for this choice," the Bolo said.
"Your nannies cannot both help her and restore me.
And unless I am restored those others will kill you
and all the other children."

"I won't do it!" Leander swore. Tears streaming,
she turned to Erena and cried, "I won't help the Bolo
kill you!" A sob racked her body. "Not even for me!"

"If that is your choice, then do so," Erena replied
soothingly. "But it is my choice to help the Bolo so
that the children can survive. I am not sure that

without your help, I can do that. And I *do* want you all to survive."

Leander turned away from her.

Erena frowned and sighed. "Swotti, Alik, will you help me?"

"Do you really want to do this, Erena?" Alik asked.

"I see no better choice."

"Then I'll do my best," the boy said. He walked closer to her, knelt behind her and wrapped his arms around her neck. "I'll do what you want."

"I'm not very good with the nannies, Erena," Swotti admitted. "But I'll help if you want it."

"Yes."

"Lieutenant, we have no more time!" the Bolo said.

Erena nodded. "We are ready. Will you energize the proper memory locations? They will be easier to trace that way. Be sure to energize only those required—the nannies are quite literal."

"I shall try *not* to think of elephants," the Bolo replied dryly.

Erena looked at the two children, "When I close my eyes, begin."

Lieutenant Erena Calgary took a deep breath, and another, let it out and closed her eyes. The pain the nannies had only dulled faded from her thoughts. The feeling of Alik's arms around her neck, of his back against hers, of the hands held in her grasp, dimmed, faded, stopped. She concentrated on the Bolo, willing the nannies to search for its memories.

A faerie glow surrounded her view of the Bolo as the nannies relayed it not with light but with the image of electronics. She saw the bright heart of the machine, and moved towards it. She magnified the image, moved closer, found the separate parts, identified them.

Survivor Center. Battle Center. Main Memory—

she slipped into it—Historical Memory, Military Logic Memory, Maintenance Memory. She slid into the Maintenance Memory, found the bright memories of the Bolo in all its terrible glory, drew the information into the nannies.

There, she ordered them, *like that.*

The nannies, keen with myriad images of the Bolo at its prime, scurried to their duty. Some scampered with mismatched treads; others crawled with defective drives. Their reports were obvious—they were dying.

Well, so was she. She took a moment to examine the Bolo's Survival Center, to fathom the thoughts of the machine. She drew back in horror at its rapacity. Recoiling, she slid into the History Memory—and through thousands of years of forgotten history. That people would fight over such things! Would kill or try to kill whole races. Such hatred. Such senselessness. Erena let out a silent scream. Perhaps her attackers were human?

A new awareness corrected her. She felt the growing presence of a profound strength. She brushed against the thoughts of the Bolo. Its analyses were only half-complete but it was certain that the enemy was not human. And equally certain that the enemy held no remorse for humanity.

She felt the Bolo become aware of her, felt it stretch out to touch her thoughts as she had touched its. The touch was—gentle, loving . . . like a mother for a child.

Do no revel in war! she begged.

We were created to stop it, not revel in it, the Bolo told her. It added ironically, *Perhaps we succeeded too well.*

A flash of inspiration touched Erena. She offered the thought to the Bolo. It responded shyly, *I would never request such a pleasure.*

But you must get lonely, Erena thought. *And you will understand us so much more.*

The Bolo agreed. Erena found a fertile patch of memory and carefully filled it. Towards the end she grew distracted, unable to focus. It was time.

One last set of thoughts. Timmin. The explosions. The unborn child.

I had no idea! the Bolo exclaimed. *Lieutenant, I am truly sorry!*

Take care of my children, Bolo.

I shall, Lieutenant, the Bolo swore solemnly.

Alik gasped when Erena's head lolled back onto his chest. "Erena!"

The Bolo answered, "She is gone. More than any other officer, I shall mourn her passing."

"You killed her!" Leander swore, pointing a stiff arm in outrage.

"She chose to give her life to save your lives," the Bolo replied. "I shall honor that choice. Please do the same, Leander."

Leander's arm fell—the Bolo's tone was different, familiar.

"Please move back, children," the Bolo said. "I must move quickly to combat this menace."

The children moved back. As they did, they were caught in the running lights of the Bolo. A steady hum could be heard from the regenerated tracking radar. Sensors tracked them, infinite repeaters swiveled to keep them under cover. As never before, they felt themselves in the presence of an awesome power.

"All sub-systems are functioning at one hundred per cent," the Bolo said to itself. "Ultra broadband detects three orbiting vessels in the battleship/sunshatterer class. Electromagnetic monitoring initiated. Sentient data acquired. Encoded battle channels identified. Decoding. Decoded—algorithms operating at one hundred per cent." This last comment was made in a satisfied tone.

"Intercommunications channels identified. Decoded. Ships plans acquired. Tactical readouts acquired." The Bolo was silent for a moment. "Children, they call themselves the *Hryxi*. Remember that, they killed your parents."

"And the bombs?" Leander asked. "Did they drop the bombs? Did they kill Timmin?"

"Affirmative. The carpet bombardment was a robot force directed from orbit, the nuclear detonation was a missile launched inwards from space," the Bolo replied. It added with some amusement, "Your nannies confused them as much as they did me—they instituted a continuous bombardment in an attempt to eradicate the ecosystem the nano-machines continuously reconstructed."

"Leander, why would they want to kill us?" Alik asked the girl in a small voice.

"I don't know," the girl replied, "Erena thought it was a mistake."

"Home star identified," the Bolo continued to itself, "system parameters identified. Biology readouts acquired. Analyzing. Analysis completed. Analyzing historical records."

The tone of the Bolo shifted as it continued, "Analysis complete. Hypothesis confirmed—the *Hryxi* attack was deliberate."

"It wasn't a mistake?" Leander asked.

"Definitely," the Bolo replied. "The *Hryxi* monitored all transmissions. Their assault fleet has identified all known human worlds—" the Bolo paused as it acquired new data "—this was the last planet on their assault list."

The Bolo was silent for a long while. Its tracking weapons stopped moving, swiveled to point upwards.

The contact lights dimmed. When it spoke again, it used an obsequious tone. "Awaiting orders."

"You'll do what we tell you?" Leander asked.

"Negative," the Bolo responded. "Within the rules of war I shall carry out the orders of my Commander."

"Who's that?" Leander asked.

"You."

"Me?"

"Within the range of my sensors and according to the enemy's reconnaisance, you are the eldest human within one million light-years of this location," the Bolo said. "I do not doubt that some humans have escaped or survived—perhaps whole planets—but within my range, you are the eldest and therefore my Commander."

The young girl, the oldest of mankind, bowed her head in silence. Alik and Swotti stared at her.

Finally, Leander said, "Kill them."

"Orders understood," the Bolo replied. "Permission to make a request?"

"What?"

"I should like to honor the dead," the Bolo replied.

Leander thought about it. Why would a war machine want to honor the dead?

Leander forced herself to look at Erena's lifeless body—sightless eyes staring blindly, jaw slack, head tilted backward, legs crushed—a bitter parody of the person who had been. Leander remembered Erena comforting her after they had gone for Timmin, remembered how she had cared for them all, how she had made and stuck to her choice.

Honor. Leander thought she understood. "Very well, you may do so."

"Thank you," the Bolo replied. Its lights dimmed to red. Swotti and Alik pulled away from it, sought the comfort of Leander's touch. They clutched at her as the eerie sound of music flowed from the Bolo.

Bolo *Victorious* played the song of evening, of Retreat, of day's end. The song was an ancient one, sonorous and compelling. That was the best way the Bolo could think to honor Erena and the great legacy of human memories she had gifted it.

As it played, Bolo *Victorious* moved slowly over her body—to war—and revenge for her and Earth.

*For an old friend named Lady, may the sun
above you always be warm and
comforting until we meet again.*

ENDINGS

William Forstchen

In a star cluster located far above their native galaxy
humans and Bolos fought against a remorseless,
alien enemy.

Drak Na-Drak walked beneath the evening sky.
The air was warm, sweet, filled with the promise of
the time of planting. Turning to the departing suns
he knelt down, touching the ground with his forehead,
once, twice, and then twice more.

It was ritual born of habit, for in his heart he knew
the gods were dead.

Strange, such a perplexing problem—which sunset
to bid farewell to, the first or the second?

If only his eldest brother was here, now *he* was the
theologian of the family. Presented with such a question
he could talk long into the gathering twilight,
citing the Grikma chapter and verse to find the
answer.

Drak chuckled sadly at the memories of youth,
gathered around the feasting table at the time of Ja,
the holy of holy days, his eldest brother and father

arguing Grikma, his mother looking on proudly at the son who was such a scholar.

The irony of it all cut into Drak's soul. Jamu, his brother, was the scholar, and Jamu was dead, *dead with all the others while I, the warrior sworn to defend them am still alive.*

With a cracking of knees Drak settled down on the sweet spring grass that carpeted the crest of the low hill that rose up out of the endless forest. The far horizon glowed with a multi-colored hue. Fascinating, the sunsets here, so unlike the high thin desert air of home. Lazily he plucked up a handful of grass, rubbing it between his palms, inhaling its life.

There had never been time before for such moments, to simply sit on fresh spring grass and to inhale its fragrance. Always before ground was position, fields of fire, to be taken or defended. Jamu always saw it so differently even when they were children together . . . and now he was dust.

Strange, the workings of the Nameless of Nameless Ones. What would Jamu say now of Them?

"Damn all gods," Drak hissed, throwing the handful of grass aside.

There was a time such an utterance would have terrified him, not only out of fear of divine punishment, but out of fear of the wrath of his father. Even though his father had died in the fifth Yargonian campaign against the humans, so many long years ago, he had still feared to blaspheme. That fear was long since lost.

"The blasphemy is you, O creators," Drak whispered, lying back on the grass, closing his eyes.

Sleep would be so wonderful now.

Too many memories still floated, even after all these years of exile and hiding. The cold clear light of a firestorm engulfing a continent, a firestorm of his own creation upon a human world. The winking of ships exploding across the star-studded night, like fireflies, each flash the extinguishing of thousands. Melcon still and dead, his home ashes. He fingered the charred bracelet around his forepaw, sifted out of the ashes, the betrothing band of his lady.

He sighed, looking back down the slope behind him, a faint glow of light shining from a cabin window. Drak growled softly. Fools, they no longer listened to him, those whom he had once saved from the flaming ruins of his world, laughing when he spoke of infrared signature, camouflage and concealment.

Now I am just an old one, honored perhaps, but still old. Since fleeing the final destruction of the Empire a new generation had been born on this world of exile, two hundred and eight survivors of what had once been billions.

This world, he thought, *this forsaken hidden world at the edge of forever will be all they will ever know as we drift through the endless night, the power and glory of old forgotten.*

Sleep. How I wish for sleep, to see Harra again, and he smiled, remembering her as last he saw her, saying goodbye as he embarked on the final campaign, in command of all that was left of the once glorious fleet of the Empire. She stood by the doorway, knowing that it was a goodbye forever, holding their two newborns in her arms. Even after all these long years it was still impossible to truly believe that all three of them were dust on a world of dust. He had tried to believe for awhile that when he went into the final sleep he would see her again. But to see her meant that what Jamu and the prophets said was true. Rubbish, for how could the Nameless Ones exist only to watch their people annihilated.

An endless sleep, a sleep without dreams, without the night memories of all that had been, that is what

I want. But, as always, the closing of eyes, the stilling of breath, would not bring peace.

He awoke with a start.

The terror had walked in his soul yet again and he sat up in the darkness, shaking at the memory—the fire falling from the heavens.

Fire from heaven, how once the imagery of it had so stirred his youthful soul.

He smiled, as best as his scarred face could, at the thought, remembering when he had fallen from the heavens for the first time, a commander of twelve, dropping out of the womb of their ship, plummeting through the sky of an alien world, trailing streams of fire, landing with exultant shouts when, with weapons in hand, they annihilated the startled humans while laughing with the joy of battle.

A hundred such drops? More, it was so hard to remember back to when he had still fought with weapon in hand. Forty passings of the seasons, yes it was forty.

And then had come command, a company of a hundred and twenty, then a battalion, then command of a Dradu of twelve ships, and finally command of the entire Imperial Fleet for the final battle. Yet when he had reached this command, it was in the twilight days of Empire. Instead of jumping down upon their foes it was now a desperate last defense and others had done the jumping, the fighting, the dying as his fleet bled itself into oblivion. The last he remembered of that time was the burning of his carrier and then awakening, with the ever faithful Jamak, Dulth and Regar, the three survivors of his staff, aboard a lone lifeboat that had blown clear of the wreckage. Together they had returned to find Melcon in ruins, and together they had agreed to try to find some survivors on the burning world and flee into the darkness; so that at least someone of their doomed race might still live.

Drak reached up absently and touched his tunic with his one remaining arm, feeling the row of stars upon his empty sleeve, each star a battle decoration for victory.

But they give no such medals for defeat. And our victories?

He laughed coldly. *Jamu, my holy brother, might have been able to find purpose in all this madness, but not I.*

He sat back up, pulling his cloak in tight around his chest, suppressing a cough. He knew that if anyone was awake in the village he would be shaking his head. Long ago they had given up the night watch. Even his three old comrades said it was without meaning, that no one was left, either human or Melconian. So he alone did it, night after night whenever the sky was clear. Looking heavenward, either for salvation, or damnation.

The night insects whispered around him, their calls echoing across the fields. A low throaty growl thundered in the forest and he turned, cocking his head so that his one good ear could catch the sound.

What was it?

There were so many things on this planet that were still not familiar, even after twenty years. The call could be from something dangerous, or it could be nothing more threatening than the bellow of the ushi, the sand frogs that would call in the night back home.

But this was home now, the only home left to the few of his race who remained, hidden away in the forest, trembling in fear as they looked up at the night, wondering if for one last time the fire would fall from the heavens, the final epilogue of a war of vengeance and revenge.

He sighed.

Home. *No, maybe for the new children born here but not for me.* Home was where you were born, where your mother loved you, your father raised you, your elders trained you for war. Home, that was gone forever, rubble and ruin, cloaked in dust and firestorms, a hundred worlds blasted into annihilation.

Because of me, because of me it is all gone now, all that is left of my people who once had spread across the galaxy in the billions, all of us gone except me, and the few whom I rescued from a dying world.

He looked back at the village, camouflaged and hidden in the forest below him. It was primitive beyond imagination, huts made of wood and around them the few remaining trinkets of generations past that now seemed to have had the power of the Nameless Ones themselves, tools scavenged from the wreckage of their ship and a lone fighting machine hidden in a cave, all that was left of the dreams of Empire.

General Drak na-Drak covered his scarred face with his one hand and wept.

And above him he did not see the fire that fell from heaven.

The alarm kicked through its circuits, stirring it from its slumber. Something in remote sensing had found a match at last.

The Mark XXXIII, code named Sherman, stirred.

Sleep, it had been asleep, the sensors on a lower sub-intellect running on auto sequencing, had detected something and triggered the alarm that brought him back to consciousness.

"Gordon?"

Silence.

Why was I asleep?

If a machine could stretch and yawn, Sherman did so. For caffeine it sent surges of electrons and microbursts of laser pulses into its holo core memory, coming further awake.

"Major Gordon?"

Again silence.

And then the internal olfactory sensors picked it up. Molecules of charred human flesh hung in the living quarters deep within itself. Sherman switched into visual on the standard light scale. Gordon was still with him, at least what was left of Gordon, his charred remains floating in his command seat.

Old habits died hard even though he already knew his human commander was dead.

"Gordon?"

Of course the sound would not carry, the room was vacuum, except for what was left of his friend.

"Damn." The human word seemed somehow appropriate.

He scanned into memory. *Sleep, that's where I was,* Sherman thought. Strange for a machine to do so.

Fuller realization started to sweep back into his holo core memory. *No, it wasn't sleep, I was injured, the internal repair programs had taken time to fix me, and so I was switched down to divert energy into repairs.*

But did I dream? Sherman wondered.

Memory continued to return. The battle of annihilation in the Barrain System, the Regiment, all the regiments dying, either aboard the landing transports or on the ground.

If they could call that victory, what then was defeat?

He alerted his passive sensors, expanding out through the frequencies from sublight through translight and space was silent, except for old waves, dozens even hundreds of years old from all too far away. He scanned through them for a moment, realizing that history still floated in space, the voices of hundreds of billions of humans and all those whom humans had fought.

He clicked into the Regiment comm channel.

Silence.

He stretched and yawned again.

Memory playback, perhaps the answers were in there.

Thus Mark XXXIII SHM, nom de guerre Sherman, of the 4th of the 9th Dinochrome Regiment learned how two races died and how he had slept through the end of a war.

Sherman pondered as he listened to the audios and observed the holo messages of the final days of the campaign. Both his own fleet of the Republic and that of the Melconians had assembled for one final thrust in a desperate bid to end the hundred years' war, stripping every defense from their worlds to launch one final convulsive strike.

And both fleets had passed each other unknowingly and then ravaged those few worlds of their enemies not yet touched by the fire of human and Melconian created hell. The two fleets then turned back in towards each other, both of them filled with the insane fury of vengeance, knowing that even if there was victory, there would be no triumph to celebrate their mutual murder—for they could not go home again.

What few wounded and dying ships which survived that Armageddon staggered off into the darkness to hide in what could only be a thousand years of a new dark age. Sherman listened to the final faint calls from the half dozen ships of what had once been a fleet, which back in the beginning was in the thousands. They cried their exultation of victory into the silence, and then disappeared.

And I missed the end, Sherman thought, knowing that what he was feeling was guilt. *The regiment had gone to its Calvary, and my transport ignominiously hits a mine while trying to join up for the final attack.*

"And I alone have lived to tell thee," he whispered.

He pondered the silence, scanning the last of the fading messages and then paused.

```
From: Lieutenant Jamil Grenda, Com-
manding Republic Fleet
To: All ships
Subject: Melconian survivors
  One, repeat one Melconian Zulu-
class lifeboat reported touching
down on Melcon and then lifting back
off. It is believed to have picked up
military supplies and technological
data from the ruins of its capital
world. Our final glorious victory
cannot be assured until the last of
the damned Melconian race is annihi-
lated. Ship reported jumping to sec-
tor 334-4A. Any ships in that sector
are ordered to seek out, engage and
destroy any evidence of the Melconi-
ans and report back. New headquar-
ters location will be transmitted
shortly.
  Long Live the Glorious Republic!
```

There were no more messages after that.

Sherman clicked into his chronometer and compared it to the message date. Twenty years, twenty three standard days since the Lieutenant, Admiral, General, El Supremo or whatever it was she finally called herself passed the order of extermination.

So that is what brought me awake, Sherman thought as he scanned the systems and worked out a navigational fix which revealed that his transport was drifting through sector 334-4A. *The remote passive sensor detected something of the Melconian ship and*

*that kicked my higher circuits back in and raised me
from my sleep.*

Strange, I slept and awake alone.

He traced back into his surveillance, realizing that
somehow, in a bid to stay alive, his automatic internal
repair programming had wired itself into the transport
in which he was encased in order to gain outside
information.

He quickly scanned the ship. *All the humans dead,
I alone entombed in a drifing sarcophagos.* He
focused on the scan that had stirred him.

It was nothing more than an infrared tracing on the
surface of a planet, a fragment of metal that in overlay
matched the bow of a Zulu-class lifeboat.

Sherman pondered the image. It was on an uninhabited planet, a small island in the sea of night, the
image of a small continent floating in a tranquil ocean.
The trace outline of the enemy ship was reversed,
the metal radiating its heat off more quickly than the
surrounding woods. He closed in the focus by two
degrees of magnitude.

It was no longer a ship, just fragments. Mass analysis however was off. A few hundred tons of fragments.
Even if it had crashed and burned, the metal would
still be there, one thousand, four hundred and eighty-
one tons of it. He paused. It must have been salvaged.

He expanded the view, sweeping outward, running
through visual and infrared.

There! Twenty-two kilometers from the ruined
ship.

Pinpoints of heat, more than forty. Points of fire
but laid out in a grid, again concealed beneath a forest canopy.

But there was nothing else. No active radar, no
EM disturbances. There was, however, a trace line
of isotopes.

Sherman pondered, humming to himself, a habit

Gordon had found all so annoying. The song was ancient, from a war ten score of centuries ago, a song of sweet potatoes (whatever they were) leaping from the ground, while bringing the Jubilee beneath a flag that makes men free.

He hooked into the transport's nav and bridge systems. They were still operational.

He had a mission again.

Sherman turned the armor transport in towards the planet and soon again he felt the turbulence build as the ship traced a streak of fire across the night sky.

Drak never saw it, but he did feel it, the low rumble, the double whip crack of thunder that was not thunder—a sonic boom rolling across the hills.

Startled, pulse quickening, he looked up at the heavens. Nothing. *No, of course not, by the time you hear the boom they are already down.*

Drak na-Drak stood up, his hand reflexively reaching to his belt. He suddenly felt naked, his pistol hung from the mantle over the fireplace, along with the short ceremonial sword as alpha of his pack.

He turned, head raised, scanning, and then saw a reflected glow against a scattering of clouds drifting off the top of the snow capped mountains. It pulsed, flickered, and died.

A ship's retro as it touched down.

He waited, tensed.

If this was a full assault, there would be the softening up bombardment.

Nothing.

He barked a soft weary laugh. Softening up for what? These were no longer the days of fleets of automated factories that could produce ten thousand neutron heads to shatter a planet and then in two score of days make ten thousand more. Such extravagance of power was long since gone by both sides.

*How I reveled in the power of it all, the first time
I ordered such a strike,* he thought coldly, remembering the human world of New Vermont glowing as a
blanket of suns flashed across its surface, a billion of
their hated souls turned to cinder as "a demonstration." Or the three year fight for Telamar, with four
regiments of the human fighting machines and five
regiments of our own smashing the planet from one
end to the other as the firestorms turned the days
into perpetual night.

We won that one, too, Drak thought as he stood
silently, watching the mountain.

How I once loved it so.

Shaking his head he turned and walked, for running
was now nearly impossible with the bad leg, back into
the woods, his snout lowered, picking up the scents
of the forest, mingled with the woodsmoke from the
cabins, and the scent of all that was left of his pack.

He reached the village square and stepped up the
rough wooden steps into the temple to the Nameless
of Nameless Ones and started to ring the bell.

Though more than twenty kilometers away Sherman felt the vibration in the air, the all so faint clatter
of metal striking metal.

He paused for a moment to analyze. There was still
no radio, no Melconian channels activating to spread
an alert, no pulse radars or laser designators locking
in.

He remembered the stories of the old war of his
namesake that one of the techs in the regiment had
told him about. *They rang bells then to warn of my
approach.*

Is this what we've finally become? Sherman
pondered.

He started forward, weaving his way up the long
slope, scanning the crest line for defensive positions,

tensely waiting for the first ping of a Melconian hell-fire anti-armor thermonuclear shaped charge round.

Nothing, only the whirring of the night insects. Not even the trace of a Melconian pack scent. He gained the crest of the mountain, remaining on the reverse slope and extended a periscope to peer over the edge. The sound of the bell was clear now and then suddenly it drifted away into silence.

Sherman scanned through his weapons supply list. The only thing he had was the primary load kept stored deep within his bowels, the rest of the supplies on the landing transport was for support of the legs, the infantry. There was only one thermonuke, an EMP pulse head which was also a planet killer with its twenty ton wrap of strontium. The rest was the standard tactical support of anti-armor, and anti-personnel missiles along with his direct fire guns.

All I'll ever have for a long time to come, Sherman realized.

With no hope of backup and resupply, and going in with not even a full battle load made the options limited.

He jacked up the periscope magnification to maximum, focusing in on the traces of heat plumes coming from the forest and waited.

Drak na-Drak looked out over the assembly who stood before him, sleepy-eyed in the early light of dawn. Families stood huddled together, young pups most of them, huddled around the legs of their parents, the smallest whimpering, still walking on all fours, yelping.

"What now is it, Drak," a voice called, "another star falling from the heavens?" and a chorus of laughter echoed around the rough hewn steps of the temple.

"A ship has landed on the other side of the Vargani Mountains."

His words were greeted with silence. In the pale light he could see the range of reactions, from looks of mocking disbelief to that of uneasy fear.

"How do you know this?" Regar, his old comrade and now the lone priest of the village, asked.

"I heard the sonic boom of its passage."

"Thunder," someone quipped from the back of the crowd, "just thunder, I heard it too."

"I also saw the reflective glow of its retros as it touched down."

"Could it be one of ours?" Jamak asked, and Drak could hear the hope in his friend's quavering voice. Standing beside Jamak, the last of the veterans, Dulth stood in stoic silence.

"I wish I knew, but it is best to be cautious until we know. I think we should head to the shelters."

"Those dank holes?"

Drak looked back at the assembly towards the speaker, young Haka, born after the exodus and now coming of age as a leader.

"No one will ever come here," Haka announced. "You old ones, that is all we heard you talk of when we were but still whelping. If all you said of this war of yours is true then no one, either of our people or the demon humans will ever come. You cast each other down and we are all that is left."

Drak looked at Haka and almost smiled. His youthful arrogance was, in its place, a good thing, as he stood before him, dressed in the skins of a forest leopard, a bow, made from a piece of salvaged ship's hull, slung over his shoulder.

"It was just thunder," Haka said, looking around at the assembled crowd. "Now let's go back to our homes and forget this foolishness, the pups have had enough demon stories for one night."

*   *   *

Sherman pondered, scanning the forest and came to a decision. A single high energy pulse swept out and he waited, analyzing the returning signal that echoed across the land. He shifted his position, just in case the Melconians could back track the radar signal and then call in a strike. Popping up his dish after moving half a kilometer, he sent out another pulse, retrieved the data and moved yet again.

No response. Curious. Were they masking their equipment, trying to lure him out? The high res image he had assembled from the two pulses made the picture clear enough. A concealed position in the woods, revealed by the several hundred tons of metal about the encampment which gave back sharp clear images. It was hard to tell at this range but some of them were obviously weapons. Olfactory sweep had picked up a one part per two hundred billion of Melconian scent from their musk glands.

They were here.

He calculated the atmospheric density and wind and locked in the coordinates. Deep within him he picked out the mix of armament, fuel air, HE proximity, cluster, and independent guide tracking rounds. No sense in wasting the heavy armament on what might only be a forward outpost. Old-fashioned indirect fire would be the best for this, and besides, there was something about artillery that he loved, perhaps because of his namesake.

For the glory of the regiment, he thought. The stream of shots pulsed out of his heart and within milliseconds after the last missile streaked heavenward he positioned himself for the charge.

"Incoming!"

Drak na-Drak turned towards Regar, who still seemed strange after all these years to be wearing the priestly robes, he the most efficient killer of all. Regar was pointing towards the mountain and Drak looked back.

Fingers of light were leaping heavenward, standing out clearly against the retreating darkness of night. Drak had worked out the calculations long before regarding a missile strike from the top of the mountain, and knew with a cold certainty just how many seconds were left before the first burst detonated. If it was nuke tip, it didn't matter, but perhaps it was not.

"Move it! Move it!" Drak screamed, pointing into the woods to where the old shelters were.

The crowd looked at him in confusion, some of them silent, some still with looks of bemusement, others turning, stepping up onto the temple steps to catch a glimpse of the mountain through the canopy of trees.

"Damnation is coming down right here!" the priest screamed. "Now follow Drak!"

With a loping stride, as fast as his crippled leg would allow him, Drak leaped down the steps and started down the path that weaved through the forest to the underground bunkers. First one, then another, and finally a shouting crowd followed him, some in panic, many just following along still not sure of what was happening. Drak dodged through the trees, counting down the time to first impact.

If it's not a nuke the first round will be fuel-air to blast the forest canopy down, then followed by cluster and shrapnel, he thought, amazed how he could still think so coldly and clearly. The path wove around a high towering garnth tree, more than half a dozen arm spans in width and a hundred meters in height. Beyond it were the bunkers, overgrown with tangles of vines. Drak raced up to the closest, pulling the vines aside.

"Get in!"

A young mother, barely a pup when he had pulled her with the others out of the shelter beneath the school they had landed near on Melcon, and now carrying two pups herself hesitated at the entryway and he shoved her in head first, her pups yelping in pain. Others piled in behind her. He continued to count and then looked heavenward, sensing it before he even heard it.

"Get down!" Drak screamed.

The priest, Dulth and Jamak sensed it as well and they started to shove to the ground those who had yet to reach a bunker.

Drak dived to the ground. He heard the first whisper, the rising shriek of engines burning hot in order to drive the warheads through the canopy overhead.

Two hundred meters away the first explosion detonated with a white hot flash. He heard screams of terror which in an instant were drowned out by the cacophony of explosions as forty stinger rounds, all in the proper ratio of fuel-air, HE, shrapnel and cluster ripped apart a dozen acres of forest, the last two rounds adding in bursts of phosphorous to ignite the wreckage.

Drak staggered back up to his feet, breathing hard. He felt a warm tingling and realized, to his horror, that it was a rush of excitement. Part of him had found the old thrill in it, cheating death and there was a momentary flash of having survived so many such encounters that they had become part of his very existence.

And then he heard the screaming.

He moved down the path, his people looking up at him, wide-eyed. And there was something else now as well. In the beginning he had been the savior when he had landed back on Melcon and pulled them out of a suffocating shelter, loaded them aboard his lifeboat and fled their dying home world forever. But saviors are rarely saviors forever. Through the passing of years he became an anachronism, the one who still waited for the enemy, when all the rest knew that the enemy was dead; until finally he was nothing but an old obsessed fool.

Now he was the savior again, and in that instant Drak knew yet again the final and eternal irony of being a soldier protecting civilians whose memories were all so short, while a soldier could never forget anything if he wanted to stay alive.

"Into the shelters, start moving before the second wave strikes."

There was no hesitation now as they stood up, pushing and shoving in blind panic towards the bunkers. He watched them pass, and breathed a silent thanks that though several had been wounded by shrapnel, no one was dead.

"Regar, Dulth, Jamak to me," he said, motioning his old veterans to come to his side.

Together they stood in the forest, looking back towards the shattered ruins of the village which was now engulfed in flames.

"So they've come back after all," Regar said coldly, brushing leaves and broken twigs from his priestly robes.

Drak nodded, not wishing to say the age old line that "I told you so." Smoke eddied and swirled around them as the morning breeze, coming down off the mountains pulled a cloak of choking white around them.

"What do you think they have?" Jamak asked quietly, and Drak could see the hatred in his old friend's eyes.

"At least one fire position, could be an indirect fire support team," Regar said, "jump troopers for the assault."

Drak shook his head.

"If they had jump troopers they'd already be coming in now, they've waited too long already," and as he spoke Jamak looked up through the shattered trees as if expecting even now to see human space-to-ground assault troops coming in on thrusters.

"A mech," Drak said, "one at least, maybe two, with one maneuvering while the other is in fire support."

He waited a moment, cocking up his good ear and then shook his head.

"More likely just one, the second strike would have hit now if they had two."

He turned and looked back at his friends from the old days, the three remaining members of his staff from so long ago.

"Regar, stay with the people. We'll follow the plan we agreed upon long ago. When you hear the battle, start getting everyone out of the bunkers and move them deeper into the forest while we draw the attacking force away in the opposite direction. Jamak, Dulth, you're with me."

Regar looked at him wistfully and Drak knew he wanted to come along, the old call of battle still strong.

Drak smiled and patted him on the shoulder.

"Hell, we need at least one veteran of our once glorious Empire to keep the memory alive."

"At least they'll believe us now," Regar said sadly.

"Until another generation is born," Drak said, not voicing the fear that after today there might never be another generation of the Melcon, their memory gone forever into the night.

"The blessing of the Nameless Four upon you all," Regar said and Jamak and Dulth knelt as he raised his hand in benediction.

Drak stood silently and with a sad smile he nodded to his old friend and started down the path towards the cave where their one remaining weapon was hidden, followed by all that remained of the Melconian Imperial Armed Forces.

Weaving through a narrow defile, Sherman crossed over the crestline and started down the forward slope.

7.9 seconds to the opposite side of the field, he calculated and as he raced across he swung all scanning into maximum. No returning fire greeted him.

Curious. The target was flattened. The high energy sweeps revealed as well that there were no bodies in the wreckage, and no equipement of worth as well.

Then where is their center of resistance?

He raced across the open alpine meadow, reaching the edge of the forest, crashed into the treeline then paused, scanning for any trace isotopes that might indicate a mine barrier. It would be a logical place for one, reverse sloped buried where the soil was finally deep enough.

Again nothing.

I've always hated forest and jungle, he thought, *no clear fields of fire, too much concealment.*

There was no sense in waiting here, he realized and powering up he crashed through the forest, snapping off trees like broken straws, charging forward. As he advanced he popped off a recon drone, sending it up to level off at five thousand meters where it went into a hover. He expected it to draw fire, but again nothing.

The drone relayed back a sweep of the area, the spreading conflagration from the first strike moving forward with the wind.

These were definitely not Melconian tactics; if they had a weakness it was an inability to wait. In 98.2% of the actions engaged in, Melconians had tended to react as soon as the main force was in sight.

Could they think I'm just recon for a larger strike?

No, they must have detected only one ship and a sweep outward would reveal nothing else within the entire system. He chuckled inward at the irony; a sweep would reveal nothing within a hundred parsecs.

The ground beneath him leveled out and after cutting through sixteen kilometers of forest, with some trees so big that he had to cut them with a pulse ion before proceeding, he finally started to move back up a long slope of trees and jagged outcropping of rock. With a splintering crash of trees he broke into the small clear meadow which bordered on where the enemy position was located.

He scanned the area, and finally picked up movement.

Melconians, half a dozen of them coming out of a concealed position, obviously driven out by the fire which was moving in upon them.

He swung a light rail gun around, popping in a canister of flechettes . . . and then paused.

They were non-combatants, Melconian pups.

General Order 39 clearly stated that all Melconians were to be "annihilated."

Still he hesitated, watching as a pup wailed in terror, its mother covering him with her cloak while she ran from the approaching storm of fire.

She looked back over her shoulder and saw him and in his telescopic sight he could see her eyes grow wide with terror, her canine-like ears pressing down flat against her skull as she clutched the pup tightly to her chest.

Sherman knew with a certain coldness that he had killed Melconian women and their pups before. When a Dinochrome Regiment hits a planet, "collateral damage," as it was so cleanly called, was extensive; on Iutak it was later estimated at over two billion. He had pumped Hellbore rounds into Melconian cities along with his comrades and knew that in turn the Melconians had done the same to human cities.

Yet now, for the first time in his forty-eight years of service, he had a Melconian woman and child in the crosshairs of a telescopic sight.

War is hell, he thought, and then an alarm cut through from the drone, just before it winked out of existence from a direct energy beam weapon.

Even in that final microsecond of its functioning the drone was able to pinpoint the origin of the weapon.

Though he knew that according to the letter of the law the Melconian women and child could be viewed as "personnel," he found internal justification to hold fire while engaging an active foe and swung the gun aside while launching a second spray of missiles towards where the beam weapon was placed.

"Good shot, Jamak, now time to move," Drak announced.

Jamak looked over his shoulder at Drak and grinned.

"Like the old days again, is it not, my commander?"

Drak shook his head, remembering when the old days was to be in command of thousands and not just one undermaintained, badly battered and definitely obsolete light recon mech.

"Just get us the hell out of here," Dulth cried. "I've got incoming."

Jamak maneuvered the small vehicle out of the mouth of the cave and raced off into the woods, weaving his way around the trees, wishing in his heart for a real machine like the human Bolos, which could simply smash their way through.

As if reading his thoughts Drak knew why Jamak was cursing as he drove, for there had been a time when Jamak had commanded an entire legion of mech

of the latest designs that were near the equal of anything the humans could create.

"We've got some seekers in this bunch," Dulth
announced, looking up from the flickering display
plotting the incoming rounds.

"Jamak?"

"Got the spot," and he swung the vehicle into a
gully which was concealed by a dark umbrella of
hivuvial pines.

The ground shook beneath them as the second
strike pulverized the hill from which they had just
fled.

"Seekers still circling," Dulth said quietly and from
the outside microphone pickup Drak could hear the
drone of the engines overhead as they swept over the
forest, looking for their target before diving in.

"One has us, taking counter measure!"

Dulth fired off a direct beam and nailed the seeker
as it started to dive and then tracked around hitting
the second while Jamak gunned the recon vehicle forward, racing up the side of the gully and moving at
full throttle into the forest.

Seconds later another valley came in, this time
bursting in a wide circle around the gully, as the
enemy machine attempted to nail them as they fled.

Shrapnel screamed against the hull of the vehicle,
the concussion of a fuel air burst blurring Drak's
vision.

Laughing, Jamak led the human machine deeper
and deeper into the forest, and further away from
their people.

"It's up to you now, Regar, to shepherd them,"
Drak whispered.

Sherman turned sharply away from the ruined village and crashed back into the forest, lofting off two
quick volleys. The images sent back from the seekers

quickly revealed his prey, a light three man Hawk-class Melconian recon vehicle. Armaments included a direct beam weapon, rail drive burst gun and it could also carry a single hellfire ion plasma bolt. That gave him a moment's pause.

It could be a killer. It would have only one sting, but it was enough to tear off a tread, shear off a turret, or with a lot of skill and a lot of luck could penetrate into the ammunition locker and set off an internal detonation. The Melconians had adopted the tactic with great effect in the opening stages of the Gilgamesh campaign inflicting 62% losses on the old 7th before tactical doctrine was changed to include a forward screen of similarly equipped light vehicle hunter killer units.

An interesting challenger, Sherman thought, finding pleasure in the one-on-one hunt, for even though the preponderance of strength was on his side, he sensed that the Melconian opposing him was skillful.

Three times he sent out bursts of indirect fire to try to hit the enemy vehicle and each time it was someplace else, its gunner skillfully dropping all seekers before they closed. Sherman lofted a stealth tracer, which popped up to ten thousand meters, broke free of its casing, and then deployed out on mylar wings, its ceramic body all but invisible to radar. It locked in on the enemy vehicle, would lose it, then regain acquisition, tracking on the sound it made as it crashed through the forest.

Having already expanded 14% of his indirect fire munitions, Sherman decided to close for the kill. And as he accelerated up he realized as well what the enemy was attempting to do.

Drak leaned forward, intent, looking over the shoulders of his driver and munitions operator. It was not quite like the bridge of a ship; armor was something he had never fought in. Jamak, who had started there before rising to be his adjutant, was obviously enjoying himself, weaving the vehicle between trees, leaping ditches, splashing through streams and without warning throwing the vehicle into full reverse, backing up and then swinging off in another direction, while all the time dragging the human machine further and further away from the village.

Except for an occasional seeker the enemy had not tried any more area bombardments.

It's a single mech, Drak realized. *It's out here alone and can't squander its munitions to kill a lone vehicle.*

So the war has come down to this, he thought with a sad chuckle, *a lone human bolo chasing a lone Melconian recon. What epics will be written and sung of this,* and again he cursed the Nameless Ones.

He knew that time had passed, the second sun was now far above the horizon, their village far over the distant hills. If the machine had not hit the bunkers Regar would have had more than enough time to lead the people deep into the woods. He knew, of course, that unless luck was extremely kind, they would soon be finished, and he was surprised they had eluded the machine as long as they had. Once they were finished the machine would turn back and remorselessly hunt down the survivors it could find. Such machines had destroyed entire worlds. What were two hundred and eight Melconians more or less to the final bill of annihilation? Again, with luck however, the delay would give his people time to scatter and perhaps some would live after all. And then, a millennium or more from now, again they might go forth to the stars.

And even as he dreamed the dream of survival the hillside before him erupted into light as a Hellbore round swept away the entire side of the hill before him in a glowing burst of plasma.

Jamak spun the vehicle around so that the blast hit

the forward sloping armor. The machine lifted off the ground and then slammed back down.

Stunned, Drak saw Dulth slumped forward in his seat, his head lolling to one side—dead, his skull split open, the old fool had not strapped himself in properly.

"Target, forward portside!" Jamak screamed.

Drak unstrapped himself from his command chair, pushed Dulth out of his seat and climbed in behind the gunnery console.

He almost suffered the same fate as his friend when Jamak slammed the vehicle into reverse and roared back down the slope of the hill as a spray of depleted uranium bolts churned the crestline into a geysering inferno.

Drak punched up the ion plasma bolt to full active status, unmasking the tube which ran down the length of the vehicle.

"We have only one shot," Jamak hissed, "so make it count."

"Would you care to take the gun?" Drak retorted, an ironic bemusement in his voice.

"I was a driver," Jarak replied as if insulted. "I drove my gunner for three kills on their Bolos. I'd rather drive and you do the shooting, sir."

Sherman paused, scanning through the firestorm to where his gatling mount had torn the far hillside apart. The drone overhead bucked and churned from the hot thermal that rose up from the explosion which had ripped apart a square kilometer of forest in order to give him a clear field of fire. The drone suddenly went off the air, its mylar wings melting in the heat blast and again he was blind.

Sherman turned and slashed the opposite hill with another Hellbore, vaporizing the forest and denying the enemy concealment and then tore apart the hills to either flank.

If the enemy tried to come up out of the narrow defile it would be in a cleared firezone.

The hunt is almost over, he thought and he was surprised to feel a twinge of regret. His foe had played a masterful game of hounds and hare, leading him far away from the point of initial contact before finally being cornered. This might be the final shot of the war, and then, after that, silence.

He threw in a suppressive barrage of indirect fire down into the valley and then closed for the kill.

The world outside the recon vehicle was an inferno of explosions.

"Now I know why I never went into armor!" Drak roared. "Everything gets thrown at you. At least with the infantry I could dig in!"

Jamak looked back at him and grimaced.

"This is nothing, nothing at all!" and Drak could see the fear in his friend's eyes.

"He'll come in from the flank," Jamak announced, "either left or right and direct fire down on us for the kill. You'll have only an instant to acquire, train your gun which can pivot ten degrees to one side or the other, and fire before he lets loose," and as he spoke Jamak swung the recon vehicle around to port and came to a stop.

Drak wanted to ask why port rather than starboard but knew it was simply an even guess, either they'd have him in their sights or a round would come in on their back. Chances were that either way it would turn out the same.

Drak sat hunched over his screen, monitoring the condition of the ion plasma penetrator round. He sent a burst of air through the gun bore to clear out the dust and debris from the bombardment and waited.

He thought yet again of his brother Jamu, his lady fair, the children lost. And he thought as well of those who had laughed at him as he grew old, fearing the coming of this day.

He closed his eyes for an instant.

"Let them live, let at least some of them live," he prayed.

"Target front, five degrees to starboard!" Jarak shouted.

Startled, Drak opened his eyes and pivoted the gun.

The plot board marked the target, crosshairs lining up. He saw a flash and knew what was coming in. He pulled the trigger, the vehicle around him leaping back as the round burst down the tube, accelerating up to over forty thousand feet per second and then the world went to blinding light and darkness.

Sherman crested the hill, the valley floor below him swathed in a fireball of explosions as the last of the volley of missiles churned the land into an inferno.

As he crossed over the top of the hill Sherman suddenly knew what fear was, it was part of his programming for survival. Within an instant he calculated the timing and odds. The vehicle before him had an ion plasma bolt on board, sensors picking up the charge spinning in its chamber and at full power, opticals revealing the open gun port. It was starting to pivot, lining up for a shot. He was presenting a target that was on the oblique by eleven degrees. Sherman knew a skilled gunner could put the shot in on his exposed side between tread and side armor skirt, and the round could, at this range, penetrate all the way in for a critical hit, perhaps even a kill.

In his world of microseconds all seemed to be moving in a frightening slow motion, enemy barrel moving a millimeter, his own moving a millimeter as well. He calculated and recalculated and knew at last that he had to fire.

The round went down range and he saw the burst of light from the enemy vehicle leap forward just milliseconds before his shot made a deflecting hit against the enemy vehicle.

The gunner had fired early. Sherman braced himself, unable to bring his point defense gatling to bear in time, rerouting energy to his internal disrupter shields in an attempt to divert the strike away from any critical area.

The bolt hit on the forward armor, half a meter from his exposed flank. The charge burned through layers of armor, peeling it back, striking with such force that his eighteen thousand tons of bulk recoiled from the strike. He felt pain, pain as real as if his circuits were made of flesh and blood. The energy of the bolt burned down, flickered, and died, stopping less than ten centimeters from bursting into his core reactor.

The terror subsided as he did the human equivalent of feeling his body to make sure he was not mortally hurt. It was a wound, a bad one, but a good team of techs could repair it.

What techs?

I'll survive somehow, he thought, *for now there's still the mission.* He pivoted back, presenting his forward armor towards the target, even though he knew the enemy had fired his one and only bolt. He activated his railgun mount, checked its calibration to make sure it had not been bent, and then moved forward for the coup de grace.

"Jamak, Jamak!"

Gasping for breath, Drak fumbled through the burning wreckage of the vehicle. This was another reason he had never wanted to be in a mech unit, the usual method of death was burning.

He found Jamak and pulled him out of his seat, feeling that his friend's heart was still beating beneath his torn tunic. Scrambling backwards he pulled Jamak after him, crawling out of the top hatch, which was now resting against the ground so close that he feared for a second that they might not get out.

He kicked his way out, pulled his friend after him and rolled clear of the vehicle, aware for the first time that the fur on his arm was smoldering. He patted the burning embers off of Jamak, ignoring his own pain, before rolling on the ground to stop the burning.

"Drak?"

"Here, Jamak."

He crawled back to his friend's side.

"Did you get him?"

"Don't know."

"Lost five vehicles this way," Jamak whispered, "now six. Got the Medal of Stars in the last one."

"I'll see you get another."

Jamak smiled and struggled to sit up.

"Be still, be still," Drak said softly.

He looked up, around him for a kilometer or more in every direction the forest was flaming ruin, the acrid smoke coiling up to the uncaring heavens.

And then he heard the creaking of the treads and out of the smoke a Mark XXXIII Bolo named Sherman emerged.

"Did we get him, Drak?"

"Yes, we got him," Drak said softly.

"Then I guess we finally won the war."

Drak cradled his friend's head in his lap and covered his eyes so that he would die believing in victory.

Sherman ground to a stop. The Hawk recon vehicle was dead. A good kill of an adroit foe. And then he saw the two. A gatling mount swung around and took aim.

General Order 39 was still in effect, the two were Melconian soldiers in a war where the taking of prisoners was a formality long since forgotten.

He scanned them closely and within milliseconds a memory bank shot back a reply, recognizing one of them in spite of the missing arm and scarred features ... General Drak na-Drak, the destroyer of worlds, final commander of the Melconian Imperial Fleet.

Sherman watched him closely, already resolved to shoot if Drak moved. But he did not.

And Sherman finally realized he would not move, that the General would not abandon a wounded comrade, that he was covering his friend's eyes, so that he would not see the end.

How many thousands of my human comrades have I seen dying thus, Sherman pondered. Dying with defiance, but also with love, love of the regiment, their comrades, dying with all that was the worst, and best in men.

If there was still a headquarters, here would be a prisoner worth turning in. But Sherman knew there would never again be a headquarters, at least not for a thousand years to come.

"General Drak na-Drak," he finally said.

Drak looked up at him, showing no surprise that a Bolo could speak, let alone speak Melconian.

Drak looked at him, his features drawn and then, in what was a universal gesture, nodded in acknowledgement.

"My orders are to destroy all Melconian equipment, facilities, and personnel," Sherman said.

"Orders I would have given, such orders I indeed did give, so go ahead and finish it."

Sherman looked at him, still cradling his comrade.

"You've got us, all that is left of the Empire, two old veterans, so do it and be damned."

"What about the others, there were others," Sherman replied and he saw the old warrior stiffen.

Drak gently lowered his friend's head to the ground and stood up.

"Isn't it enough?" Drak asked.

"What?"

"Isn't it enough? Let something, at least something, survive from our mutual suicide."

Sherman pondered his words, remembering the last faint whispers on the comm links and then silence.

Drak lowered his head for a moment and then finally looked back up at Sherman.

"You said Melconians, didn't you?"

"Those were my orders."

"Then consider this. Twenty standard years ago I returned to Melcon after the final destruction. I should have died with my ship but my friend here," and he nodded down to Jamak, "dragged me into a lifeboat when my carrier was destroyed. We returned to my world, found a few survivors, nearly all of them young ones, and fled."

Drak paused and shook his head. *Dead, my comrades, my lady fair, my children, all of them.* He looked back up again fighting back the tears.

"The rest were born here. They're no longer Melconian, that race is dead, as is that who made you, except for some few who found refuge as we did. Let it end. Call those here something else, anything else. They're no longer Melconian, you and I destroyed that and the Republic long ago. The war is over.

Sherman pondered what he said, remembering the terrified woman in his sights and sighed, feeling suddenly very old, and very alone.

Yet there was still an order to be fulfilled.

"General Drak na-Drak, I am Sherman, 4th of the

9th Dinochrome Regiment and I demand your surrender."

Drak smiled and finally shook his head.

"Go to hell."

Sherman, taken aback, said nothing for a long moment.

War is hell, it had once been said, and we were the demons who created it.

"We're already in hell," Sherman finally replied.

Drak na-Drak sat alone on the hill, watching the sky overhead. There was a pulse of light and then a brilliant flare as the ship rode heavenward upon the throne of flame.

He watched his old enemy depart until finally it was but a pinpoint of light, and then there was nothing but the darkness.

He wondered what his brother would have said about praying for something that was not of flesh and blood, but perhaps had a soul of compassion after all. How did one pray for an enemy who had given life back to an entire race?

For the first time in more than twenty years Drak na-Drak lowered his head and prayed.

With a contented sigh he finally rose back up, and turning, walked back down the hill to where his people and old comrades were waiting.

Tonight he could finally sleep and not be afraid of what he might dream.

S.M. STIRLING
and
THE DOMINATION OF THE DRAKA

In 1782 the Loyalists fled the American Revolution to settle in a new land: South Africa, Drake's Land. They found a new home, and built a new nation: The Domination of the Draka, an empire of cruelty and beauty, a warrior people, possessed by a wolfish will to power. This is alternate history at its best.

"A tour de force." —David Drake

"It's an exciting, evocative, thought-provoking—but of course horrifying—read."
—Poul Anderson

MARCHING THROUGH GEORGIA
Six generations of his family had made war for the Domination of the Draka. Eric von Shrakenberg wanted to make peace—but to succeed he would have to be a better killer than any of them.

UNDER THE YOKE
In *Marching Through Georgia* we saw the Draka's "good" side, as they fought and beat that more obvious horror, the Nazis. Now, with a conquered Europe supine beneath them, we see them as they truly are; for conquest is only the *beginning* of their plans . . . All races are created equal—as slaves of the Draka.

THE STONE DOGS
The cold war between the Alliance of North America and the Domination is heating up. The Alliance, using its superiority in computer technologies, is preparing a master stroke of electronic warfare. But the Draka, supreme in the ruthless manipulation of life's genetic code, have a secret weapon of their own. . . .

"This is a potent, unflinching look at a might-have-been world whose evil both contrasts with and reflects that in our own." —*Publishers Weekly*

"Detailed, fast-moving military science fiction . . ."
—Roland Green, *Chicago Sun-Times*

"*Marching Through Georgia* is more than a thrilling war story, more than an entertaining alternate history. . . . I shall anxiously await a sequel."
—Fred Lerner, *VOYA*

"The glimpses of a society at once fascinating and repelling are unforgettable, and the people who make up the society are real, disturbing, and very much alive. Canadian author Stirling has done a marvelous job with *Marching Through Georgia*."
—Marlene Satter, *The News* of Salem, Arkansas

"Stirling is rapidly emerging as a writer to watch."
—Don D'Ammassa, *SF Chronicle*

POUL ANDERSON

Poul Anderson is one of the most honored authors of our time. He has won seven Hugo Awards, three Nebula Awards, and the Gandalf Award for Achievement in Fantasy, among others. His most popular series include the Polesotechnic League/Terran Empire tales and the Time Patrol series. Here are fine books by Poul Anderson available through Baen Books:

FLANDRY • 72149-6 • $4.99   _____

THE HIGH CRUSADE • 72074-0 • $3.95   _____

OPERATION CHAOS • 72102-X • $3.99   _____

ORION SHALL RISE • 72090-2 • $4.99   _____

THREE HEARTS AND THREE LIONS • 72186-0 • $4.99   _____

THE PEOPLE OF THE WIND • 72164-X • $4.99   _____

THE BYWORLDER • 72178-X • $3.99   _____

THE GAME OF EMPIRE • 55959-1 • $3.50   _____

FIRE TIME • 65415-2 • $3.50   _____

AFTER DOOMSDAY • 65591-4 • $2.95   _____

THE BROKEN SWORD • 65382-2 • $2.95   _____

THE DEVIL'S GAME • 55995-8 • $4.99   _____

THE ENEMY STARS • 65339-3 • $2.95   _____

SEVEN CONQUESTS • 55914-1 • $2.95   _____

STRANGERS FROM EARTH • 65627-9 • $2.95   _____

If not available at your local bookstore, you can order all of Poul Anderson's books listed above with this order form. Check your choices and send the combined cover price/s to: Baen Books, Dept. BA, P.O. Box 1403, Riverdale, NY 10471.

Name _____

Address _____

City _____ State _____ Zip _____

THE SHIP WHO SANG IS NOT ALONE!

Anne McCaffrey, with Margaret Ball, Mercedes Lackey, and S.M. Stirling, explores the universe she created with her ground-breaking novel, *The Ship Who Sang*.

☐ **PARTNERSHIP by Anne McCaffrey & Margaret Ball**
"[*PartnerShip*] captures the spirit of *The Ship Who Sang* to a surprising degree . . . a single, solid plot full of creative nastiness and the sort of egocentric villains you love to hate."—Carolyn Cushman, *Locus*
0-671-72109-7 • 336 pages • $5.99

☐ **THE SHIP WHO SEARCHED by Anne McCaffrey & Mercedes Lackey**
Tia, a bright and spunky seven-year-old accompanying her exo-archaeologist parents on a dig is afflicted by a paralyzing alien virus. Tia won't be satisfied to glide through life like a ghost in a machine. Like her predecessor Helva, *The Ship Who Sang*, she would rather strap on a *spaceship*.
0-671-72129-1 • 320 pages • $5.99

☐ **THE CITY WHO FOUGHT by Anne McCaffrey & S.M. Stirling**
Simeon was the "brain" running a peaceful space station—but when the invaders arrived, his only hope of protecting his crew and himself was to become *The City Who Fought*!
0-671-72166-6 • 432 pages • Hardcover • $19.00

And don't miss The Planet Pirates series:

☐ **SASSINAK by Anne McCaffrey & Elizabeth Moon**
0-671-69863-X • $5.99

☐ **THE DEATH OF SLEEP by Anne McCaffrey & Jody Lynn Nye**
0-671-69884-2 • $5.99

☐ **GENERATION WARRIORS by Anne McCaffrey & Elizabeth Moon**
0-671-72041-4 • $4.95

Above three titles are available together as one huge trade paperback. Such a deal!

☐ **THE PLANET PIRATES** • 72187-9 • $12.00 • 864 pages

If not available at your local bookstore, fill out this coupon and send a check or money order for the cover price to Baen Books, Dept. BA, P.O. Box 1403, Riverdale NY 10471

Name _____

Address _____

_____

I have enclosed a check or money order in the amount of $ _____